BOSTON BLACK OPS

A Jack 'Tinlegs' Taylor Thriller

ERIC MEYER

First published in the United Kingdom in 2013 by Swordworks Books.

ISBN 978-1-909149-15-1

Typeset by Swordworks Books
Printed and bound in the UK & US
A catalogue record of this book is available from the British Library

Cover design by Swordworks Books
www.swordworks.co.uk

BOSTON
BLACK OPS

A Jack 'Tinlegs' Taylor Thriller

ERIC MEYER

CHAPTER ONE

They were almost invisible, silent, bringers of death. He paused and searched the ground ahead through his NV gear. Taylor had put Anderson on point. They were creeping into a village, virtually a suburb of Kabul. So close, it was hard to determine where the city ended and the village began. But the enemy knew. The Taliban. Here, in the wastelands that lay outside of the immediate surveillance of ISAF, they operated at will, until now. The Seal Team was assigned a simple mission. It was time to demonstrate the long reach of the Allied forces. For the hostiles, there would be no peace, no place to hide. Taylor's squad had a message to deliver, a message of fear, and of death. His earpiece came to life.

"Charlie Six to One, no sign of any hostiles. We're clear to proceed."

"Copy that."

He waved his men forward, although he didn't like it. The village was the usual ragtag collection of crumbling stone houses, many repaired with rusting sheets of corrugated iron. There was a light breeze, enough to carry the stench of last night's cooking fires, combined with the usual accumulation of filth and human waste; and the ever-present rich scent of opium. Just your average Afghan village, nothing more than a collection of decaying dwellings providing basic shelter to their hardscrabble inhabitants; and something more. Over the miasmic stink that shrouded the entire area, he could almost smell the enemy. Taste them. They were there.

"Charlie Six, anything."

"Negative. We're good."

"Copy that."

He watched them darting from shadow to shadow, their Multicam camo making them almost invisible by day and mere ghosts by night. The bulky armored vests, weapons, and equipment packs they carried were also shrouded in camouflage, so their bulk was as invisible as the uniforms. He gripped his MP7 submachine gun and touched the pistol in the leg holster, just once for luck, as he always did before a firefight. His two personal weapons, the carbine length lightweight MP7, and the P226 Sig Sauer 9mm pistol, were in his opinion the best tools in the world for this kind of work. Killing work. The MP7, short even for a submachine gun, fired specially made 4.6mm rounds made of hardened steel penetrator, even able to penetrate thin armor. Its light weight and powerful penetration had made it popular with many of the Seals. Others preferred the heavier HK416, also made by Heckler and Koch, for its longer range and greater accuracy. He stared through his NV goggles, searching for an answer to what bugged him.

Nothing, but they're here.

"Listen up, people. There's something not right here, so stay doubly alert. Any sign of movement, shoot first. That's an order."

"Copy that."

This was a known Taliban village. They should have sentries out, for they were no fools. They knew there was always the chance of a raid, and they'd be prepared. Yet there was no one.

Are we walking into an ambush? There's no way they saw Charlie Platoon coming. The only way they could have anticipated us is if intelligence leaked the mission.

Even as the thought came into his mind, the first gun-flashes lit the night from a building fifty meters ahead. He dived for cover, shouting, "Everyone down, get under cover. Wes, go locate that shooter, Jerry, cover him. Dave, Tito, I want that SAW in action. Hose that position down good. Joe, use the launcher! Plaster that building! Move people, we got a situation here."

He ducked as a stream of bullets rattled on the stonework inches above his head, and some of his men opened up, starting to return fire. Their shots weren't aimed. They couldn't see anything to shoot at yet; the purpose was to keep the hostiles' heads down while they made their move.

There!

He saw a gun barrel poking out of a second floor window. He sighted at the dark opening where he knew the shooter was preparing to fire again, but he kept his finger off the trigger. There was no need to force the gomer to make a move. The sharp report of Joe Fenelli's M203 launcher announced the first grenade on the way. A second later, it exploded in front of the building, and he heard a scream from inside.

"Boss, I think he's down. Do we hold fire?"

"Yeah, Dave, it may have been their sentry asleep on the job. He just woke up, saw us, and opened up. Anyone hurt?"

A chorus of negatives.

"Roger that. Move on up to that building. We'll check it's clear. Ray, standby with the LTD. As soon as we've confirmed there aren't civilians in the area, we'll call in the air strike."

"Ready when you are, Boss."

They pressed forward until they surrounded the house the shooter had hidden inside to pour fire down on them.

"Barry, check it out inside."

Barry Waters, Charlie Six acknowledged.

"The rest of you, cover him. People, are we clear to proceed? Any sign of noncoms?"

Another chorus of negatives, no non-combatants were in the immediate vicinity. The Taliban frequently used women and children to surround their operations centers. They were disposable. Men weren't, they could fight. Besides, women and children caught and killed in the crossfire were good publicity. But not this time. It was wrong, but he didn't know why.

"You see the target, Ray?"

"Sure, I got it. No sign of noncoms, it's a clear shot."

"Light it up. I'll call it in."

He stared ahead. The headquarters building, once the seat of the tribal elders, the village council, looked quiet.

No, wait!

Another series of flashes; someone was inside shooting at them. He switched to the secure satcom.

"This is Charlie One. Target is lit. You are clear to proceed."

The voice came back almost immediately, clear and unemotional, like an announcer in an airport departure lounge. But this was no friendly Boeing 757 about to take passengers off to some sunny destination, or to visit close relatives. The aircraft were Marine Corps F/A 18 hornets, flight of four, and each armed Paveway-series laser-guided bombs. More than enough to follow their Laser Target Designator, turn the target building to rubble, and send the people inside to wherever those people went. Paradise, maybe? Maybe not. The building contained the regional Taliban commanders who'd been such a thorn in the side of the ISAF forces based around Kabul. They had managed to rack up an unenviable record of brutal atrocities; many of them against their own people who hated and feared them. When they'd been assigned this mission, it had felt good to be on the side of the angels. This Taliban outfit was one that everyone, American and Afghan wanted eliminated. Their mission was to double check the situation inside the village, and flush out and kill any loose groups of hostiles who may be lurking on the outskirts. And to make sure there wasn't a Boy Scout jamboree in progress, or a meeting of the local women's committee.

Straightforward. So why do I still have a nagging feeling in my brain? Something I missed?

"Diamond Leader to Charlie One, we see your target. Confirm launch order."

"Charlie One to Diamond Leader, you are clear launch. I say again, you are clear."

"Copy that. Stand by. Estimate ten seconds to impact."

"Roger that."

Another series of flashes lit up the night, searing bright light into his NV goggles. It came from the target building. The other shooter was still firing. Heavy firing came from only a few yards from where he was crouched behind the shelter of the stone side of a half-ruined building.

He keyed his mic. "Five seconds to impact, heads down people."

He tucked down in the lee of the thick stone, waiting for the explosions. And then he had it. It came together in a lighting flash of understanding. There were only two shooters inside the target.

They knew we were coming. Ambush!

"It's a trap! Fall back, fall back!"

The explosions were awesome in their immensity, and it was like falling though the gates of hell. The Taliban mines placed in the surrounding buildings detonated. By some freak of fate, the ordnance from the attacking F/A 18s hit the target at the same second. The combined force was like a volcano erupting.

He felt the ground lift beneath him as the buildings all around him exploded, blowing out great chunks of stone and lumps of broken timber. He was tossed into the air, and with incredulity realized he was looking down from about fifteen feet up on the devastation beneath him, of the village, and of his squad. He was falling, down, down, back to earth. When his body struck the hard packed earth, all he could think of was his men. The butcher's bill would be terrible, and he blamed himself.

Dear God, why didn't I see it coming?

It was a relief to know nothing more.

* * *

"Lieutenant."

"No, no…" He could hear shouting, and then he understood. He was making the noise. He opened his eyes, so he wasn't dead. This was a hospital bed, so white, so clean. It stank of antiseptic. The transition from the explosions in the village to this was an assault on the senses.

Senses!

He felt numb, couldn't feel a thing. He was heavily bandaged so that he couldn't move his arms or his legs, not even his head. A doctor hovered over him and began using his stethoscope on the small area of his body, his chest, that wasn't covered in dressings. He forced himself to calm down. He'd been injured before.

"How am I, Doc? Am I gonna live?"

The man nodded. "Sure, you'll live, once we've finished patching you up. There's something…"

His face was grave, yet he was not much more than a preppy kid, maybe mid twenties, so it looked odd. As if you had to be older to look so somber. And then it hit him.

"Tell me."

The man sighed. "You were badly injured in that explosion. Some of your internal organs were ruptured, and we had one helluva job getting everything working again."

"But you managed it?"

He nodded carefully. "We did, yes. But some of the damage, look, I'm sorry, Lieutenant." He'd raised his voice, couldn't help it.

"It's, er your legs."

Taylor felt the panic start to rise up inside him. "What about my legs?"

"They were both shredded in the explosion. We had to amputate what was left. Otherwise you wouldn't have survived."

He tried to calm himself. He'd lost a leg. His career in the Seals was over.

"Which leg?"

"That's the thing. Both of them."

Aw, fuck, no! My life is over, finished. There's nothing left, nothing! Not for me.

He blanked it out for a few moments as his mind automatically sifted through the priorities.

"What about my squad? Are they okay?"

The doc looked awkward. "I'm not sure, I…"

"Doc, give it to me! What happened to them?"

"I don't know the details, but there were four men killed in the explosion."

"And the others?"

"They're, er, recovering."

"What's that mean?"

"Concussion mainly, we'll know how bad it is later. Some of them are being treated right now in the psychiatric wing, but I'm sure they'll, well, get over the worst of it. I hope so, anyway."

He smiled weakly.

Oh, Christ, no! Wes, Jerry, Ray, Dave, Joe, the others.

He knew the doctor was shining him. What had he taken them into? He resolved to look them up as soon as he had the strength to get out of this place. And do whatever he could to help them. They were his brothers in arms, and he owed it to them. They'd assigned him to take responsibility for a platoon of Navy Seals, and as far as he was concerned he had outstanding business to attend to.

They talked about artificial legs, prosthetics, they called them. He'd be walking in no time, they said.

Yeah, like a fucking robot. No way. There's an alternative, there always is.

His parents came to visit twice during the long weeks of his incarceration in the VA hospital. His dad; the erect, ramrod straight naval officer. A retired US Navy Captain, he could hardly look at him. Taylor recalled how his father had raised him since birth to follow him in a naval career. Taylor senior had earned the command of a missile cruiser, his father before him a battleship. He looked forward eagerly to his son earning his first command. The Navy Seals was a disappointment to him, and he struggled to get over it. He'd tried to explain it.

"I'm sorry, Dad, but it's all I've ever wanted, ever since I first read about them in action in Vietnam. Surely you can see that they're an elite unit, the best of the best."

His dad should be proud he'd chosen such a difficult challenge. He wasn't.

"I guess it's still the Navy," he'd said hesitantly, but his eyes had been distant, his expression cold. It wasn't his fault. He'd been raised old navy, blue-water, a family tradition. But now his son was a cripple. Mom wept until she was red-eyed, and eventually both his parents talked of how they'd take care of him when he'd recovered enough to go home, as if he'd be a helpless cripple.

Well, that's what I am now, isn't it?

But they couldn't meet his eyes, and before long he asked them, as politely as possible, to stop visiting. He knew they were grateful and relieved. Taylor senior didn't need to be reminded of how his hopes and dreams, every ambition he'd worked so hard to achieve for his son, had disappeared like water down a drain. He didn't blame them. They were shattered. Parents try and bring up their kids in their own image, to do the things they'd wanted to do themselves when they were young. His dad saw him as rising to eventually command a Carrier.

"Just you make sure to send me an invitation to come along and visit for your first cruise," he'd said excitedly.

It wasn't going to happen now. He recalled reading about a famous Navy Seal amputee, Bob Kerrey, who'd lost a leg in Vietnam and went on to date a famous Hollywood actress. He famously said, 'She swept me of my foot.' They'd all laughed.

Tough guy, yeah. And a nice story, but what if they didn't leave you with even one foot?

His girlfriend came to visit him too. They'd planned to get engaged the following year and get married soon after. She was all gushing sympathy, and he knew it was well meant. He just couldn't explain it to her. She treated him like a fragile, sick kid, all false smiles and words of encouragement. Like she could make it better with a kiss and a cookie. He couldn't stand it. He didn't want her cloying attention. He didn't want anybody's sympathy.

I'm a man, a Seal, or used to be, anyway. I'll stand on my own two feet. I forgot. I don't have any.

That gave him a smile. He sent her away, breaking off the relationship. She left in tears, and he could tell she didn't understand any of it. How could she? But she'd thank him in the future, not to be saddled with a man with no legs, and with no life.

He almost laughed out loud when they fitted the prosthetic legs. Like a fucking pair of miniature undercarriage struts, covered in pink vinyl. One of them even squeaked where it had been poorly assembled. He hated them, hated wearing them, and preferred to roam the VA hospital in a wheelchair.

They called him into the office one dark, gray day, to see the hospital manager, the head honcho. He'd never forget. It was raining outside, torrential rain and even the heating boiler in the basement had failed, so the hospital was cold, damp, and dank. The man sat behind a desk as he wheeled himself into the office. His face was as gray and miserable as the weather. He told him his parents were dead, killed in an auto crash late at night on the freeway. No one else was involved. They just ran off a bridge into a deep ravine. Faulty brakes, maybe. There was no evidence his father had been drinking. But he knew. Knew they blamed themselves, in some crazy way. So they were gone, and it was as if he could feel every inch of that terrifying, long, lonely final drop. It left another part of his life wrenched away. Missing, gone for good. His parents had taken the only way out they saw left to them, in their bitter misery and shame.

Sure, Dad had been a real fighter, and my mother went with him all the way. But there are some battles you just can't win.

He planned his exit strategy, like he knew his parents had done. Every good soldier, every commander, had to have an exit strategy for when things went awry. And they couldn't go more awry than this. It was then the pain began to hit him in shattering waves that left him literally gasping for breath, as they started to wind back the meds.

He worked it all out. It was just a matter of timing. And that was when Doc Hermann found him sitting in the rusting Chevrolet Camaro he could no longer drive, a gun in his hand.

He'd asked them to bring the car to the hospital parking lot. He told them it would help his rehabilitation, to be able to look forward to driving it. Hermann van Rhoos, a doctor at MIT, researching the new frontiers of neuroprosthetics, came across him in there and talked him out of it. And gave him his life back, or as much of it as he could.

* * *

His newly restored Camaro, 1967 vintage, the best year in his opinion, turned heads as it braked to a halt. The paintwork, Bolero Red, and the 350 cubic inch power plant under the hood, marked it out as something very special. The sleek, shiny, classic Chevy was out of place here, almost as much as a NASA shuttle would have been. The car was a rare oddity in this neighborhood of sadly neglected homes, overgrown front yards, sagging roofs, and peeling paintwork. Most were in desperate need of more than a little tender loving care. Much more. Demolition may have been one option. Except that they were people's homes, or were before recession ripped the heart out of the community. They were the kernels of people's lives, the pinnacle of their ambitions. Now, many were little more than lop-sided shacks, the graveyards of broken dreams. The glossy mall that overshadowed them in the next street was a stark contrast. Even in daylight, the neon-lit, garishly painted hoardings mocked the poverty they overlooked. Their brash shadows illuminated cars sagging with age, sitting low on their worn-out springs, tired and in need of maintenance. Some of them were jacked up on bricks. Weed grew through the fenders. Even the dark, angry sky seemed as if the weather gods looked less favorably on this part of the city. Viscous clouds raced past, and puddles of water in the street were evidence of an earlier downpour that settled on the rutted tarmac. It could have been rustbelt America, another victim of the economic catastrophe that had brought ruin to so many aspiring families. Yet this was not the remains of Detroit's auto industry, or Pennsylvania's steel mills, abandoned to become rusted skeletons of once mighty factories. It was Boston, cultural capital of middle-class New England, home of MIT and Harvard; images of sophomores rowing on the Charles River and dawdling in the golden sunshine around the harbor and old town, theater, music, history, and culture. Yet this was the other Boston, the one that never featured in the guidebooks, the one the touring orchestras never reached. Never wanted to. In this place, the red car stood out like a late model Cadillac in a junkyard, the paintwork too clean and the engine too smooth. The man climbed out of the car and looked up at the sky. He appeared to wait a moment or two while he savored the wind and then glanced around at his surroundings, as if his vivid blue eyes constantly checked for…what? A careful man, and as much an oddity around here as his car. Anyone coming face-to-face with him would form the impression of a once decent-looking guy, yet now somewhat battered. The skin of his face looked oddly stretched, as if he'd had a long, hard life. Yet he was no more than thirty years old, not enough time to account for the signs of stress. His mid-brown, wavy hair, which fell loose to his shoulders, had started to show strands of gray, despite his comparatively young age. He was tall, about six one, with broad shoulders and narrow hips, the erect, trim body of an athlete, or a soldier. Probably the latter, the three-inch scar on his face, just below his right eye, suggested he'd seen his share of action.

He walked with a swagger, or maybe it was the suggestion of a slight limp. Whatever, it hadn't dented his confidence, his self-worth. He looked like a man who was in control, who knew how overcome any obstacle. It would have been a false impression. He crossed the front yard of the house like a soldier marching into battle. He spared a quick glance for a guy who was busy hammering a stake into the ground, a pole bearing a realtor's sale board. Then he moved on. He marched up to the front door and surveyed his surroundings once more. Jack Taylor was a soldier, or had been, before the bomb that shattered his body and his mind. The habit of checking his surroundings died hard. He banged on the door and waited. It opened a few inches.

"Yes?"

It was a tall, thin, stooped woman who spoke. She looked as tired as the rest of the neighborhood. Her once proud, beautiful black face was now careworn, her clothes shabby, and she looked to be growing old before her time. He was puzzled. He knew Evie Harper wasn't old. In fact, he recalled she still hadn't made it to thirty. But her lined face told a different story, that somehow she'd passed forty. Her expression was unwelcoming, suspicious.

"Evie? It's Jack, Jack Taylor. You remember me? I served with Wesley. I thought I'd call and see how he was doing."

Her face showed relief, and she visibly relaxed. "Jack, yeah, come on in. He'll be glad to see a familiar face." She looked him over and gave him a puzzled look, "But I thought you..."

He nodded. "Long story, Evie. I'm okay now, really."

She looked doubtful but moved aside, and he stepped into the house. Wes waited inside. He didn't look any better than Evie. His forehead was creased with deep worry lines, and he looked older than his wife. Yet Taylor knew he was a year or two younger than Evie. His face was deeply etched with the lines and scars of Post Traumatic Stress Disorder, PTSD. The black Petty Officer been sent home from Afghanistan after a distinguished career that had been the envy of most of his comrades in the unit. More than once he'd put his life on the line for his comrades, and he had a heap of medals and citations to prove it. But when the dark blanket of PTSD clouded his mind, when he couldn't escape the thick fog swamping his psyche after the explosion that destroyed the platoon, he was shipped home without a second thought. Taylor was still in hospital at the time, recovering from the devastation of his own shattered body, but he'd made dozens of calls and written scores of letters, fighting hard to keep Wes in the service. He knew he needed his comrades around him to help fight off the invisible enemy, the one that was in his head. The platoon, the Seals, they were his second family. He needed to be in the field, like getting back on the horse after a fall. You leave it too long, and a man's courage deserted him, forever. But his efforts went nowhere, and the bureaucracy had their victory. Petty Officer Wesley Harper was discharged to endure his suffering alone.

That was the military. Now Wes, almost a stranger, came forward slowly. His movements were stiff, and he held out his hand. He tried to force a smile, but it came out lopsided as if some of his facial muscles were frozen, like a stroke victim.

"Lieutenant Taylor! It's great to see you, man. Damn, I thought we were out of friends in this hard ole' world. Jeez, this is so good." His eyes looked down, and he adopted the same puzzled expression as his wife when he'd arrived. He squinted at Taylor's legs. "Lt, what gives? Your legs, after that blast, I thought you…"

"Long story, Wes. And I'm not in the service, not any more. It's Jack." Taylor pasted on a smile, "I'm fixed up now, that's all that matters. Tell me about yourself, how's everything going?"

As he spoke, he looked around the room, just moving his eyes, not making it obvious. The Wes and Evie Harper he recalled were proud folks, and they kept their home spotless. Now it was shrouded in dust, the couch torn where a spring had come through the fabric and not been repaired, and the windows overlooking the unkempt yard were way past due for a clean. The glass was cracked too in a couple of places. The place smelled musty, uncared for. Poor.

"We're, er, okay, Lieutenant, uh, Jack." Wes tried and failed to return the smile. His voice was slow and ponderous, as if talking was an effort. "Yeah, we're getting by."

"Horseshit!"

They both swiveled to look at Evie as she snapped out the single word. She stood by the kitchen door; hands on hips, her mouth tight with fury, and Jack recognized

ERIC MEYER

something of the old Evie, the tall, proud black princess that Wes had thought himself so fortunate to marry.

"What do you mean, Evie?"

Wes looked away; clearly embarrassed by his wife's interruption, or by the way they lived? Or both.

"What do I mean, Jack? You see that leech out in the front yard? He's putting up a sale sign. When he's done, he'll tack the foreclosure notice to the front door, and we'll have the vultures come clamoring around, looking for easy pickings after we're forced out of our home."

"But, why? What's the problem?"

The Harpers were proud, hardworking folk, who paid their bills on time and never got into debt. Something was very wrong.

She snorted. "Why? Because we didn't pay the damn mortgage on time, that's why. Wes' pension covered it okay, and I work for an insurance company in the city, so we got by. Then we had some medical bills that the VA refused to pay, and we fell a month behind. One damn month! So they foreclosed."

"They can't do that, surely, not for a month."

She grimaced. "Yeah, they can do it, Jack. They can do what they damn well please. They have done it. It's all up front and legal, like it says in the agreement."

"But why? I don't get it. It won't do them any good. It'd be better for them if you kept making the payments in the future."

She snorted. "Yeah, we can do that, but they won't let us. You saw the mall in the next street? They want to expand the parking lot, make it bigger and use some of the space for new showrooms. It's worth more money to knock this place down and level the site, so the mall developers can use it for parking cars. It makes more money than people."

She was almost in tears, so he looked away and out the window. The guy had almost finished banging in the sale sign. He looked back at Evie.

"You want me to talk to these people, Evie. It's not too late. You haven't gone yet. Maybe they'll see sense."

He looked across at Wes, but his old buddy showed little interest. She shrugged.

"I don't know, man. You think it would help?"

"It might. I can at least try and get them to listen, and maybe they'll see sense. Let me get rid of that guy outside. He shouldn't be doing that to you. I need to go somewhere this afternoon, an appointment I have to keep. I'll go see the developer who holds the mortgage first thing tomorrow. I'm sure they'll be okay."

Her eyes conveyed the doubt she felt in her mind. She made no reply, just gave him a slight nod of her head. Wes finally looked at him.

"You always did take care of the guys in your platoon, Jack." His voice was dulled and croaky, little more than a whispered murmur.

Maybe the poor guy's on psychotropic drugs for his PTSD.

"That was my job, Wes. It still is, man, nothing's changed. You want anything; I'm here for you. I haven't forgotten that when I needed someone to watch my back, you were always there for me. Always. It's SOP, my friend." Evie looked puzzled. "Standard Operating Procedure," he explained.

She nodded her understanding. "Yeah, but I doubt it'll do any good tomorrow. In that company, SOP stands for Shit On People."

He smiled. "Let me talk to them first before you give up hope. People are not always as bad as they appear."

She tried and failed to hide her skepticism. "Yeah, right. Thanks, Jack. Hey, it's good to see you on your feet. How the hell did you manage it, I mean, after the explosion? Your legs…"

He grinned. "I got fixed up. I'm okay now. I'll call by tomorrow when I've had a chance to talk to these guys. You take care now, you and Wes."

She shook her head doubtfully, looking at his legs. "You too, Lieutenant."

"Jack."

She nodded. He went to walk back out the front door, wincing as fresh agony lanced through him. An outsider would barely have noticed the slight hesitation.

It's just a bunch of nerve endings screwing with my mind. Fuck 'em! There is no pain.

But he knew he'd need to score pretty soon, something pretty strong. It was bad.

"Hey, feller."

The man looked around at him, his expression bored, uninterested. He was big, well over six feet, maybe six and a half, and red-faced from too much drinking with his buddies in the local bar. A tank-brain. Hired muscle, he looked like he had his share of Native American ancestry. The man had olive skin, dark squinty eyes, and black hair tied in a ponytail. Scuffed cowboy boots, working jeans, and a Carhartt jacket that looked as if it had gone around the world more than once. He wasn't impressed with what he saw, so he ignored Taylor and carried on thumping in the pole.

"Friend, would you to stop that. Please, leave it alone."

He shouted this time, putting a hard edge to his voice. Maybe the guy would get the idea, but he still carried on banging the pole into the ground.

What is he, a robot?

Taylor finally confronted him directly. He stood only a foot away from the muscle's face, crowding him so he had to stop using the hammer.

"Listen, I've asked you politely. Now I want you to stop. I'll see your boss in the morning, and all this will be resolved. There isn't going to be any sale." He tried the man with what he hoped was a winning smile. "So there's no need for the sign. Save your energy, buddy. What the hell, why waste your time?" He glanced up at the sky. A fine rain had started to fall. "It's crappy weather, not worth you getting yourself wet for."

Except he needs a wash, he stinks of sweat, tobacco, stale booze, and unwashed clothes.

The man stared back, his face a mask of granite disinterest. Finally, he spoke.

"Get out of my way, Mister. I have a job to do, and you're starting to annoy me. Either move, or I'll move you."

Even his voice was robotic, like Arnold Schwarzenegger on Prozac. He put his hand on Taylor's chest as if to push him away, but at the last second sucker punched him with the other hand. His knuckles grazed Taylor's jaw as he narrowly missed connecting with a vicious blow.

Why do people have to make life so difficult? Did he see the limp and guessed he was dealing with some cripple who'd happened along? Wrong guess, buddy.

Taylor's fist snapped out, so quick it was like the lightning-fast strike of a rattlesnake. The hard bone of his

ERIC MEYER

knuckles caught the big man square on a vital artery, and
he gasped with pain as he struggled to draw breath. He
went down but only on one knee, and then he came right
back up. His eyes blazed, betraying a window to the black,
murderous intent in his soul. Taylor didn't miss the look.
He'd seen it many times before, was waiting for it, ready
for it. He chopped the guy, not too hard but enough to
temporarily paralyze him, to show that he meant business.
The man sank back down on one knee. This time he
stayed down, breathing heavily, snorting, shaking his head
like a prizefighter that'd been one too many rounds with
the champ.

"I don't want to hurt you, buddy, but you're not going
to put that sign into the ground. I told you. I'll call your
boss, so take it easy. Let's see what he says before anyone
does anything stupid."

The guy shook his head to clear it and wobbled to his
feet. He stared at Taylor, a menacing glance that displayed
his murderous fury. He wanted to take this limping
man apart, piece-by-piece. Would have, it he thought he
could. For a few moments, Jack thought his message still
hadn't got through, but finally the muscle saw sense. He
put a hand up to his head, flicked his ponytail back, and
straightened his battered Carhartt, darting Taylor another
vicious look, as if to say, 'Look what you did to my coat!'

Yeah, you're a real fashion icon, pal.

He winced and grunted with pain as he moved away
from the confrontation. Then he pulled up the sign and
carried it back to his beat-up Dodge. As he climbed into
the cab, he turned back and spat out, "The next time I see
you, motherfucker, that pole won't go into the ground. I'll
stick it up your ass. If I were you, I'd keep my nose out of

other people's business, feller."

He slammed the door, started the engine and roared off, leaving a few dollars of black rubber tire marks on the tarmac, and a cloud of exhaust smoke lingering in the street like the puff of smoke that signals an Indian attack. Maybe that's what it is, a smoke signal, the guy sure looked part Indian. Or is it Native American? The guys in my platoon were happy to be called either Indian or Native American, didn't give a damn either way.

Taylor looked back at the house where he could see Wes and Evie watching from the window. He smiled and nodded, then got into his Camaro, and drove away. The rain started to beat down in earnest as he floored the gas pedal. He put the windshield wipers on high speed and headed into the city. He had an appointment to keep at MIT, a very important appointment.

He found a parking slot close to the Massachusetts Institute of Technology. The rain had stopped, the sun was shining again, and he felt almost good to be alive as he walked the block and a half to the annex of that venerable institution. Its tree-lined campus and pillared façade were familiar to him after so many visits, almost like home, but not quite. He wasn't here for the learning. It was something far, far more important than a post-graduate degree in engineering science, to him, anyway. He walked around to the outbuilding where Hermann had his laboratory; the lab that had given him his life back. The pain was searing, firing razor-sharp darts of raw agony through his body.

I'd sooner face a hostile raghead with an AK-47 on full auto than this incessant, invisible assault on my nervous system.

It kept hitting him with fresh, hot waves of agony,

and he felt a keen anticipation of relief as he paused outside the door of his old friend, Doctor Hermann van Rhoos. He stretched his lips into a smile as he looked at the sign fastened to the door. It was a kind of mission statement. 'Two legs good, tin legs better.' Doc Hermann was a neuroprosthetics specialist. No, that was an understatement, like saying Einstein was good at sums. Hermann was an unsung genius, a man who devoted his life to bringing back hope to those who thought they'd lost it forever. He knocked on the door. It was locked as always. The people who came here were not usually comfortable to advertise their shortcomings to the world. Hermann opened it and gave him a smile of greeting.

"Jack, how you doing?" He looked at his wristwatch. "By my reckoning, you're about a half-hour late. Problems?"

"Nothing I couldn't handle. What have you got for me today, Doc?"

"Is it bad?" Van Rhoos stared into his eyes, searching for and finding the signs he suspected would be there; pain, a bombardment of exquisite torture. Hermann could work miracles with lost limbs, but he couldn't achieve everything his patients desperately needed, most of it, but not all.

"Yeah, not so good."

"You want a shot?"

"Like you wouldn't believe."

Hermann gave him the blessed injection of Oxycodone, straight into the vein. It was way too little, too seldom, but it was all he was allowed to give, and when it was so bad, the release from the agony was as good as a major lottery win. Then he set to the real work, the reason Taylor had come. Van Rhoos had developed new software that promised to give Taylor even greater reliability and mobility with his new legs. His tin legs.

The downside was the pain. He knew was dependent on the drugs, illegal drugs. Preferably shot into the vein. Heroin, morphine, Oxy, it didn't matter as long as it did the job. Officially, he was prescribed with painkilling tablets, but taking oral medication was like pissing on a burning building. It achieved little. He injected frequently, despising what he did even as he stabbed the needle into his vein, and so he'd become reliant on approaching sellers on littered, dark, grime-encrusted street corners. Buying from the lowest forms of life, the dealers who were at the bottom of the food chain, the bringers of death. They were scum, for sure. Yet for him they brought life, the only way he could keep his sanity. He floated between mind-fuddled delusions, weird dreams, and the all-too-real world of the doped up cripple, as his life seesawed between comfort and pain. But the respite became more infrequent. It was only a short journey to a suicidal slough of depression, and he reached it when the meds finally wore off, and in a lucid moment he understood where he was going. Nowhere.

Hermann was a brilliant yet controversial figure, often at loggerheads with his more conservative colleagues at MIT. His brand of research, which combined prosthetic limbs with a new, sophisticated and radical technology that linked the latest microelectronic devices directly to the nerve endings that fed to the brain, gave hope to many desperate amputees.

The science was known as neuroprosthetics. Utilizing a brain-computer interface to capture electrical signals through the nervous system, scientists developed tiny microelectrode arrays smaller than a square centimeter.

Hermann was one of the pioneers who implanted the new electrodes to decode neuronal signals and generate electrical activity in the robotic creations, enabling the construction of a microscopic transducer to send information to the sophisticated artificial limb. Each cybernetic limb was a marvel of ultra-miniaturization, enabling them to pack in enough discrete electronics and servos to navigate the space shuttle. Hermann spent a great deal of time and resources developing his space-age limbs, constantly revising both the control software and the hardware to give new life and new hope to amputees. So far, his ambition to develop limbs that were better than the originals was a dream that was about to come true.

Many branded his research dangerous and potentially life threatening to those patients in his care. Hermann van Rhoos ignored them all. He fitted Jack with the latest artificial limbs, equipment which he managed to connect to Jack's nervous system by means of radical surgery. And yes, it was dangerous. Jack smiled as he remembered being warned.

How dangerous can anything be to a man who has nothing left to live for?

The new devices weren't perfect, and Hermann continually adjusted the systems that interfaced his brain with the new legs and controlled them by means of embedded, programmed discrete chips. As a result, he had almost as much freedom of movement as he had before he'd lost his legs. Each visit brought new improvements that made things that bit better, and his new legs that much stronger. Hermann insisted they were better than they'd ever been, and maybe he was right. They were still improving as he tweaked them with each visit, but the pain was always with him too, except for those few blessed hours of relief when he fed his drug habit.

Hermann was a person who genuinely cared for his fellow man, as he strived to heal what troubled them. Taylor was a fraction under six feet tall, but van Rhoos towered over him, at least two inches taller and almost twice as broad as the former Seal. He had smiling blue eyes in a smooth face sporting a broken nose, a reminder of his footballing days. Nowadays he kept in shape with a daily row along the Charles River. In spite of the blue eyes, his skin was olive, and his head topped with curling black hair, doubtless a legacy of unknown ancestors. Surprisingly, he affected a gold ring in the lobe of his right ear, making him look even more like a Latino, or maybe a gypsy. It was a startlingly dramatic face, vital and full of compassion, but what one noticed most was that it radiated life.

Van Rhoos looked him over, frowning. Taylor knew that nothing escaped him. "I've made some adjustments to the control algorithm. I think you'll find the legs will respond much faster than before."

"How many microseconds this time? Taylor grinned.

"I estimate 1.5 at least. It may not sound a great deal, but believe me you'll notice a difference, especially in your response times. Climb into the chair, and let's take a look at you."

He knew the procedure. He pulled off his pants and sat in the former dental chair van Rhoos used when he was making adjustments to the limbs he'd created. The legs had titanium knee joints that for some reason the doc insisted had to be left uncovered. He told people it made him feel like C3PO. At the top of each of the limbs was a socket where van Rhoos could insert a plug to interface the limbs with his mainframe computer. There were also inspection ports, plastic caps, two on each side that allowed Hermann to insert a range of probes and equipment to monitor the connections between the human and the artificial.

Taylor didn't know how it worked. Only that since his association with Hermann, his life had taken on new hope, and a new meaning. He could walk, so he could stand proud and take his place, stand beside anyone as a fully functioning human being, more or less. It was a dream come true for him, and he gave up all thoughts of ending his life. He watched as Hermann manipulated the plugs and sockets, all the time humming a piece of Mozart while he made the connections. The other love of his life was opera, and it was SOP for Taylor to listen to the soaring notes of Mozart's The Magic Flute while Hermann worked. It was a strange feeling as he began uploading the new algorithm. One moment his legs were functioning almost normally, and then they were dead, refusing to respond to the commands his brain fired at them. He waited patiently while Hermann worked, and then he heard the sixty-four dollar question.

"How are you doing with the medication?"

"It's okay. I get by."

"Yeah, sure. Have you managed to cut down that stuff? You were hitting that crap pretty heavy last time I saw you. What was it, about two weeks ago?"

"It was seven days, Doc, and you know it. I'm still working on it, trying to cut down."

Trying and failing.

"So you're going to those sellers, are you? You know it's a one-way street, Jack. It'll kill you, sooner or later."

"Yeah, I know where it's headed, but I keep working on

cutting down. It's just a matter of time."

Hermann grunted. He hit a button on the keyboard and said, "Try it now, see how it feels."

He sent the command from his brain to lift his leg from the knee, and while he held it up, moved his foot from left to right. Hermann ordered him to go through a range of basic diagnostic exercises and nodded his approval.

"That looks good. Good response times."

"It feels good, Doc. Better than good! I can feel the legs responding to my brain signals quicker than ever. It's strange, almost like it was before I lost them, but in some way even better."

"Don't get too carried away. There's a way to go before they're perfect. I did notice one glitch when I was checking through the machine code. For some reason if you were turning quickly with your legs bent and something hit you on the knee, the legs could freeze. To be honest, it's an unlikely scenario, and I doubt it'll ever happen. But if it does, you'll need to call me, and I'll come out and reinstall the software."

"I'll be careful, Doc. It's worth anything to be back on my feet."

Hermann nodded. He seemed content with what he'd achieved. "I'll keep working on them, Jack. Believe me, when I've finished with you, you'll put the Six Million Dollar man to shame." Then his voice changed, and he sounded grave, "That other business, the drugs, that's something I can't help you with. I realize the pain must be shocking at times, and I don't admit to having all the answers. I only wish I did. But you've got to keep working at it, and try cutting down on the doses. If the cops arrest you, you'll be in real shit. You won't get any analgesics in

State prison."

Taylor nodded, stepped down from the chair, and put his pants back on. The legs did feel good. They took his weight, and he took some steps around the laboratory to check them out. He felt as if he could run twenty miles without stopping. He felt strong, powerful, and he had his life back, except for the pain.

"This is great, Doc. Thanks a million. I'll work on the other thing, believe me."

"Yeah I know you will. You're more than welcome, Jack. Back again in a week, unless you run into any problems; just let me know."

They shook hands, and he left the laboratory, walking through the dark labyrinthine corridors of MIT and out into the street. He felt good. He felt strong and renewed, human.

He drove into the city center, careful to keep his speed down until he was more used to the different sensations in his legs. He drove into the parking garage he rented, nodded a greeting to Chuck, the attendant who kept an eye on his wheels, and walked the five hundred yards to the cramped ground floor apartment he rented in a converted warehouse in the North End. By the time he sat down with a cold beer from the icebox, he knew the new programming would give him a quantum leap in his mobility. He'd watched his reflection in store windows as he walked past, and the limp had all but disappeared. He'd work on that. Outside the evening was approaching, and the light was fading. He should stir himself and make a meal from the tiny kitchenette just off the lounge, but he wasn't hungry, not for food. The session with Hermann van Rhoos had left him exhausted as it always did, and the problems Wes Harper and Evie had with their mortgage company left him worried. He'd done his best to reassure them, and he'd continue to do his best in the morning when he approached the finance company, but he wasn't under any illusions. These people were like sharks, basking in the murky waters of low-income families and high profits developments. They'd do anything to turn a fast buck. The only thing that would concern them when a decent family was thrown out on the street was whether they could turn an extra buck or two, by maybe robbing them of even more. He tried to concentrate his mind on working through the problem, but in the end it was useless. Only one thing was foremost in his head. The pain.

There is no pain. Yes there is! Fuck, it hurts like hell.

He felt the increasing misery that always came when he knew exactly where he would be going, what he would be doing, and how low he'd feel for doing it. It was as if he was nothing more than a slavering dog, answering the imperative ring of Pavlov's bell. Yet he had no more freedom of action than those poor canines in the old Imperial Russia.

It's too much, the pain, if only it would stop.

And yet, there was only one way to make it end. At first, he'd been prescribed Oxycodone. As his tolerance increased, he needed more and more, until finally the physician called a halt.

"Jack, you have to realize this is no way to deal with your pain. We have to find another way to help you without turning you into an addict."

At first, he'd been naive enough to believe the doc at the VA hospital had been on the level. It was only afterward, when the agony became unbearable, and he spent countless nights lying in a sweat soaked bed, conscious of his missing limbs, that he realized the guy had been feeding him a line. The government insisted on a clampdown on the prescribing of powerful drugs, and Taylor had fallen victim to the VA physician following the government edict. They never did find another way to help him. In fact, they left him to cope on his own, in any way he could.

And tonight, I'll be out looking for my next fix.

He strolled along Chelsea, still checking his gait in the store windows, and turned into Paris Street to the playground. He knew that at this time it would be empty, and the tree-lined play area gave sufficient cover for the people who took over the park when the children had gone home. Cars were parked nearby, and he recognized some of them. They were always there, always the same cars, always the same dealers. Sometimes the cops ran them in, and they would be off the streets for a day or two, but then they'd be back. He knew the system. The Man, Quint, would be seated safely in the black Hummer, protected by one of his men with an Ingram or a Mac 10. The front guy, Derek, waited in the park, and Jack strolled through the trees to find him. He was black, his face wasted and lined with the ruin of years of abuse. He wore Nike Airs on his feet, the ones with the built-in electronics to monitor your running, shiny nylon training pants drooping from his ass, black with a white stripe down the leg, and an expensive black leather Armani jacket. His hair was twisted into rats tails, threaded with bright colored beads. When he smiled a greeting, Taylor recoiled at the man's obvious problem with halitosis, seeping out of a mouth that showed blackened and missing teeth.

"What can we do for you, my man?"

"The usual," Taylor replied flatly, hating himself.

"I got you some nice smack if you fancy something stronger, man."

He shook his head. "I'll just take the Oxy. Fifty dollars."

The man shook his head, tried, and failed, to smile apologetically.

"Nah, fifty don't cut it. Motherfuckers been all over us lately, and that Oxy shit is hard to get. Price is eighty, man."

Taylor hid a grimace. He knew it was no good showing these people what you felt. Of course the price was eighty dollars. He was hooked, and they knew it. Their business demanded they jack up the price accordingly, until he was reduced to penny ante stick-ups in mom and pop stores to feed his addiction. It was the way of the world, their world.

"No way, my friend. You want me to dig out a new supplier, that's fine. But eighty dollars, forget it."

The man named Derek gnashed his rotting teeth as he thought it through. Probably Quint had put the price up to sixty dollars, and his man was making a few dollars on the side to help feed his habit. Eventually, they settled on seventy dollars, and Taylor knew he would have to begin the process of finding a new dealer; with all the risks it involved, impure product, and the constant risk of the cops busting in and arresting him. Something inside him shivered when he thought of being banged up in a cell with no access to the drugs he needed. It wasn't going to happen.

There is no pain. It's just an illusion.

He walked away, heading for home with the Oxy hidden away in the lining of his coat. It was probably the thought of the blessed relief that made him careless. He didn't notice the cruiser parked out of sight in a dark alley, or the homeless man leaning against a storefront ahead of him. He kicked himself for his stupidity. Back in the old days, he would never have missed either of the telltale signs. The homeless man was just that bit too perfect, his posture too upright, and his shoulders a little too broad.

"Hey, buddy, any chance of some help, here? I could do with a few dollars," he said hopefully, "or maybe you could spare some of that shit you got from the guy in the park."

The alarm bells in his head shrieked. He ran, twisting away from the plainclothes cop, and heading diagonally across the street to avoid the uniforms stationed in the cruiser. He heard a shout from behind him, and the car doors slam shut as the uniforms leapt out and ran after him. As he threaded his way through the narrow lanes and alleyways of the North End, he suddenly realized he was enjoying himself. The new software upgrade on his legs had made a difference, and he was running as swiftly as he could remember doing before the explosion that changed his life.

Except that when I stop after this amount of effort, the agony will be unimaginable. Thank Christ for the Oxy.

"Stop, Mister, police. You stop there or I shoot."

They may as well shoot. He wasn't about to give up and spend days of mind numbing agony in a police cell. A shot in the back and a quick end was the better option by far. He darted into yet another narrow lane behind a Chinese restaurant, waiting while the cops charged past out on the street.

What was it that alerted me to that fake homeless man? Right, the guy didn't stink. Not the acrid stench of dirt and decay of stale booze and urine.

He'd never have been caught out like that in the field. He'd run missions in a number of theaters and come across plenty of hostiles pretending to be something else. In Iraq, the blind beggar, the too-eager cab driver, and many more. He'd seen them all and killed more than a few.

I should have spotted that cop a mile off. I need to think about that. I lost my legs, not my wits.

The street was clear, and as the cops kept moving away from him, he made his way back home.

"Hey, Mister! Stop right there."

He swiveled quickly and saw the fake homeless man only a few yards away.

Fuck it! I should have shaken that guy, dammit! I must be slower than I thought.

Even worse, as he swiveled around, he'd felt something in his legs. He remembered Hermann's warning about being careful not to bring on a software crash if he swiveled sharply and something hit him on the knees at the same time. He made a mental note to be careful, even as he started running again.

"Stop! Police. Stop or I shoot."

He ran on and was at least satisfied that he appeared to be gaining on the cop chasing him. And then the shot rang out, a single shot that experience told him was from a 9mm pistol, probably a police issue Glock. The bullet whistled a few feet over his head. The guy was aiming to miss. Automatically, Taylor grabbed for his own gun, as he had done a hundred times before when in action, but this time he had no gun. He had no armored vest, no commo system. No platoon of skilled and heavily armed Seals in close support and a gunship hovering overhead. This was

New York City, and he was a civilian fleeing from a cop. A cop who knew he'd been involved in an illegal drug buy.

I have to get away, have to!

The possibility of losing his newly acquired stash was something too horrifying to contemplate. He had to have the blessed relief of the Oxy, and no fucker was about to take it off him. He saw a narrow gap between two buildings, a dark alleyway, and dived into it. He kept running, hearing the footsteps and heavy breathing of the cop who was about ten yards behind him, and then he came to the end. There was no way out, nothing. He'd run into a cul-de-sac.

He cursed himself for the amateur he was. He'd come a long way from the Navy Seal who'd successfully returned from so many operations, until the last one. The cop was only five yards behind him. He knew he could take him, but it was the last thing on his mind to injure a guy who was just doing his job.

"Hold it right there, buddy. Turnaround and put your hands in the air."

Taylor mentally shrugged. He had to get out of it, had to. He had no choice. He turned to face the wall and put his hand up high. It was the only way to disarm the cop without hurting him real bad. The cop came up behind him, and once again Taylor smiled to himself at the absence of the giveaway stink that should have warned him before. The cop holstered his Glock, and Taylor heard the jingle of steel as he pulled out his cuffs and went to clamp one on his right wrist. That was enough. As soon as he had a picture in his brain of the position of the cop's hands, he turned. It was a lightning fast movement, and probably the man didn't even see what was coming. But the knowledge that his suspect was not where he should be was enough to alarm the man. He went to take a step back and un-holster his pistol, but he was too slow by at least half a second. Taylor's hand snaked out, and he found the pressure point on the man's neck. It was a machinelike motion, one he'd trained for so many times, and there never was any doubt of the outcome. His thumb pressed the carotid artery, and the cop fell to the ground like a sack of grain. Taylor made sure the guy's head didn't hit the concrete, and then he stooped and grabbed the Glock, and took off again. The guy would be out for maybe five minutes, but in that time there were plenty of chances for someone to happen by and seize the gift of a free Glock 9mm. He tucked it out of sight and walked away. He had no need of another pistol. He had plenty of his own hardware, enough to start a small war. Besides, he'd always found the Sig Sauer P226 a much better weapon. Once he'd wiped his prints off the Glock, he'd make sure it was returned to the local precinct. It would be easier to ditch it in the Charles River, but some instinct made him value firearms as tools to fight fanatics and bullies with, rather than essential equipment for stickup artists and drug gangs.

He put the key in the door and walked in. The pain was knifing through him in waves, like a frontal assault from a heavily armed enemy. It wasn't a bad analogy. It sure was the enemy, and the hurt was as bad as any of the gunshot wounds he'd taken in the field. Four in all, during his career on active missions, but they'd healed quickly. He rummaged in the drawer where he kept his kit, and seconds later was shooting up. The blessed warmth pumped through him, and the pain took a hike. He was about to clear away when his cell rang. He checked the display. Wes.

"Yeah, what is it, Wes? Anything wrong?"

At first, his former Seal buddy didn't speak. Then there was a sob. "They've been back, Jack."

"Who? That property outfit?" He checked the clock on the wall. It was 0100 hours, late for a commercial concern.

"Yeah."

Another sob.

"What is it, Wes? What happened?"

"It's Evie."

"Evie! They hurt her? Dammit, Wes, I'll come right away. You at home or in hospital?"

"I'm at home."

"Okay, I'll be right there. How is she?"

It came again, another sob. "Jack, they killed her. My Evie is dead."

CHAPTER TWO

The scene in the Harper's shabby house was not unfamiliar to a man versed in the kind of behind the lines warfare which for so long was part of Taylor's life. And Wes' too, during the time when they were part of the same unit, and engaged the enemy in scores of towns and villages across the battle scarred landscape of the Muslim fanatics. But this was no Third World shithole, nor part of the desperate struggle to gain ascendancy in what American soldiers knew as sandland. They were in Boston, admittedly a poor part of Boston, Dorchester. But still, a part of the Continental United States, and yet it was the same shabby squalor, the same cries of anguish and despair. Evie's family had arrived and was drenched in tears, apart from her brother who muttered angrily about revenge. Wes had almost entered a state of catatonic shock. He was standing just inside the front door, staring at the blank wall, with eyes that were red rimmed and deep pitted. Taylor joined him.

"Wes, I'm so sorry. How did it happen? Do you know

who did it?"

Wes turned to him, and the eyes were mirrors into the depths of his tortured soul. "It was them, that fucking property development company."

At first, Taylor tried to persuade him that despite his sorrow and anger, it was unlikely. Maybe they were a bunch of money grabbing thieves. Sure it was nothing new, but murdering a client they were about to foreclose? It was a hard one to swallow.

"Maybe it was an accident. These things happen, Wes. Kids on drugs, you know. They get high, drink too much, and start popping off their guns. You know what it's like. It happens all across America from time to time."

Taylor was brought up in a neat, middle class American home. How could his strict, buttoned-up naval officer father have contemplated anything less? Taylor senior expected to live the way he went to work, tight discipline and no misbehavior. Neat front lawns, and cars polished religiously as on a Sunday as going to church. They all knew about the drive-by shootings in poorer districts, the drugs, and the knifings. It was on the network news, daily headlines calculated to shock, the American nightmare.

"No, Jack. It was no accident. Neither was it any kids. It was those fuckers who want us out of here."

"I don't get it, my friend. How does killing Evie change anything?"

"We were resisting them, so they decided to send a warning. They want us out so they can bulldoze this place and develop the site. It's a clear message. I'm next if I don't get out."

"It's incredible, Wes, but listen, man, you must consider the alternatives. It could equally have been an accident, some kids playing around with Saturday night specials and popping off a few shots."

Wes stared at him for long and hard. Taylor could see he was reliving those last fateful moments.

"I was with her, Jack, in the same room. She was talking to me about how we may be able to hang in here. She said about you going to see the finance company might make a difference. Then the glass in the window shattered just as I heard the sound of two shots, and she was thrown backward. Tossed down, like a fucking piece of garbage! The blood, Jack, I tried to stop it. It was all over me. Oh, my Christ," he exclaimed from the depths of his agony, and then lapsed into floods of tears. Taylor waited, giving his friend the benefit of a few minutes to grieve. He was about to say something when Wes spat out the last part of his wife's death.

"It was an execution, no question. They hit her with a double tap, and it weren't no .38 pistol. It's not confirmed yet, but I've seen enough battlefield wounds. They hit her with a 7.62mm rifle. Maybe an AK-47, or one of the more modern NATO sniper rifles that use the same caliber round. They slaughtered her, butchered her as if she was worthless." Tears streamed down his tired face, and he tried to wipe them away. "Oh, fuck it, what can I do?"

Taylor turned away, to give his friend time to recover himself. If what he said was true, this was no drive-by shooting. The use of the military caliber rounds was an indication of a professional hit. It was true there were more and more AKs in the US as people were attracted to their mystique. Designed and built in the Soviet Union, the original AK-47 was one of the first true assault rifles to be manufactured. Even after sixty years, the model and its variants were the most widely used infantry rifle in the world, principally due to their low production cost and ease of use. The AK-47 was manufactured in many countries and had seen service with Third World armed forces, as well as irregular forces worldwide. More AK-type rifles were produced than all other assault rifles combined. But using a military assault rifle didn't prove a thing. The clincher was the double tap. It was a conventional and common technique of the military sniper, to ensure that when they hit a target, it stayed down, period. But his suggestion that the developer who held the mortgage was behind it still seemed fantastic. He felt a stab of guilt in his guts.

Maybe if I'd gone to see them today instead of keeping my appointment with Hermann, Evie would still be alive. What was that sign on Truman's desk? 'The Buck Stops Here.' Yeah, it's time to stop the buck passing and give my old buddy some practical help. They signed me up to lead these men, and I never chose to resign.

"Wes, tell me about this developer that holds the mortgage on this place. What's the name of the company?"

His friend looked up, and there was a spark of interest in his eyes. He scratched his head and said, "Shit, I can't remember. It was Evie who dealt with all the paperwork. Wait, I'll check out the file of letters she kept from them."

He went to a cardboard carton that was placed on the floor next to an armchair, which was undoubtedly where Evie would seat herself to go through the sheaf of documents she had received from the developer. He went to sit down while he rummaged through the box, but he couldn't bring himself to occupy 'her' chair. Not yet.

"It says here MMP Mall Corp." He was reading from

one of the many letters he'd removed from the carton. "I guess the M stands for Mehdi. He's the guy that owns the outfit, according to this. Mehdi Hussein."

They exchanged a glance. There was no need to say anything. The kind of name was familiar to any American who'd fought overseas. Fought the fanatical Islamic terrorists. Mainly Arabs.

"Now hold on, they're not all terrorists," Taylor reminded his friend. "I wouldn't draw any inference from the name."

"I don't," Wes grunted, "but it sure makes you think after what we've been through."

He nodded. "Listen, Wes, I'll pay them a visit in the morning. You can believe me, if I think they have a name to do with this, I won't let it rest."

"You'll call me, as soon as you find out anything?"

Jack stared at him, his mind racing as he tried to decide how to play this. His friend was seeking vengeance and was more than entitled to take it. But maybe he should remind him of the old Chinese proverb, 'Let him who seeks revenge dig two graves'.

"I'll have to call the cops first. That's the way to deal with it, Wes, but you'll be next on the list if I have any suspicion they're involved. If not, I'll do everything I can to find out who was behind it. Hey, why not come back to my place? You don't want to be on your own tonight."

He shook his head.

"I'll be fine, thanks. The cops will be back soon for a statement, and I have to take care of Evie's folks. Call me, Jack."

"I will, and that's a promise."

* * *

He stopped the Camaro a couple of blocks from the downtown Boston address listed as the head office for MMP. Parking so far away was a cautious move, the result of long and bitter experience in the field. He recalled that the guy knocking in the sign outside Wes' place might have seen the Camaro, so why help them out with a reminder? He was unarmed, and he considered for a moment unlocking the trunk and taking out his Sig Sauer, but he wasn't ready to carry a concealed firearm. Not yet, anyway. Maybe later. He opened the glove box and took out the trusty old combat knife he'd carried on many missions overseas. He looked at it for a moment, the battered hilt and razor sharp blade, still dulled and blackened to prevent any light from reflecting from the exposed steel. He tucked it inside his coat and climbed out of the Chevy. His first surprise came at the building. MMP occupied the top floor of a neat, six-story office block. The top floor, that meant the executive floor. They were doing well. The guard in the foyer directed him to the elevators.

"Top floor, buddy."

"Thanks. They're doing well, this MMP outfit."

"You'd better believe it. They own the whole building and lease out the other floors." He glanced around to make sure no one was listening. "They've got more money than Fort Knox, yet they still pay me minimum wage."

"Right. Let's hope it puts them in a good mood today, I'm asking them for a favor."

The guard laughed. "I wouldn't bet your shirt on getting it. You got an appointment?"

Taylor shook his head. "No."

The man looked doubtful. "They don't normally see anyone without an appointment."

Jack smiled. "I'm pretty sure they'll see me."

"Your funeral, buddy."

He turned away and continued reading the sports pages. He was obviously there more for show than for any security he offered the occupants of the building. Taylor rode the elevator to the top floor and walked out into a reception area. A girl was seated behind the desk with a telephone headset in her ear and a nail file in her hands. She didn't look at him as he waited for her. Instead, she continued talking to someone the other end of the phone. Taylor gathered from the sign on her desk she was named Millie. He cleared his throat, but there was no response. He tried talking to her over her conversation.

"Ma'am, if I could have your attention for just one moment."

Nothing. He reached over, lifted the headset from her head, and tossed it across the office. She stared at him in shock.

"You can't…"

"If I could just have a moment of your time, Ma'am, I need to speak with Mr. Hussein."

Her nose flared in a juvenile attempt at a put down. "Mister, before I call the cops, I can tell you Mr. Hussein doesn't see anyone without an appointment."

She got to her feet and flounced across the office to retrieve her telephone headset, maybe to call the cops, maybe to continue talking to her friend. He couldn't care one way or the other. He stepped around the reception desk. There was a door nearby which bore the sign 'Manager'. He heard her screaming at him to 'Stop right there', but he ignored her, pushed open the door and went in, closing it behind him.

In front of him a guy was seated behind a large desk, covered with an assortment of papers and junk. It seemed the man who owned the desk was not possessed of a tidy mind. He jumped to his feet in alarm as he saw the intruder. The man was well dressed, if you liked 80s kitsch; a cream linen jacket, tailored pants, sunlamp tan, and shirt unbuttoned to show lots of chest hair. It matched the carefully styled black curls arranged on his head to hide his premature baldness. He was of medium height, a man trying, and failing, to appear fit and healthy. He had watery blue eyes and a thin, undernourished chin. A carefully trimmed black mustache snuck across his upper lip.

So is this is the creep who runs the outfit?

"You can't..."

"You're the second person to say that to me in the space of a couple of minutes." He smiled to reassure the guy that he came in peace. "Are you Mr. Mehdi Hussein?"

The man's mouth had dropped open in astonishment at the intrusion, and he shook his head. He was also one hundred percent Caucasian.

"I guess not. So where is he, this Hussein?"

"Not here, and if you know what's good for you, you'll get out before you get hurt."

Jack smiled as he noticed the push-switch on the desk. Evidently, this was a high-risk business where it paid to have a means of calling the cavalry.

"I guess I'll have to take my chances. So where do I find this Mehdi Hussein?"

"He's not in the country, Mister. He travels a lot. If there are any questions about MMP, I deal with them. My name is Grant Williams, and I'm the general manager. But right now, I want you out of here. You want anything, you make an appointment."

Taylor heard the door open behind him. He turned in time to see three men enter the office. They were big.

So this is the MMP muscle. That's interesting, why do they need them?

Williams nodded at the biggest of the three.

"Gunter, get this motherfucker out of here! Show him how we deal with uninvited visitors."

The man who stood in the front of the new arrivals smiled. It didn't make his face appear any more inviting. All it did was show his broken teeth and cause his broken nose to twist like a bent wall plug. He was a huge man, tall, with massive shoulders, bulging biceps, and a powerful body that looked like its owner worked out. A lot. He had a small mouth, and thick, bushy eyebrows on his swarthy face. His pitch black eyes could only be described as plumb mean.

"It'll be my pleasure, Mr. Williams." He turned to his two partners, both big men, but dwarfed by him. "It's time for this son of a bitch to leave, the hard way. Get him out of here. Toss him down the staircase."

He watched while his two subordinates moved in. Taylor waited for the moment. It came when the man on his right swung his fist to smash it into his stomach. He telegraphed the movement way in advance, and Taylor moved slightly. The fist connected, but only with fresh air. As the guy was regaining his balance, he swiveled and took hold of the other man's hair, and yanked it down hard so his head collided with the adjacent desk. Taylor pushed him slightly to one side, and he fell to the floor, dazed.

The first guy had recovered, and launched another huge punch at Taylor's jaw. He threw up his hand to deflect the blow, hitting the guy with an uppercut that took him in the throat. The thug joined his colleague on the carpet, gasping to catch his breath. Taylor looked up quickly to see what their leader was doing, but so far, he hadn't moved. He just watched carefully, and when Taylor looked at the hard, cold eyes, eyes that were dark pools of evil, he knew in his heart that he wouldn't need to look much further than this for the man who'd killed Evie. He'd met men like this in the field, many times. He was a killer.

Finally, the big guy nodded and smiled, "So you know how to handle yourself, my friend, but you haven't tangled with Gunter Metz yet. You're finished, motherfucker. I'm going to take you apart piece by piece, before I throw you headfirst down the stairs."

He took a step toward Taylor, but his boss, Grant Williams shouted for him to stop.

"Wait, Gunter. I don't want a fucking war in my office. Help your guys out. They look like they need it, useless bastards." He fixed his eyes on Taylor. "Okay, Mister, you got my attention. What is it you want? I'll give you five minutes, and then this guy really will deal with you, and believe me, he's not like the two you just put down. Most people don't like to cross Gunter Metz. If they do, it's not a mistake they make twice. He'll nail your ass to the floor."

"With an AK-47?"

He saw Gunter and his boss exchange a quick glance. It was only a millisecond, but it was as good as a confession of guilt.

"I've come about Wes Harper," he continued. "I guess it's not news to you that his wife was shot dead last night."

Grant Williams tried to put on a contrite face. Jack almost laughed out loud; the expression was so contrived.

"Yeah, I heard. A terrible shame, give my condolences to Mr. Harper when you see him."

"I can do better than that. He doesn't need to lose his home at a time like this. I'd like to go back and tell him we can stop foreclosure, and he can keep it."

Williams spread his hands in a gesture that was supposed to say there was nothing he'd have liked better. He put on a sickly smile.

"It's out of my hands. The paperwork has all gone through, and it's just a question of him packing his things before the bulldozers go in."

"We can always send the bulldozers in while he's still there, Boss," Gunter Metz grunted.

"Can it, Gunter." He looked back at Taylor. "No, I'm sorry, they have to get out, and the sooner the better. The place is being redeveloped."

Yeah," the man called Gunter sneered, "and I guess Harper knows how dangerous these redevelopment sites can be."

"I said, can it," Williams reiterated.

He'd thought at first it was just grief talking when Wes told him this outfit was behind Evie's killing, but these cocky assholes were doing everything except admit what they'd done. They were almost making a joke of it between themselves, they were that confident of their cleverness.

"It won't be dangerous if you stop the foreclosure. His house won't be redeveloped."

Williams shrugged. "Time is up, buster. Get out of here. Don't force me to ask Gunter to show you the exit."

"I really want you to reconsider," Taylor said softly.

"Don't get me wrong, Mr. Williams. I'm asking you nicely, but the next time I ask it won't be so nice."

The manager chuckled. He looked at his hired muscle. The first two men had recovered and were scowling at Taylor.

"Toss him out, Gunter. And you two, do it right this time."

"My pleasure, Mr. Williams," Gunter replied.

Taylor raked them with his eyes, noting each man had a bulge under his coat.

They're carrying; it's as well to be forewarned.

He started toward the office door as if he was surrendering and about to leave. The three men moved in on him, their eyes glaring with hate, determined to take revenge. As their hands closed on his arms to hold him, he turned, stepped forward, and head-butted Gunter in the face, hearing an audible crack as the big man's already broken nose was broken yet again. He sidestepped as the guy struck back with a huge fist, and he chopped him on the side of his bull neck. Gunter gasped and went down on one knee. The other two men were grabbing at him again, and he felt a stunning blow to his kidneys that forced the wind out of him. The pain was terrible, but pain was something he was very familiar with. He ignored it, ducking a heavy blow that the other guy aimed at his head. Then he swept his leg around in a sliding kick that took his first assailant in the crotch and sent him screaming to the floor in agony. He ducked under another attempted punch from the second man, swiveled, and smashed his elbow into the man's solar plexus. The muscle was left gasping and choking, while Taylor readied himself to face Gunter again. The monster was staring at him with an expression of hate out of a face that had turned into a sodden, red mass of blood, snot, and broken tissue. Then he attacked, catapulting forward like a charging Andalusian bull. Taylor handled him just like the Spanish matadors would have done. He swiveled his hips and evaded the charge by a hair's breadth. At the same time, he took hold of the man's coat and helped his forward momentum, straight into the solid brick wall of the office. He could have sworn the building shook as Gunter's massive weight smashed into it, and he crashed to the floor. He was satisfied the man would not cause him any problems for the immediate future, so he looked back at Grant Williams, hoping the man would see sense. Instead, the manager's hand was snaking toward the drawer of his desk in an unmistakable gesture. He was about to pull a gun. Taylor was unarmed. Almost. He snatched out his combat knife by the hilt, changed the hold to the blade, and threw it in a move he'd practiced often. The huge, heavy blade flew unerringly at the man's hand, and went all the way through, to pin it to the desk.

"What the fuck!" he screamed. "Oh, Jesus fucking Christ, my hand, Fuck! Help me, it hurts!"

While he struggled, whimpering in agony, Taylor walked over and looked in the drawer. Sure enough, tucked in the drawer was a .38 Colt automatic, short barrel, a handy pocket pistol; handy enough to threaten any of MMP's clients who came to complain, and even handier to blow the head off anybody who attempted violence. He picked up the pistol and tucked it into the pocket of his coat. Williams was trying to pull out the combat knife to release his hand, without success. Taylor left it there.

"Have I got your attention, Mr. Williams?"

The manager was sweating with pain and fear. He nodded eagerly. "Yes, yes, tell me what you want, and get this fucking knife out of my hand."

Taylor put his hand on the hilt and ripped it out of the desk, freeing it from the tissue of the man's hand. Williams screamed, and blood welled out of the wound and began to form a pool on the desktop.

"Now you're being reasonable. First, I suggest you put something around that hand. I don't want you to bleed to death before we finish our business."

"There's a towel in the bathroom." The man nodded toward a door behind him.

Taylor walked over, and keeping an eye on the four men, put his hand inside and ripped the towel from the rail, throwing it at Williams.

"You know what I want. The foreclosure has to be cancelled. Someone's going to answer for the murder of Evie Harper, but I guess we'll let the cops deal with that one. In the meantime, I want my friend to keep his home."

Williams had been trying to stop the bleeding, but now he looked up at Taylor.

"Look, man, you've made your fucking point, and if I could stop this happening, I would. I don't want you chasing my ass every time Mr. Harper gets a letter through the post. But I can't! The only legal power to change anything belongs to Mr. Hussein, and he ain't here."

"Where is he?"

Williams hesitated for a few moments, obviously terrified of revealing too much about his boss.

Who the hell is this Mehdi Hussein? It may be I need to look into this mystery man's affairs more than I thought.

"I swear to God he's not here. He's in the Middle East.

56

He has business interests over there and won't return until the middle of next week. He's due back Tuesday evening, so I guess he'll be here Wednesday morning if you want to talk to him."

"Listen, you piece of shit. I'll talk to him. But in the meantime, I want you to reach him and tell him to get moving on putting a stop to that foreclosure. Don't give me any crap about you don't know his cellphone number. Just make sure you give him the message. Clear?"

"I'll do my best," Williams nodded sullenly.

"Good. You can also tell him that if anyone goes near Wes Harper's house, it'll be his or her last day on this earth. That's not a threat, that's a promise. If this little bar fight worries you, I can tell you it's nothing. Don't make me get serious about you people. That's the last warning you're going to get."

The man nodded. He slumped back into his chair, still trying to staunch the blood, and it looked like he was beaten. Taylor gazed around the office and noted the three men were all beginning to stir. Gunter was climbing to his feet, shaking his bloodied head. He looked at Taylor, gazing up and down as if sizing him up. Then his gaze went back down to Taylor's pants.

"What the fuck is that?"

He looked down and saw that his pants had got ripped during the fight. They gaped where the seam had opened at the knee. But instead of skin, there was the gleam of the knee joint that Hermann insisted had to stay uncovered.

"What are you, the fucking Terminator? Jesus Christ, the son of a bitch has got an artificial leg. He's a fucking cripple!"

Taylor went cold. He was on an equal footing, literally,

with any man, except when they caught sight of his artificial limbs. These men knew only one law, the law of the jungle. The law of who could bring the most violence to a confrontation. His artificial limbs were, in their eyes at least a sign of weakness. That meant he'd handed them a psychological advantage. It couldn't be helped, and it was time to leave. He didn't bother to comment on Gunter's observation, just walked steadily toward the door and opened it. Before he left, he turned back to Williams.

"Don't forget, you tell this Mehdi Hussein to do the right thing by Wes Harper. Otherwise, I'll be back."

It was the wrong thing to say. He could have bitten off his tongue.

"Right, he thinks he's the fucking Terminator," Gunter gloated. "Don't come back here, motherfucker. The next time I see you, I'll rip the fucking chip out of your brain."

Taylor gave him a cold stare and then left. He deliberately took the stairs down to the first floor. He'd almost left the misery and stigma of his lost limbs behind him after the genius of Doc Hermann's creations made him a man again. But pride dictated he demonstrate to these low lives he was anything but a cripple.

He made it back to his Camaro and climbed into the driver's seat. He needed to get home and change his pants, but he owed it to Wes to go see him and explain what they were facing. There was plenty to talk about. The most important being that MMP was undoubtedly a very violent and dangerous organization. Wes had called it right. He was now sure they'd killed Evie as a warning to get him out of his house. He started the engine and drove back to Dorchester, watching the urban landscape change as the gleaming high-rise buildings of downtown Boston gave way to the decay of the poorer suburbs. He was still pondering the threat of MMP when he pulled up outside the house. As he climbed out of the car, he was surprised to see a young woman in the front yard, taking photos with a digital camera.

If that don't beat all, they're figuring out the redevelopment even before they've kicked Wes out.

"Miss, what are you doing?"

She looked back at him coldly. One thing was for sure: she wasn't intimidated. Not in the slightest.

Whoever MMP is employing, this is one classy lady.

She was short, just over five feet, with short auburn hair styled to fall over one eye in a way that looked as sexy as hell. She reminded him of his girlfriend, Fay Helsing. They'd planned to spend their lives together, and yet he'd sent her away in tears. She'd never understand how he'd done it for her, so she could find herself someone who wasn't condemned to the life of a pain-wracked cripple.

I hated myself as I watched her walk out of the hospital room, her shoulders shaking as she sobbed uncontrollably. Christ, the guilt was almost too much to bear, but it had to be done.

He looked at the girl again. Vivid green eyes dominated a face that featured a snub nose, smooth, creamy skin, and full luscious lips. In his opinion it looked like they were made for kissing, not doing the dirty work of people like MMP. She wore narrow jeans and a tweed hacking jacket over a cream silk blouse. Her only jewelry was a necklace, and it looked like antique silver. She wore no ring he noticed, then wondered why he'd bothered to look. Despite her cold glance, her eyes sparked anger.

"What business is it of yours?"

He was impressed; she looked at him with a direct stare, suggesting it would take a lot to intimidate this girl.

A pity about her employer.

"I'm a friend of Wes Harper. I've made it my business to keep the scum who want to foreclose on him away from his home, so I'd suggest you put that camera away and hightail it out of here. You can tell you boss it's not going to happen."

She stared at him, and he felt her gaze penetrating like a powerful laser. Then she smiled.

"You really think I work for MMP?"

Taylor nodded. "It sure looks that way."

"You're wrong. I'm trying to help Wes, not harm him. He invited me here. You heard about Evie?"

He realized he'd miscalculated. "Yeah, I heard about Evie. That's another piece of unfinished business. I'm sorry about linking you to those scum."

They both looked as the front door opened, and Wes shuffled out onto the veranda.

"I see you've met Miss Donovan," he said to Taylor.

He looked at her, and she came toward him with her hand outstretched.

"My name is Kate Donovan. I work at the local law center. We're trying to help Wes find a way out of his trouble." As he shook her hand, she continued, "I guess you must be Jack Taylor, his friend from the Navy."

"That's right."

He felt the warmth and energy of her in that handshake.

My God, she's some woman, especially for a lawyer.

Wes called over to them.

"Why don't you come inside, and I'll make some coffee? We're all on the same side, so I guess we should all get acquainted." He looked at Taylor. "Did you get anywhere?"

"I went to see the developer, Wes, but I didn't get very far. I'm sorry, but I'm still working on it."

"Now you know they're not easy people to deal with. Come on in, both of you, let's hear the worst."

They were seated around the table in the kitchen. Wes had it covered with documents relating to the foreclosure.

"I guess I'd better explain," Kate began. "I'm keeping a photographic record of the houses in the area threatened with foreclosure, just in case they try any tricks like partial demolition and passing it off as vandalism or storm damage. I don't know if it will help," she said tiredly, pushing the lock of hair back in place that fell across her eye, "but I feel at this stage it's worth trying anything. Although it's hard to know what underhand trick they'll try next."

Taylor looked at Wes. "I don't need to tell you they're bad people, my friend. The type that will use any kind of underhand tactics they can get away with. I'm real sorry about Evie. It must be damn hard for you without her."

Wes nodded and wiped at a real or imagined tear in his eye. "I'll get by. Tell me what happened when you went there."

He explained the confrontation he'd had at their offices. He made light of the exchange of blows. Wes had enough on his mind without having to know about any more violence. He looked at his friend closely. He looked different. Since he'd joined the fight to help save his home, and his wife had been shot dead, something had happened to Wes Harper. The shuffling, zombielike PTSD victim of yesterday had transformed overnight into someone who looked like he had something to fight for. Maybe Wes had thought there was nothing he could do about the house, but it was obvious that MMP had made a huge mistake when they killed Evie. They'd turned a frightened, beaten man into one who was fast recovering his strength and looking for satisfaction. He looked back at the girl.

A lawyer, well, well. They sure make them pretty in these parts. More than pretty, she's gorgeous.

"What about you, Miss Donovan. Is there anything you can do from your law center?"

"It's Kate," she corrected him.

"Jack, Jack Taylor," he belatedly introduced himself, holding out his hand.

She gave him a small smile. "We're in a fix with this one, Jack. Mehdi Hussein knows the law. In fact, I suspect he could be a lawyer himself. He sure knows every trick in the book. The situation is he stands to make millions of dollars by developing this area. It's not just the parking lot. The city has produced a re-zoning plan, and they've agreed that if MMP can buy out the owners, the site can be redeveloped as a mixed retail and commercial area. I doubt that millions fully describes the money they'll make from the deal, more like tens of millions."

"So all he has to do is get people like Wes to leave, and they're home and dry?"

She nodded. "That's about the extent of it, yes. This company, MMP has interests all over Boston, and as far as we can tell, they're one of the biggest developers in New England. But they're crooked, like a cancer, a blight on the area, preying on poor people. Our law center has a number of cases involving them on the books right now, and we're trying to stop them from ruining people's lives. But how can you stop a company that is prepared to murder the families of people who oppose them?"

"There are ways," he mumbled, almost to himself.

"Not legal ways," she corrected him firmly.

Wes glanced at her. "If those bastards come back, I have a couple of surprises for them. I loaded the old Remington 12 gauge, and I put the Makarov I brought back from Iraq in a handy place."

Kate Donovan looked shocked. "Wes, you mustn't use guns. It can only lead to more trouble."

"More trouble? They've already killed my wife, there's only me left. If I have to go to join her, so be it. At least I'll take some of them with me. I'd remind you that I didn't start shooting at people. They did, but I intend to finish it."

She stood up, her face angry. "Jesus Christ, this is such macho bullshit. You guys need to remember you're in Boston. This is the cultural heart of New England, not some backwoods village in Afghanistan. You can't go charging off with loaded pistols to fight it out at dawn."

Taylor gave her an unimpressed glance. "It's too late for that, Kate. Last night they killed Evie, and this morning they pulled a gun on me when I visited them. If you want to give anyone free advice about the law, I'd suggest you start at the offices of MMP."

She calmed down. "Yeah, I take your point, but this has to be resolved legally, not with violence. I guess the first priority is for Wes to talk to the cops and find out where they're at."

"I tried them earlier," Wes mumbled. "Bastard detectives in charge of the case were too busy to come to the phone."

"Maybe they are busy, Wes. Perhaps they're overloaded with cases. Why don't you give them another call now, and we'll wait to see what they tell you?"

He nodded and went off into the hallway to make a call. Taylor and Kate sat in silence for a short time. Then they both spoke at once.

"Do you..."

"I think..."

They both laughed at each other, slightly self-consciously. "Go ahead," Taylor insisted.

Christ, you're beautiful.

"Okay then. We need to make more of an effort to contact the owner of MMP, this Mehdi Hussein. Somewhere along the line, he needs to put in an appearance so we can talk to him face-to-face, maybe even subpoena him if he refuses to show."

Taylor explained what Grant Williams had told him, that he was away until the following week on business. She shrugged.

"In that case, we have to wait. It could even work in our favor, him not being here. It means we can serve papers on the company, which he'll be unable to reply to. Any delay for us helps Wes to stay in his home that much longer. You were about to ask me something, what was it?"

"It's a straight question. What chance does Wes have of fighting this? Legally, I mean."

She worked the problem through, her eyes screwed up in concentration as she worked out the options. When she replied, she wasn't smiling.

"I guess you should know his chances aren't great. This company seems to have a lot of clout in the city. I've tried a couple of legal moves, but they always seem to be one step ahead of us. I get the idea they've made huge sums of money buying up properties on the cheap, foreclosing, and somehow pushing through the necessary zoning changes to redevelop the sites. It's big business, multi-million dollar business, and when those kinds of figures are concerned, they'll fight like hell to succeed. All Wes has on his side is our law center, which means me."

Taylor stared at her. "He also has me, Kate. We fought together in the service, and that kind of loyalty doesn't end when they toss you out onto the scrapheap. I'm not a legal expert, but if these people are going to play rough, that's my area of expertise." She was about to reply, but he pressed on, "Have you noticed Wes? This whole business had pushed him to the very depths of despair, but killing Evie is likely to rebound on them. He looks to me more like the old Wes I used to know. He loved that woman, more than you could know. He wants them to pay. I promise you that."

Her eyes flickered with interest. "He does seem different. Tell me, what was he like?"

"Before the incident that destroyed my squad?" She nodded. "He was an okay guy," Taylor went on, "but people took him for a pussy. When he went into action, he turned into a regular tiger. I've seen him single-handedly charge a score of hostiles, and these Islamic nutcases are tough fighters. He turned them into mincemeat. He was fearless, one of the toughest guys I've ever known. That's what's so painful, seeing him like he is now, whipped and beaten. Except maybe he's coming out of it."

She nodded again. "May I ask you a personal question?"

He'd been dreading it. Ever since he'd seen her eyes stray to the rent in his pants where the gleaming stainless steel and titanium of his knee joint showed through. He shrugged mentally.

What the hell? That's the way I am. Take it or leave it.

"Go ahead."

"I understand you lost both your legs in Baghdad. I can even see that joint showing through the tear in your pants, yet you walk and act like an athlete or a soldier. How come?"

He explained about Hermann van Rhoos and the pioneering neuroprosthetics work he carried out at MIT.

"So, you're pretty well back to normal. That's good."

He shook his head. "Hermann has a sign over his office door. 'Two legs good, tin legs better'."

He explained the philosophy. How Hermann was determined there would be no more part-repaired cripples. Instead, there would be men who would be compensated for the loss of their limbs by becoming stronger and faster than they ever were before.

"It's not there yet," he cautioned. "He still has a long way to go, but I feel pretty good."

Her eyes were wide with astonishment, as she looked him up and down.

"You look pretty good too."

Then she reddened, realizing she'd fed him something of a come-on. He smiled it away as Wes returned to the kitchen. His face was grim.

"It's not good news. The two detectives handling the case have got nowhere."

"Tell me their names," Kate replied. "As soon as I've finished here, I'll visit them at the precinct and see what I can find out."

"I only know the name of the lead detective," Wesley

said. "A guy called Malouf. Wasim Malouf."

Taylor and Wes stared at each other for long moments. Surely it was a coincidence that the lead cop shared the same ethnicity as Mehdi Hussein, a prime suspect in Evie's murder. The murder they were supposed to investigate. Both men were Arabs, and therefore most probably Muslims. There couldn't be a connection? Could there? Finally, Kate nodded her understanding.

"Okay, I'll check it out, Wes. As soon as I know anything, I'll get back to you."

Taylor suddenly remembered he had to get home and change his clothes. It was time to replace the torn pants before he suffered any more embarrassment. He stood up to leave.

"I'd best be getting along. Wes, give me a call when you know any more. In the meantime, I'm going to do some checking around. I know a couple of people in the city, so I'll see what I can do. I'll talk to you later." He looked at Kate, and their eyes met briefly. "Nice talking to you."

"Me too."

Her smile was warm and brief, and as she turned her head toward him, he caught the flash of her beautiful green eyes as they locked onto him. He didn't trust himself to prolong the moment. She was a young, pretty professional with her own life. He was a beat up ex-Seal who was trying to recover his life after coming close to losing it. He didn't feel sorry for himself, not one bit, but he was realistic and knew he had to let this one go. She was beautiful and desirable, and he'd have to content himself watching her from afar. Just like his old girlfriend Fay, the last thing she'd need was to clutter her life with a legless war vet. He walked out of the house and to the Camaro. As he drove back to the North End, he went through a mental checklist of people he knew who lived in Boston. There was Doc Hermann, of course. A girl he used to date, and who now worked in City Hall. He seemed to remember her name was Ruth, but that was a long time ago. Then there was one of the guys from his unit, Jerry Yates. He kept a careful eye out for the cops while he scrolled through the list of numbers in his cell. There it was, Jerry Yates. Jerry had been the unit demolitions wizard. He could almost destroy an entire block with little more than a couple of grenades and a pencil fuse. He was one of those guys that had the knack for destroying things, and Taylor recalled that he loved his work with a passion, before that fatal explosion which tore them all to pieces. Jerry, as he recalled, had survived relatively unscathed. He was one of the lucky ones, unless he suffered the hell of PTSD, like Wes, but when he'd spoken to him a few months before, a call he'd made from the hospital, he'd seemed okay.

He pressed the speed dial and waited for an answer. When it came, he barely recognized the voice.

"Yeah?"

Cautious. Even frightened. Not Jerry, surely?

"Jerry? This is Taylor, from the platoon."

"Jack? Jesus wept! It's good to hear your voice. You still in the VA hospital?"

Taylor sighed. He'd have to go through it all again.

"It's a long story, Jerry, but I'm okay now. I'm in Boston. I wondered if I could come and see you. One of our guys, Wes Harper, he's got some problems."

"Yeah, Wes, a great guy. How is he?"

"He's not so good. He needs our help, Jerry."

The grating laugh was the last response he'd expected.

"Help? Don't we all need some of that?"

There's something wrong, for sure, badly wrong.

"What's up, Jerry? Things not going so well?"

A pause. "They've been better, but look, I'm sorry, Jack, you're more than welcome. Come around, it'll be great to see you."

He gave directions, and Taylor turned at the next junction and headed out toward Jerry's place. When he reached it, he felt like he'd arrived in a war zone. Most of the businesses were boarded up. On the corners, sullen gangs of youths, black, white, and Latino hovered in feral bands. He finally pulled up next to an apartment block that was definitely in the twilight of its years. It reminded him of Wes' house in Dorchester, the neglect, the peeling paintwork, and the air of hopelessness in residents who shuffled along the sidewalks. The only sign of life or defiance was in the gangs. Three hundred dollar trainers and Armani and Prada coats were their symbols of success and prosperity. They watched him through narrowed eyes with hard, cold expressions that had seen everything, youths for whom life had nothing more to offer. Taylor had no doubt most of them were carrying, and if they thought a new face was a threat to them, they'd have no hesitation in pulling out a Mac 10 or an Ingram and using it to deadly effect.

What the hell is Jerry doing in a place like this?

The apartment he sought was on the fourth floor. The sign on the elevator said 'out of order', so he took the stairs. When he reached Jerry's floor, his friend was standing at the door waiting for him. From a distance, the lithe, handsome, dark haired former Seal was unchanged. But close up, he was a shadow of the man he'd once been.

Unlike Wes, he was white, but that was the only major difference. The stretched skin, the wrinkles, the scared eyes; it was the same story. Taylor knew Jerry's body was covered in scars from the explosion, hidden beneath his clothing, and there was a long inkvine scar just visible on the top of his neck. The veins of one eye were bloodshot, so it had still not recovered from the blast. But the serious damage, the damage to the mind, would be invisible.

"I saw you drive up, Jack." He walked forward, with his hand held out. "We best go back downstairs, move the wheels, and find someplace for a coffee."

He saw Taylor's puzzled look. "It's that Camaro, man. You leave wheels like that out in this street, and there won't be much left when you get back. We better move fast. The local thugs don't waste time."

Taylor led the way back down the staircase and out into the street. Jerry was right. A young black man was about to insert a thin steel lever into the driver's door.

"Hey, you! Get out of there!"

The young man turned around to him, slowly casually, eyes sullen, and clouded with the downside of his last fix.

"You gonna make me?"

The hard stare was challenging. He'd already made up his mind. These wheels were his. The shiny Camaro offered the chance of several days' supply of crack. Taylor swallowed his anger. The guy was more to be pitied than blamed.

"Get out of here, kid. That's my car."

The young man pulled aside his designer leather jacket to show the butt of an automatic tucked into his waistband.

"This here piece says they're my wheels, motherfucker."

He felt a sense of sadness. He'd have to deal with

the kid and teach him a hard lesson. A lesson he should have learned from his father, if he had one. Or from his teachers, if he'd ever attended school. The chances were he'd done neither. Taylor moved gently forward, arms held out at the sides, palms up. As if to say, 'hey, I don't mean you any harm'.

The kid's eyes narrowed. At the last moment, his hand flashed inside his coat. But even had he not been befuddled with drugs, the kid would have been too slow; too slow by a mile. Taylor took another step forward, and his fist flashed forward to take the punk in the kidneys. He bent double and for his trouble received an uppercut that crunched into his face, lifting him off the ground. He fell in a sprawling heap on the sidewalk, blood streaming from his nose. Taylor bent down and retrieved the kid's gun, reflecting that this was becoming something of a habit, taking other people's weapons off them after they'd used them to threaten him. The kid was screaming.

"Motherfucker, you broke my nose! Shit!"

"You're still alive, kid. Take this as a lesson, and stay away from people's cars. Get yourself into drug rehab."

The kid sneered at him through eyes that were weeping tears of pain. He got to his feet and quickly walked away. Jerry looked terrified.

"Jack, something you should know. Around here, there ain't no drug rehab. It's just a dream. When these kids get hooked, it's a death sentence. That kid, he'll find some friends, and there's a good chance they'll come back for revenge."

Taylor nodded. "In that case, they'll just have to learn the same lesson."

He unlocked his car, and they drove to a mall about a

mile away where the Camaro would be safe from predators. They found a Starbucks and a quiet corner inside to talk.

"Jerry, what the hell is going on? I just came from Wes Harper's place, and he's got serious problems. His wife was killed, and a crooked property developer is trying to seize his house. I come here and find it's not much better. What gives?"

Jerry sighed deeply, "You ain't been out of the hospital long, have you Jack? Where's your place?"

"The North End."

He laughed. "Yeah, I might have known. Tell me, how come you're walking? Did you grow new legs or something? The last time I saw you, all you had after that explosion was a pair of stumps."

Taylor told him of Hermann van Rhoos. About how he'd given him new legs and handed him back his life.

"That's why I came to Boston in the first place. When I went to help out Wes, I thought of you, thought you could lend him a hand too. But it looks to me as if you have enough problems of your own."

"Yeah, it's not so good where I live. The scum have taken over the neighborhood. As if that isn't enough, someone is trying to turn the area into yuppie apartments. The cops do damn all about it, the drugs and the violence."

So it's happening here as well. But this is Boston, not some Islamic shithole! Why?

"But Jerry, surely they can see what's going on?"

His friend closed his eyes, and a bitter expression came over his face. "There are some local cops who turn a blind eye, and we've seen more than one payoff go down. That's the problem."

"You know who's behind it? What's the name of the

company?"

Could it be MMP, playing the same game as they were with Wes' place?

Jerry shook his head wearily. "I dunno, but they've got a lot of muscle. One of 'em's a huge guy, twice your size. If anyone complains, he tears them into pieces."

Taylor nodded. Gunter Metz, it had to be. Jerry stopped suddenly and looked out the window. Taylor followed his gaze. A pair of Japanese motorcycles had pulled up, and two teenage black boys were staring in through the window of Starbucks, right at them. Jerry saw them too and licked his lips. Taylor hid a grimace. The Jerry Yates he'd once known would have been capable of sorting them out if they tried anything funny.

"Jack, I'd better get home."

"Trouble?"

"Might be. That kid in the street, he may have got those guys on the cycles to come looking for us for revenge. They're all crazy about respect, you know. They get dissed, and they come after you with an M-16. No, I need to get home and keep an eye on my place. Let this settle down. I'll give you a call in a couple of days."

"But why not talk to the cops?"

Gerry chuckled. "The cops? I just told you. They're here to protect and serve, but the guys they protect and serve are like that big guy that comes around and threatens to rip apart anyone who complains. They want us out of our homes, and they're more than happy to see the dealers and crack heads wreak havoc where we live. As long as these people keep paying off the local law, their asses are covered. The rest of us, we just try and keep our heads down. It's hard to understand what's going on. We just try and survive."

Taylor finished his coffee. He thought he did know what was going on, the question was what to do about it. They went back out into the parking lot and got into the Camaro. There were no further signs of the punks on motorbikes, so he slid out of the exit and took Jerry home. Feral youths were still lounging on the corners, but they may have been different ones. It was hard to tell; they all looked the same. The good news was there was no obvious interest in Jerry's apartment. He let him out and drove away, and they agreed to keep in touch. He was troubled. Wes, Jerry, these were brave, tough, bold men who'd given their all for their country; only for their lives to be held hostage by wild gangs, swindling corporations and crooked cops.

Something is badly wrong. It's like a disease that's infected the entire area, a disease with a name, Mehdi Hussein. But what the hell anyone can do about it is beyond me.

He spent a troubled evening, drinking beer and trying to watch an old film to take his mind off the troubles of his old buddies, but the images didn't and wouldn't go away. Wes, a decorated Navy Seal who'd seen his wife executed and was threatened with the loss of his home. Effectively, his life was almost over. And Jerry, the clever demolitions man who lived in terror of hordes of junkies who staked out his neighborhood, while the cops stood by and did nothing. Then there was the mysterious Arab who owned MMP, the company trying to redevelop Wes' street. An Arab who'd bought off the cops and used a band of low life muscle to inflict pain and suffering on once proud members of the United States Navy. His thoughts strayed to Kate Donovan. He couldn't help himself as he wondered what it would be like kissing those full, luscious lips. Caressing her firm breasts and seducing her during a night of wild and abandon sex.

He smiled inwardly. I'll have to put a stop to that. She's the wrong girl, I'm the wrong guy, and we're both in the wrong place.

He went to the icebox to pull out another beer when his cell phone rang.

"Taylor."

"Is this Mr. Jack Taylor, friend of Jerry Yates?"

The voice sounded official, with a pseudo politeness that was the mark of cops the world over.

"Yes, is there a problem?"

"You'd better get over here, Massachusetts General Hospital. That's 55, Fruit Street. You know where it is?"

"I know. What's the problem? What's happened?"

"He got beat up. You'd better come over."

He pressed him for more, but the cop hung up. As he pulled on his coat ready to leave, he knew immediately what had happened. With a sinking heart, he realized Jerry's assessment had been right on the ball. One of the punks had been dissed, and someone had to suffer.

Why didn't I listen? What the fuck is going on here? It's like a fucking war zone! Is this what we fought for, shed blood for?

He fought to control his anger as he drove through the Boston evening traffic. Since the explosion in Baghdad, by sheer luck his life had begun to recover, but some of the other survivors from his platoon were going downhill fast.

Something has to give. As I live and breathe, if Jerry's been hurt bad because of what I did, those fuckers are going to get a war they wouldn't believe. What does that make me, a vigilante? What would my father say? The strict, by-the-book captain of a missile cruiser will be turning in his grave; too bad. I made my own life. I'm a Seal. One way or the other, I always will be until the day I draw my last breath.

CHAPTER THREE

Jerry lay on a hospital bed. He'd been the oldest member of the platoon, dangerously close to the maximum age before they put you out to grass. Now he looked ten years older, almost like a senior citizen. The ER room was like a battle zone. Doctors, nurses, and medics ran around. Relatives and friends shouting questions and screaming in tortured anguish. Uniformed cops standing around looking bored, waiting to question wounded and bleeding victims. His friend was submerged beneath a forest of tubes and wires that hung down over the bed. Behind him, a series of monitors were tracing the path of his vital signs, and a monitor beeped its electronic note. As long as the beep continued, Jerry was at least alive. If the beep went silent...

Taylor put his head close to Jerry's, which was covered in bandages like an Egyptian mummy.

"Jerry, this is Jack. Can you hear me?"

He didn't reply, and Taylor looked closely at his eyes. They were vacant, open wide, but showing no sign of any understanding. He looked around for the nearest nurse. She was attending to a patient in the next bed, putting a dressing on what looked like a gunshot wound. He'd seen enough of those in the field to recognize the signs. She was an older woman, with deep, shadowed, tired eyes, probably hitting the nightshifts to help pay off the bills after her husband was laid off. Or maybe he'd gone away to screw the younger woman. Jack ended the speculation.

"Ma'am, could you tell me how my friend is? He doesn't look so good."

"It's Miz."

"Excuse me?"

"Miz, not Ma'am."

"Right, sorry."

So much for speculation, he smiled inwardly.

"How is he doing? He looks to be unconscious."

She glanced at him and back to the patient she was attending. He waited, and eventually she looked back at him and decided to speak.

"Mr. Yates is on life support. He's in a coma. You're wasting your time trying to talk to him. At least you are if you want a response. I doubt he can hear you. It's by no means certain he will recover."

"You mean he could die?"

"That's right. He's real bad; they sure did a number on him. It's a miracle he made it here alive. The cops brought him in, and they said to let them know if he ever woke up, but I wouldn't hold your breath on that one."

He nodded and looked back at Jerry. The injuries to his body were covered in bandages and dressings, but he could see they were extensive, and that was just on the surface. God only knew what internal wounds he'd suffered. He sat for the next hour by the bed, murmuring quietly to his unconscious friend, hoping he may hear him. Maybe if he heard a familiar voice it would help. It was the only thing he knew how to do. An unfamiliar voice made him look around.

"Who are you?"

He glanced at the new arrival. A guy wearing a battered brown A2 flight jacket that Taylor recalled he'd seen last on Jerry Yates. He was twenty or maybe twenty-one, short and powerfully built. Under the jacket he wore a creased blue button down shirt, with khaki pants and stylish brogues. His hair was long, cut with a parting over one side. He had fine youthful features; decorated with a small beard he'd grown in the modern way, just a wisp of hair on his chin. A good-looking guy, he was almost a ringer for Leonardo DiCaprio. The similarity was striking, and he knew Jerry had a son of about this age. He stood up and offered his hand.

"Name's Taylor, I served with Jerry in the Service. You must be his son."

The man relaxed and put out his hand. "That's correct, Levi Yates. Any word on my father?"

How the hell can you tell a kid his parent is hovering on the cusp between life and death? There's only one answer to that question, with extreme difficulty. But I won't lie to him, no way. He deserves the truth.

"It's not good, Levi. They gave him a real hammering."

He looked scared, and his eyes crinkled as he fought back the tears.

"Will he live?"

"I honestly don't know. Right now, it's a tossup. There's no way of knowing the extent of his internal injuries. I

79

guess the best that can be said is the docs are doing their best. They're good people."

"Those motherfuckers!"

Taylor was taken aback. "The doctors? Why would that be?"

Levi shook his head, "No, not the medical staff. I'm sure they're working hard to save him. I mean those guys who beat him. I guess they're putting pressure on all of them to get out of their apartments."

He shook his head and explained about the punk they'd clashed with in the street. "In some ways, it may have been my fault. I'm real sorry, Levi. If there is anything I can do to help, I will."

Jerry's son looked at him strangely. "You don't get it, do you? Those gangs that run around loose in the streets like packs of wild dogs, they're not doing it for nothing. You've heard of gentrification?" Taylor nodded. "Yeah, well think about it. If they can redevelop some of these sites, they make millions of dollars. All that's standing in their way are the tenants of the buildings they want to remodel. There's a kind of chain I've noticed, the way it goes down. The gang bangers and big dealers boot out the small-time pushers. The area deteriorates, and the cops turn a blind eye. Eventually, most people get out one way or another. A few of them are bought out. Then, hey presto, some smarmy corporate executive chalks up a few million more dollars in his offshore accounts when they redevelop."

"I'm helping out one of our guys right now, Wes Harper. That's what's happening to his place in Dorchester."

Levi nodded. "It's a racket, and it's not just in Boston. Anywhere the demand for quality apartments has pushed the prices through the roof. Cities like Boston, New York, and I guess a few others are ripe pickings. They're like the carpetbaggers who raped the South after the Civil War. They move in and pick over the bones of people's smashed and ruined lives."

"I hear you. There's a company called MMP. They're involved with some of these scams. Ring any bells?"

Levi shook his head. "Not really, no. I haven't had much to do with it. I only picked up little bits of the story from Dad, but he was always too proud to tell me everything. It could be the same outfit. I don't know."

Taylor sat with Levi for two hours, both men keeping a watch over Jerry, talking to him, trying to let him know they were there. Who knew what he could hear and what he couldn't?

"You never know, people in a coma often hear and remember everything while they were out." Taylor explained. "It could help him if there's any chance he may recover consciousness."

But even as he said the words, he knew it didn't look too good for his friend. Jerry was only breathing through a ventilator that hissed and sucked air in and out of his body, aided by a forest of wires and tubes feeding him nutrients and monitoring his vital signs. His face was pale and clammy, devoid of any life or apparent feeling. There was always hope, but both men knew the truth was staring them in the face. Levi stared at him for a moment and then nodded, "Yeah, right."

Finally, Taylor got up to leave. He jotted down his cell number on a piece of paper and handed it to Levi.

"Call me if anything changes, anytime. And if I can help, you only have to say the word. I mean that. Your father and me went through a lot together, and we don't walk out on each other when things are bad. Not ever."

He took the paper. "I'll let you know, and thanks for being here. I know if he can hear us, it'll mean a lot."

Taylor left and climbed into his Camaro. He didn't start the engine at first, just sat there mulling over the events of the last twenty-four hours. Was it survivor's guilt? He didn't have an answer to that question. He wasn't a psychologist. All he did know was they'd all suffered badly in the blast that had destroyed the careers of so many fine Navy Seals. He'd started to get his own life back on track, but now he found his buddies had lost out too, in different ways.

I have Dr. Hermann van Rhoos on my side. Who do they have? Until now, no one. That's about to change.

As he sat there, he got a few odd looks from cops coming and going to the ER room, probably they thought he was a drunk sleeping it off before he drove home. But he finally started the engine and drove home. He edged the car into the parking lot, nodded to the attendant, and walked back to his apartment. He felt sore and knew the pain was returning. He'd have to do something about that, and soon. He put the key into the lock of his front door, tensing as two men came up behind him. He turned his back to the door, checked the area for any more threats, and then glanced at the two strangers. One, the older man, was an Arab. The other was white, blonde haired, with the face and build of a Californian surfer. His clothes had the crumpled surfer look too, but he still looked like a cop.

"Mr. Taylor? Jack Taylor?"

Cops. The way they speak, that pseudo-polite tone is an immediate give away. Do they honestly think because they called you Mister, or Sir, they're being polite? That you won't realize they see the public as hostile, interfering busybodies, who neither appreciate nor understand them?

"I'm Taylor."

The man who'd put the question, the Arab, held up a gold shield.

"I'm Detective Wasim Malouf. Major Case Squad. This is my partner, Detective Brad Stutz."

"What can I do for you, Detectives?"

He watched them carefully. So this Detective Wasim Malouf was the guy investigating Evie Harper's murder, or was supposed to be investigating. So far Taylor had less than total confidence in the ability of these cops to locate Evie's killer. Wasim Malouf looked as Arabic as his name sounded, with smooth, coffee colored skin. He was of medium height, with a stylish haircut, and dark eyes that looked at him with a look of intensity. Maybe suspicion. After all, he was a cop. He was also well built, with the hard appearance of someone who worked out.

Probably he works out by beating up on his suspects, Taylor smiled to himself.

He was also a snappy dresser. He wore a sharply tailored suit that looked like Armani, together with a shirt and tie that were enough to complement the suit. On his feet, he wore fashionable black brogues that would have done justice to Prada.

Obviously, the pay of a Boston PD detective is enough to fund that kind of lifestyle. Armani, Prada, does he have, an apartment in Beacon Hill?

He smiled, showing neat white teeth that had to have been capped.

"You're a friend of Wes Harper, I believe?"

He shrugged. "Yes, I'd call Wes a friend. We served

together, U.S. Navy."

"You were both squids," Malouf commented.

Taylor nodded. The term 'squids' was incorrect. It was a slang reference to officers and men in the regular U.S. Navy. Taylor and Wes Harper both belonged to the Navy Seals. Technically, a part of the Navy, but the slang term for a Seal was a frog. He didn't correct the cop.

"We're concerned you may interfere with the investigation into the murder of Mr. Harper's wife. I understand you went to visit a company called MMP."

Taylor waited a few moments while he got his thoughts together. There was no immediate threat, and he wanted time to phrase his answers carefully.

"Yeah, I went to see them. How's the investigation going?"

"We're looking into it. Why did you visit MMP?"

Taylor stared at the Arab detective, meeting his eyes to convey a silent message.

You're full of shit. You know it, and I know it.

"I asked you how the investigation is going. I went to see MMP to ask them to stop the foreclosure. I appreciate you looking into Evie's murder, Detective. Have you made any progress?"

"That's police business, Mr. Taylor. I talked to the folks at MMP, and they said when you called round, you threatened them with violence. Is that true?"

He thought back to that visit first thing in the morning. The way he recalled it, they attacked him and pulled a gun on him. All he'd done was defend himself, but there was no point in telling these cops. Whatever the agenda of this swarthy detective, Taylor doubted that any facts would interest him. Not, where MMP was concerned.

"No."

The younger man, Brad Stutz, stepped forward, his face hostile.

"What does 'no' mean, Mister? Are you screwing us around?"

Taylor looked at him long enough for the guy to understand he wasn't intimidated in the least. These two were cops probably armed with 9mm Glocks.

Try staring down ten or twenty ragged-assed insurgents armed with AK-47s and RPG rocket launchers. That sure is a lesson in life, and often in death. You have a lot to learn.

"Your friend asked me a question. It sounded like a yes or no question. I gave him my answer. Or were you guys looking for some conversation?"

Even as he spoke, he cursed himself for winding up the two detectives. He had two old friends who were in need of help, and it may just be that these two cops may be able to do something. Unlikely, but possible. Rubbing their noses in the dirt wouldn't make things any easier for Wes or Jerry. He hurried to smooth things over.

"Look, Detectives, it's late, and I'm tired. I'm sorry, but one of my friends was hurt tonight, and I've just been to visit him in Boston General. He's pretty bad."

Malouf nodded and did his best to look sympathetic. He almost succeeded.

"We're sorry about your friend, but that's another matter. We'll catch the guy who killed Evie Harper, I can promise you that. Just stay away from MMP, otherwise you could wind up spending time in a cell, should they decide to make a formal complaint. I understand Mr. Hussein returns next week, and he may not be so forgiving as his manager."

So he knows the name of the owner of the development company. Interesting! Do they go to the same mosque together? That would be worth checking out. I bet I already know the answer.

"I hear you, Detective."

Malouf nodded. "Leave police business to the police, Sir. We'll get our man." He turned to his sidekick. "Let's go, Brad. I think we understand each other."

Taylor watched them leave and then went inside. It took him a long time to get to sleep that night. His career had meant working with men who took care of one another. It was a lesson that was written in tablets of stone as far as he was concerned. And now two of his friends were in trouble. Serious trouble. It would take more than a few harsh words from an Arab detective and his surfer buddy to warn him off. Was it his imagination, or did the junior detective look embarrassed with Malouf's obvious threats? Taylor got the impression that when the younger man pushed hard, he'd been trying to impress his superior. Maybe he was wrong, but it was information worth knowing for the future. He went inside and managed to root around to find an unopened bottle of Bourbon and a part-used packet of Oxycodone. He was exhausted, too tired to go looking to score. He washed the tablets down with booze and fell into an uneasy sleep, fully dressed. In the morning, he felt like hell.

He showered, dressed, and started to eat breakfast. He had the impression today was going to be busy, and he almost smiled when his prophecy was proved true, and his cell phone rang even before he'd poured his second coffee of the day.

"Jack, it's Wes."

"Wes, I was going to call and see you later. Is everything okay?"

"I'm not sure. That guy, the one who was putting up the sign when you called round, he just arrived, a few minutes ago. He's got the sign again. He's about to put it back up."

These guys didn't waste any time. They think they have Wes and his friends on the run.

"I'll come right around, but don't try and tangle with them on your own. We'll deal with this together. Have you contacted Kate Donovan from the law center?"

"Yeah, I called her before I called you. I was hoping she might have some way of stopping them, doing this legally. She said her car is in the garage today, so she'll get here as soon as she can get a lift from a neighbor."

"Give me her number, Wes. I'll pick her up on the way."

He made a note of Kate's cell number and saved it to his phone. He called her, and she answered straightaway.

"This is Jack Taylor, Wes Harper's friend. I'm going there now, and he told me you might need a lift. If you give me your address, I'll pick you up."

She didn't reply for a few moments.

Maybe she's trying to work out if there was anything in my words that might have a double meaning. Jesus Christ, but she's some girl. Way out of my league.

A few seconds later she came back to him and gave the address.

Evidently, she decided I present no threat to her. She was right.

"I'll be there in ten."

He locked up the house, almost ran around to his parking lot, and got into the car. He gunned the engine of the Camaro, screeched out past the startled attendant, and drove her hard towards Kate's address. When he braked to a halt outside her apartment block, she was already on the sidewalk, talking to another girl of a similar age. She glanced at Taylor, turning her attention back to her companion. They chatted for a few moments, and then Kate put her arm around the other girl and kissed her.

So that's the way it is. Well, well, that's one that got away, not that it's any business of mine. So why do I feel so angry and frustrated?

He watched as she broke away, opened the door, and climbed into the passenger seat. He didn't wait for her to fasten her belt, just slammed his foot down hard on the gas and raced away. She looked sideways at him, her eyebrows raised in surprise.

"You in some hurry, cowboy?"

He shook his head. "Not especially."

She shrugged at his brusque reply and fastened her belt. He kicked himself for being so childish. After all, he already knew he stood no chance with a girl like that. A couple of years with a poverty law center, and then she would no doubt be snapped up by some blue-chip Boston outfit and spend her time doing expensive lunches with wealthy corporate clients. At least it would keep her and her girlfriend in the style they were doubtless accustomed to. For the first part of the journey, they sat in silence, and Taylor could sense she was working something out. Maybe his rudeness, and he made a note to apologize sometime. Finally, she chuckled and when he looked at her, she was smiling.

No, Jesus, she's laughing, at me.

"What? What is it?"

"She's my older sister. She's a year older than me, and she came to stay in my apartment for a couple of days while she was visiting a friend who lives just outside the city."

He tried to play cool. "Uh huh."

She was still smiling when she continued, "You thought I was a lesbian."

"It's not my business."

"Maybe it isn't, but now you know."

He nodded. "Okay. Now I know."

He could sense her continuing to look at him as he drove, but he kept his eyes on the road, trying to ignore the flush of embarrassment he knew had spread over his face.

As they drew up outside Wes' place, it was obvious that trouble had arrived in spades. The sign was up in the front yard, and a couple of burly men were dragging Wes' possessions out of the house. Taylor recognized them as the two guys he'd tangled with at the offices of MMP. He looked around for Gunter, but there was no sign of him. As he and Kate stepped out of the Camaro, another car door opened, and two men got out; the two detectives from the night before, Malouf and Stutz. They ignored them and walked up the path, just as Wes came out. He wore an expression of bitterness and anger, his face suffused with blood.

"They're taking my home! Everything I've got! They won't listen to me. I tried talking to them, but they said it's the law."

Before he could reply, Kate went up to Wes and put a reassuring hand on his arm.

"I assure you, Wes, it's not the law. Don't do anything

stupid. I'll deal with this."

As she was talking, the two cops walked up and stood by them.

"I've told all of you," Malouf said sourly, "Stay out of this. You have to let the law take its course."

Kate Donovan was ready for him.

"I'm pleased to hear that, Detective Malouf." She handed him a printed document. "This is a court order asserting the right of Mr. Harper to occupy the property until such time as a final decision is made about the legality or otherwise of the foreclosure. As you are so keen to let the law take its course, perhaps you would arrest these two gentlemen who are obviously in breach of that law. I assume that is what you're here to do," she said calmly, "To arrest the criminals who have broken the law."

Malouf didn't say a word. He snatched the paper out of her hand and read it through. Finally, he flushed red with anger and stared at her.

"How did you get this?"

"I don't think that's any affair of yours, Detective. Surely, your business is to make sure the order is obeyed."

He murmured a curse under his breath. Taylor couldn't hear it, but it sounded something like 'fucking whore'. He turned to the two men from MMP and shouted at them.

"You men, get out of here. You're trespassing. This house is covered by a court order order, forbidding you to take possession."

They looked astonished and glanced at Malouf for clarification. He gave them a brief nod, and they turned and walked away. They clambered into their vehicle, a minivan with MMP Developers painted on the side. As the vehicle sped away, Malouf looked at Taylor.

"If I were you, buddy, I'd help your friend find another place to live. These guys will be back as soon as that order is rescinded."

He was trying to make it sound like friendly advice. It came out more like a warning.

"Thanks for the tip," Taylor nodded.

He stood with Kate and Wes, watching the detectives clambering back into their car. They roared away in a cloud of exhaust smoke from their unmarked Dodge sedan. Taylor smiled when he saw how someone had previously graffitied the trunk, and it had been sprayed over to hide it. But the original lettering was still visible when the sunlight struck it at the right angle. Four letters, P I G S.

They helped Wes take his furniture and possessions back inside. When he assured them he would be okay, Taylor offered to take Kate Donovan to her office where she needed to prepare more legal documents for filing. They drove in silence, and he found himself enjoying the brief journey. Just being with her was a pleasure. He found a parking space on the street, about a mile from his place in the North End. The law center was a former storefront, and part of the original owner's sign was still in evidence, 'Fine Drapery and Yarns'. He went in with her and found it was a single room cluttered with scratched desks and sagging chairs. The computers were vintage, probably the rejects from some wealthy local company who gave them away in a moment of philanthropy. She introduced him to a guy who came forward from his desk right at the rear of the room. He smiled at Kate.

Or was it something more than a smile?

"This is my boss, Jeff Martins. He's the center manager."

They shook hands, and Kate explained to him the

events of the morning at Wes Harper's place.

"Does Mr. Harper want to move? I mean, if he plans on getting out, we could be putting time and resources into this for nothing."

Taylor felt a faint dislike for the man.

You're talking about a man's home! It's not like a used car he might be trading in for a different model.

He was about his own height, good-looking, even handsome, although a little pasty and pudgy, his shoulders slightly hunched. Probably the result of too much time spent at a desk, with not enough fresh air or exercise. He had carefully combed blonde hair, held in place with gel to give him a faintly preppy appearance. An appearance he fostered with cord pants and a tweed coat. A Ralph Lauren blue button-down and heavy, brown brogues completed the image. He looked more of an academic than a lawyer, and Taylor smiled inwardly. He'd decided not to like the guy before they'd exchanged more than a couple of words.

Maybe it was the way he'd looked at Kate. That's crazy, it's none of my business.

"He wants to stay in his home, Jeff," Kate assured him. "Remember, they killed his wife. If he moved out now, they'd have beaten him."

Martins grunted, "Okay, go ahead and put together a new filing, but run it past me before you take it over to the court."

"I'll do that, Jeff."

He walked away, and she smiled at Taylor, "What do you think of the place?"

"I've seen worse," he grinned, "but I guess it's good experience before you move on to a real law firm."

He knew instantly he'd said the wrong thing.

"A real law firm? What the hell do you think this is? Our clients come from the poorer section of the community, and we can make the difference between them keeping or losing everything. This is as real as it gets, buster."

"I'm sorry. I didn't mean…"

She ignored him and walked over to her desk about twenty feet away. He followed her and watched while she expertly prepared the new court documents. At the same time, he listened to the conversation at a nearby desk. It was unintentional, but the room was so small and so crowded, it was impossible not to overhear.

They were a couple who looked to be in their forties. Apparently, they were due to attend court in connection with the outstanding debt on their home, another foreclosure, and the same company was involved, MMP. The guy was a former Marine Corps noncom, Lincoln Moss. He'd left the Corps early and settled in South Boston where he had a small house in the area of Andrew Square. His job as a welder had ended when the company ceased trading, and now he worked part-time as a short order chef in a downtown burger bar for minimum wage. Another vet. Taylor worked out he'd probably seen service in such theaters as Grenada, Iraq, and probably Afghanistan.

What the fuck! It's like this corporation has declared war on former servicemen.

Kate finished working on her court filing, got to her feet, and walked over to him. She followed the direction of his gaze.

"They keep coming; sometimes it's all we see."

"Are many of them from the military?"

She nodded. "Quite a few, yes. Too many."

Then she gave him a smile, and Taylor heaved a mental

sigh of relief. It seemed she'd shrugged off her earlier coldness.

Maybe it was my fault. I jumped to stupid assumptions when I should have waited.

" How will you handle Wes' problem?" he asked her.

"Apart from this filing, which will give him a little breathing space, I guess it's time to contact the media. I have a friend who works on the local paper, and I just called him. He should be here soon, and with any luck, he'll drum up some interest with our politicians. How about some coffee, or did you have somewhere to go?"

So I'm definitely forgiven.

"I'd love some coffee." As long as it gives me some time with you.

They sat at her desk; sipping the coffee she'd had an office junior bring in from a nearby coffee house.

"The coffee in here is like horse piss," she grinned.

He nodded. "That manager of yours, Jeff Martins, he seems a nice enough guy."

"He's okay, yeah. He works hard, and does a good job. Not really my type, though." She stared at him, "if that's what you meant."

"No, of course not."

She relaxed, and they sat chatting while they waited for the reporter. She told him she had a burning ambition to mend many of the wrongs that cursed poor people to a life of misery.

"I'm not trying to help people evade their responsibilities," she said quickly. "From time to time we get obvious deadbeats in here, and I send them packing. But when someone is busting their gut to pay their way, and a crooked corporation is doing everything in its power to take their home off them, I get angry."

"So there are more companies like MMP in the Boston area?" he asked.

"Not really, no, they're the worst," she replied, "but when we do come across these cases, it takes a massive effort to counter the underhand tricks they get up to. And worse."

"Like murdering Evie Harper?"

She grimaced. "I don't know if they were behind her death, but it's not the first time it's happened. Where millions of dollars are at stake, people are prepared to go to extreme lengths."

A man came in. He was about forty years old, short, maybe five feet four, and wore the unmistakable stamp of a news reporter. A laptop bag carried on a shoulder strap, a warm lined windcheater enabling him to stand around chilly crime scenes while he hunted for witnesses to interview, and well worn boots that had trudged through many a cold and rainy street in the quiet hours of the night when many crimes and other newsworthy events occurred. He came over to them. Taylor would have called his appearance 'rumpled'. His sandy hair was overdue for a haircut, his skin freckled, and his face bore several days stubble. But his dark eyes were sharp and curious.

"Hi, Kate, how's things?"

"I'm okay, Dan. Dan Blass, meet a friend of mine, Jack Taylor."

They shook hands, and Dan sat down with them. Kate explained what had happened with Wes Harper. When she finished with the murder of Evie, he was about to comment when Taylor interrupted.

"It's not just Wes. Another friend of mine who was with

me in the service is on life support, right now. While the cops stand by and do nothing, his neighborhood is turning into a clone of Helmand Province. Like that couple that came in to the law center," he turned to Kate. She nodded, "He's a Marine Corps vet with similar problems. It's a crap situation."

"Yeah, I agree, it's bad. A man gives everything for his country, so he deserves more. But these crooked corporations are not easy to deal with. Some reporters I know have tried in the past, and they wind up with broken legs and their houses torched. I'm sorry, but I have a living to make, and I can't make it from a hospital bed."

He stood up to leave, and Kate looked at him through astonished eyes.

"You mean you won't do anything? You won't even write an article in your paper and draw attention to what must be a huge scandal?"

He shook his head. "Won't? Can't, would be more like the truth. Even if I tried, my editor would pull it. Some of these companies, they're big advertisers, and they'd pull their business if they got wind of it. I'm sorry, Kate. I wish I could help." A slight expression came over his face. He stared across at Taylor. "Hey, is that right, you're helping these people out and you haven't got any legs? I mean," he added hastily, "you have got legs, but false ones, you know. That would make a great story, if you'd let me write it up."

Taylor stared at him. With an effort, he stopped himself from reaching across and slamming the reporter's head down on the desk. Maybe Blass understood he'd taken a step too far. He got up, made for the door, and left. Kate looked across at Taylor.

"I'm sorry, I felt sure he'd be interested in helping us."

"Maybe he had his reasons. Listen, Kate, I have to get to the ER room and check on Jerry, see if he's conscious yet. I'm worried about him."

"I'll come with you, if I may. I just need to collect some documents."

He looked at her, surprised, and more than a little pleased, "Sure."

They walked out into the street, and he led the way to his Camaro.

"Jesus, you must have worked hard to make that car look the way it does," she exclaimed. "It must be really ancient."

But Taylor wasn't listening. His senses were on alert since the enemy had showed their intention to play dirty, and he'd spotted a couple of guys leaning against a battered Dodge parked a few yards away. He recognized the vehicle and one of the guys, Gunter, Grant Williams' chief muscle. He stood leering at them. Taylor looked toward the other end of the street and saw Gunter's two assistants, the ones he put down in the offices of MMP.

"Kate, get in the car."

She gave him a strange look, then looked up and down the street and understood immediately.

"Do you think they mean to start trouble?"

"They're not here to admire the scenery. Get in. This is something I have to deal with."

"No!" she objected. "If there's going to be trouble, I'm staying right here."

Taylor nodded, measuring the options, and then everything changed as Gunter pulled aside his jacket to reveal a big automatic he had tucked away in there.

So that's the way they're going to play it.

Taylor was still carrying the gun he'd taken away from Williams, but the unknown pistol would not be in the same league as the Sig Sauer P226 he had in the glove compartment of the Camaro. He swiftly unlocked the car, opened the glove compartment, and pulled out the Sig, making sure to keep it out of sight under his coat. Then he climbed back out onto the sidewalk. If there was going to be gunplay, he didn't want to be trapped inside the car, an easy target. He was about to push Kate to the ground when he heard a faint noise, and a bullet kicked up dirt from the sidewalk inches away from his feet. They were using a sound-suppressed pistol, and as he looked back up the street, his assessment was confirmed when he saw a fifth man inside a minivan, with the large fat barrel of a silencer stuck out through the window. They wanted blood, and then another shot whistled through the air and creased his arm, taking a huge rip out of the sleeve of his coat. The shooters flanked them, and there was no option but to fight back.

This is a gunfight. In a Boston street, for Christ's sake!

He turned to Kate. "You know how to use a gun?"

She smiled grimly. "I had three brothers, and none of them were Democrats. I grew up with guns."

He thrust the spare gun in her hand. "You may need this, and you'd better find some cover. These people mean business."

The distance to the law center was too far. If either of them tried to make it, the hidden gunmen would likely shoot them down before they were halfway. It was a simple plan. The two men either side had shown they were carrying, yet they wouldn't shoot. It was too public and too risky. So their mission was to corral them, to contain them while the hidden shooter with the suppressor did the damage.

Does he plan to kill us, or is this another warning? What the hell, it's a firefight. Time to do battle.

He pushed Kate toward the doorway of an empty store where she was hidden from incoming fire. Another shot had buried itself in his left leg, his artificial leg. He didn't know if it damaged the electronics or the sensitive servos and cables that made it all work, but naturally he didn't feel any pain. It still worried him. If the shooter knocked out something vital, it could stop his legs from functioning completely. That would make him an easy target for these scumbags. He ducked behind the Camaro, regretting having to use it as a cover. He knew what was coming next, and a volley of shots drilled holes through the shiny red bodywork. At least it could be repaired. A shot to a vital organ would be the end for him or Kate. Two shots fired unnaturally loud, very close, and he glanced across to where Kate had stepped half out of the doorway and snapped off two rounds at the shooter. The bullets buried themselves in his minivan, and the man stopped shooting to take cover. Taylor realized it was raining again, a heavy shower that soaked the street, but he couldn't see any way it gave him an advantage. Visibility was good despite the rain, much too good to hide him while he flanked the shooter. He glanced up and down the street, and the two men still covered either end. He knew if he and Kate tried to leave, they'd be cut down in a fusillade of shots. He heard a scream as a bullet ricocheted in the doorway where Kate sheltered.

"Are you hit?" he shouted.

"No, I'm okay. How can we meet these bastards?"

He smiled to himself. One thing's certain; she's full of spunk. She may be a liberal-minded lawyer, but when it comes to fighting back at these people, she's ready to take them on.

"The four guys in the street may hold their fire. They'll be worried it's too public for them to start a war in plain view of every passerby. All they're trying to do is drive us toward that other guy. As it is, those two shots you fired may be enough for someone to call the cops, but they might not make it in time. Check your clip, and tell me how many rounds you have left?"

He waited a few seconds, and then she called back to him.

"There are four rounds in the clip and one in the chamber. Tell me what you want me to do."

"Fire off three shots, that'll still leave you with two bullets. Try and hit the hidden shooter. He's keeping his head down, so the chances are you'll miss. But while he's behind cover, I'm going to take him."

"No, it's too risky."

"It's too risky if I don't. I'm ready, Kate. Do it!"

Three shots cracked out. She spaced them evenly, about two seconds apart, enough to keep the shooter's head down, and to give him time to reach the minivan. He jumped to his feet and started to run. Immediately, he knew something was wrong. His left leg was dragging slightly and not coordinating with the right. It slowed him down, but he still had time to roll behind the vehicle as Gunter and his partner noticed the threat he posed, and snapped off a couple of shots that almost creased his hair. The guns they used were not sound suppressed, and Gunter's big pistol sounded like a cannon going off in the street. If the cops hadn't been called already, they sure would be now. Then a thought crossed his mind.

Malouf and Stutz. If those two detectives turn up, and it's certain they'll come when they hear I'm involved, they'll likely run me in, maybe Kate as well. No way they'll be interested in any explanation. Malouf made it pretty clear whose side he's on, and it isn't the side of the law. Time to wrap this up and get out of here.

A movement caught his eye. About forty yards away Gunter was racing toward him. It was like watching a charging tank. He'd have to move fast. He heard a slight movement inside the minivan. The shooter was close to where he lay on the wet tarmac. Then the handle of the rear door started to turn.

The guy's coming out!

As the door opened just a fraction, Taylor raised his gun and squeezed off four shots from the Sig. He had the satisfaction of hearing a scream of pain inside the vehicle. The door opened wide, and the shooter tumbled out, falling to the street where he lay still.

Score one for the good guys.

But when he glanced up, Gunter had almost reached Kate. Taylor catapulted to his feet and raced in a limping run toward where she was concealed in the doorway. He shouted to divert the racing man, and Gunter looked up, alarmed. He reached the doorway and grinned, just as his feet slipped on the wet sidewalk, and he went sprawling on his ass. His gun skidded under a parked vehicle, and the curbstones seemed to tremble as Gunter's massive skull made contact with them. Incredibly, he was still conscious but sufficiently dazed to be out of action. Taylor surveyed the street, but the other three men were staying well back. What had seemed like an easy hit had turned into a nightmare, and he judged they'd offer no more threat, not while their leader was down. Their priority would be to help him up, clean up the evidence of the shootout, and get away before the cops arrived. He grinned; it was his and Kate's priority too.

"Get in the car. We're leaving now."

She obediently ran out and climbed into the passenger seat. He jumped into the car and sped away, noticing with dismay the rain coming through the bullet holes. As they raced along the wet streets, his mind ran through the options they had left to them. He realized his clothes were soaking wet. There was also the problem with his left leg. The bullet that went through it had done serious damage to the sophisticated mechanisms, which made them work. He needed to get home, change his clothes, and talk to Hermann about the damage. He turned to Kate.

"I need to get home and change my clothes, then get the leg seen to. I wondered if I could take you somewhere first."

"I'm okay, but I'll stay with you. I'm afraid I've underestimated them. They're much more dangerous than I guessed."

"I'm to blame for this. I underestimated them too, and I should have known better. Someone needs to do something about those bastards."

"You made something of a dent in them," she smiled.

He nodded. "We may not be so lucky next time. It's time to take care of our defenses."

He drove into the parking lot and waved a greeting to Chuck.

"Parking is nigh on impossible in the North End," he

explained. "I like to keep the Camaro in here, and it has the added benefit of being away from scumbag car thieves and graffiti artists. Not that it did me much good today."

She nodded. He saw she was shivering. "Jack, I was scared today. Really scared. I felt that if you hadn't been with me, I might have been killed. Thank you for taking care of me."

He looked across at her. "It's no problem, always happy to help."

She smiled at him, a warm smile that sent a tingle up his spine. Lately, most of the smiles he got were of pity, but this wasn't that kind of a smile. Her eyes met his.

"That's okay then."

They walked around the corner and neared Taylor's place. A fire crew was damping down the building, spraying a hose through the front window. He walked closer, stopped, and stared. Everything he owned. They'd torched it.

"The bastards," he muttered.

"Jack, I'm sorry," she said gently.

"I'll get over it."

"Yes, I know you will. You're that kind of guy."

He turned to stare at her. "No, you don't understand. I'll get over it, but they won't. They've declared war, and war is my business."

CHAPTER FOUR

"I can put you up at my place. It looks like you'll need somewhere to stay."

They were returning to the parking garage, after he'd ascertained that most of his gear was burned beyond recovery, including all his dry clothes. He turned to look at her.

"Look, you don't need to, Kate. I can find…"

"Stay with me, Jack. I want you to…"

She paused. Her eyes were shining, bright with fierce energy after the brush with death in the street.

Want him to what? Take care of her, of course. It was a close one.

"Sure, for a couple of days, that's all. Until I get fixed up. I don't want to…"

"We'll talk about it. I suggest we start by driving to a mall where you can buy some clothes. You're soaking wet, you'll get…"

"Rusty?"

Her jaw dropped, and her eyes filled with anguish. "No,

please, I didn't mean to…"

Then she saw his mouth drooping at the corners as he tried to hide his smile.

"You bastard!"

"Yeah, well, if I can't make a joke about it, who can?"

She finally relented, and her mouth bent into a crooked, knowing smile.

"I guess I can't argue that."

He led the way to his parking space. His brow furrowed in anger as he saw the bullet holes in the bright red paintwork. As fast as possible, he needed to get those fixed. Since the blast that wiped out his platoon, there were few things he still cared about. The Camaro was definitely one of them. She noticed his expression.

"Bit of a bummer," she said tonelessly.

He grinned at her comment. "It is that."

"It means a lot to you, the car, doesn't it?"

"Yeah, and now they've burned my place down, it means a whole lot more."

"There other things in life, you know."

"Like what?"

"Maybe you ought to get yourself a girlfriend, enter into a new relationship."

He gave her a searching gaze.

Is she trying to be a counselor? I hate fucking counselors and their cloying advice and remarks. What the fuck! Most of them wanted me to sit around in a community center with other wounded vets, weaving baskets or painting fucking pictures.

As quickly as it came, he squashed his anger.

Maybe she meant something else. That's too much to hope for, but she's trying to be helpful, offering to put me up. I need to control my anger, especially with a girl like this one. I enjoy being with her, and the last thing I want is to push her away.

"Maybe you're right," he grunted noncommittally. "What about you? You got a boyfriend? I mean, now I know you don't have a girlfriend."

"That's correct, I don't have a girlfriend. Nor do I have a boyfriend. Not yet."

She stopped and let the remark hang in the air. Taylor asked her to stand back while he moved the car. She looked puzzled but did as he asked. He started the engine, engaged reverse, and rolled back twenty feet, exposing a mechanic's pit underneath where the car had been standing. It was covered with diamond pattern, locked and reinforced steel plates, securely bolted in place. She assumed it was to prevent any accidents, should kids ever get into the parking area and go exploring. Taylor unlocked the shackles and grunted with the effort as he opened the hinged, steel hatch and swung it right over. It hit the concrete with a crash, and Kate craned forward to see what was inside. She gasped.

"Mister, tell me I'm dreaming."

He climbed down the half-dozen steps into the pit, except that it was no longer a simple mechanic's pit. The walls, fitted with niches for tools and spare parts, were racked with an array of guns and military ordnance. If Kate Donovan had known much about guns, she would have recognized weapons as the HK 416, the MP7, RPGs, the second most prolific terrorist weapon worldwide. And the terrorist's number one weapon of choice, the AK-47. First built in the Soviet Union, Russia, in 1949, that auspicious year which saw the coming of another weapon intended for mass destruction. The Soviet atomic bomb had never, as far as Taylor was aware, been responsible for killing anyone. Yet the AK-47 that shared the same birthdate was perhaps the most prolific killer in the modern world. The Kalashnikov, in all its variants, the AK-74, the AKM, and the carbine models, were part of terrorist lore, perhaps the most iconic part. Any terrorist without his AK-47 was like a Wall Street trader without his pants. There were handguns stashed in their boxes, a couple of Sig Sauer P226s, several military Colt 45 automatics, and other exotic handguns he'd taken in the field from various hostiles; who no longer had any use for them. The arsenal also included a pair of RPG launchers, a variety of grenades, and even an M203 grenade launcher.

He began pulling out weapons, an HK 416, an MP7, and a pair of Colt 45s. After a moment's thought, he added a snub-nosed Makarov, the solid, reliable Russian built automatic, and the M203, together with a case of grenades and boxes of ammo. He packed them into canvas holdalls, zipped them closed, and began carrying them up to the car. He popped the trunk and dumped everything inside, then looked across to Kate. She was still looking between him, the car, and the armory, totally dumbfounded. Shocked may have been a better description. He darted her a smile.

"What?"

"What? Are you serious?" she exploded. "I mean it's like the headquarters of the local militia down there. Why do you have so many weapons?"

He shrugged. "It's just a few bits and pieces I brought back from various missions; some of them were gifts, others were war trophies. You just never know when they'll come in handy."

"Handy!"

"That's right. You've seen what MMP is capable of. There's good reason to assume they have the cops on their side, so we can't look there for any help. When people come chasing my ass with guns, I like to have the means to shoot back. Get in the car, it's time to move out."

He went to close up the steel hatch and realized she hadn't moved.

"What's up?"

"I need a gun."

"A gun? You have a gun! You used it back there in that shootout."

She grimaced. "I intend to get rid of it as fast as possible. The cops will have forensics swarming all over the scene, and besides, who knows what history it has. I'm a lawyer remember? I have to be careful."

"I understand, but Kate, this could get a lot nastier than it already has. Carrying a gun could make you even more of a target."

"So how do I defend myself from these animals?

He nodded. "Yeah, I guess that's fair. How does a 9mm Makarov sound?"

She smiled. "I've no idea what that is."

"It's a Russian-made gun, solid, reliable, and pretty compact. The clip carries eight rounds, and it's a 9mm caliber. Not a lot of range, but close-up there's plenty of hitting power. I can always…"

"Stop, enough of the technical literature! Just give me the damn gun."

He went back into the pit and emerged seconds later with a medium size automatic pistol. He handed it to her.

"I have a box of 9mm ammunition and a couple of

spare clips, bring them along."

She stared at the gun in her hand. It was clean, immaculately clean, and well oiled, but obviously not new.

"Where did you get it, Jack?"

He thought about that for a few moments, and then his face clouded, "You don't want to know."

He had one more task before they left. He strapped on his ankle holster, the one he'd used when he was undercover in the field. It carried a Glock 26, the so-called 'Baby Glock', loaded with ten 9mm rounds. Compact, easy to hide, it was a weapon that had an element of surprise. At close range, the Baby Glock was as capable of killing a man as his Sig Sauer.

He locked the steel cover, and they climbed into the Camaro and drove away. They stopped briefly, and she helped him choose new clothes, shirt, pants, underclothes, and a coat. New shoes were no problem. His prosthetic feet were no different from any other feet, except his new ones were a whole heap tougher; their chassis was built from titanium. They carried the wrapped parcels back to the Camaro and put them on the back seat. He drove to her apartment block, cruised past, and circled around to find a parking space in the next street.

"I don't want them to know where I'm staying, and the car is a giveaway."

"That sounds sensible. Let me help you with those holdalls," she smiled. "It's a lot to carry up to my place."

"I can manage. It's okay."

Her smile faded. "Stop right there, buster. We're in this together, so we share the load. This is not me talking to an injured vet; this is me telling you we do this together or not at all."

Before he could answer, she lifted two of the holdalls, grunted with surprise at the weight, but started walking toward her apartment. He grinned as he picked up the remaining two bags and followed her. Her home was in an old building that had probably once been a warehouse. It was tastefully laid out, and decorated in a style that could be summed up in one word. Expensive. Beautiful, thick rugs were thrown carelessly on the varnished wooden floor, and the furniture all looked old, well used, but tastefully chosen. The kind of things that people called heirlooms. The walls displayed an equally tasteful selection of paintings, both modern and old, and they all seemed to blend in well with each other and the rest of the apartment.

"Nice place," he murmured offhandedly.

"It belonged to my aunt. She left it to me when she died. I love it here. It always feels like home. Jack, you need to get out of those wet clothes. Why don't you take a hot shower, and I'll see if I can dry them for you." She suddenly looked embarrassed, and averted her eyes, "I mean, is it okay for you to shower. I'm not sure…"

"I guess you think I'm like the tin man, and a shower will make me rust and seize up."

He regretted his words the moment he'd spoken them. She had no way of knowing. He tried to make it right.

"Look, Kate, these legs can do pretty much everything normal legs can, and then some. A shower would be good."

And so would a hit of Oxy. It's getting bad, and she may worry if I start banging my head against the wall.

She showed him into the guest bedroom and went away to find some towels. He stripped off his wet clothes and stood in only his shorts while he looked around for somewhere to put his wet stuff. He turned suddenly as Kate bustled back in carrying an armful of fresh towels.

"Oh, I'm sorry."

He cursed inside. He hated anyone seeing his artificial limbs, and the idea of this girl seeing them was even worse. At least with his pants on, he looked normal. Well, almost.

"That's okay."

He looked around the room, confused, and unsure. She came to him and touched his arm. She put her head close to his.

"Jack, it's okay."

He pushed her away and rounded on her, suddenly furious, "Look, dammit, I know what I am, and I know what you see standing in front of you. I also know it's not okay, so there's no need to try and placate a limbless war vet."

She was shaking her head, and he could see a tear tumbling down her cheek.

"You don't get it, do you? I'll tell you what I see standing in front of me, Mister. I see a guy who's going out of his way to help his friends. I see a guy who's served his country and had to fight and struggle all the way when his country almost turned its back on him after he was wounded."

He went to reply, but she put a finger to his lips.

"Let me finish. I also see a guy who I fancy a great deal. A guy I'd like to kiss me and take me to bed, and it doesn't seem like he's going to ask me."

He stared at her, "Er..."

"Look, you fool, you turn me on. Fuck me, Jack, now. I don't give a shit if your legs are real or artificial, or made of paper and sealing wax. You're one hell of a sexy guy just as you are, and you're making me very, very horny."

He moved his head slightly toward hers, and their lips touched. He felt as if a bolt of electricity had jolted him, and all of a sudden the agony didn't seem so bad. Their kiss aroused him like he wouldn't have believed possible, and then he found himself caressing her tits, her ass, and then he started to undress her. Finally, her body was naked, and she stood before him, beautiful and magnificent. She knelt down, pulled down his shorts, and found his penis with her tongue. He shivered as she licked it, opened her mouth, and enclosed it completely. He stroked her hair, almost unable to breathe with the magical vibes that encompassed his body. Almost before he knew it, she stood up and allowed him to guide her toward the bed. He touched her everywhere a woman should be touched, and she moaned with pure, healthy pleasure. He slid his hand up between her legs and sampled the moist warmth inside her, feeling her tremble as he found her secret spot. He kissed her on each nipple and slid up to join her in another long, passionate kiss. She guided him inside her, and the world, his world, was changed. Their lovemaking was urgent, a voyage to Paradise, one which he never wanted to end. They climaxed together, and he rolled off her, panting with exertion, and lay beside her body, enjoying the scent of female perspiration and musk. It had been a unique experience, almost beyond belief.

Finally, she spoke, "Well, you sure know how to treat a girl."

He grinned at her. "It all depends on the girl. In your case, you'd only have to whistle and I'd come a running."

"I might hold you to that, Jack Taylor," she replied contentedly.

They lay together without speaking; each enjoying the novel sensation that is so unique when one first meets a partner to whom they feel so totally attuned. His good mood faded as he felt the pain returning, and knew he had to find his wallet where he had some Oxy tablets stashed. It wasn't the same hit as he got when injecting, but it was enough to keep the pain within tolerable bounds.

"I need to find something. I won't be a moment."

She watched as he took his wallet from his pants and walked into the bathroom. He closed and locked the door, and then looked at his meager stash. He counted sixteen tablets. He needed four then just to keep him going, to survive, and if he couldn't shoot up, he'd go through the rest in the next few hours. He flushed the toilet and went back into the bedroom.

"Is it bad?"

He glanced at her, surprised.

"Is what bad?"

She sighed. "Jack, I'm not a fucking halfwit. I can only begin to imagine the pain of losing both legs and being fitted with artificial ones. It must be terrible. You were taking strong painkillers in there, weren't you? I assumed you'd need them sooner or later. Tablets? Or were you shooting up?"

He was about to tell her to mind her own business, but he looked at her firm, tender body, and her face, so pretty and sincere. He choked off the comment.

"Tablets."

She nodded. "If there's anything I can do to help, let me know. I've read enough stories about wounded vets crashing headfirst into the government's anti-drug program and coming off worse. For what it's worth, guys in your situation need what they need, and fuck the consequences."

The word ' fuck' when she said it didn't sound in any way coarse. She used it purely to make a point.

"Why don't we put some clothes on and have a coffee. I'll make a start drying out your stuff, but in the meantime, I can find you a dressing gown."

"As long as it's not Barbie pink," he grinned.

"No, it's navy blue and about your size."

I bet it belonged to a live-in lover. I wonder what happened to him.

Once again, she seemed to read his mind. "Don't even ask."

They spent hour after hour talking, and it was if they'd found something in the other that each had been searching for. His mind wandered, and he heard her ask him something. He turned back to her and felt something give in his leg. He remembered the gunshot that drilled him earlier. He'd need to see Doc in the morning to get it fixed, suddenly realizing the day had almost gone, and he still had much to do. He jumped to his feet.

"Kate, I have to go out. I need to rent a car."

"What do you mean? You have the Camaro."

"No, it's going back in the garage for the duration. It's too recognizable. I need something fast but anonymous. These bastards won't give up until we make them give up. Until that time, they'll keep harassing people like Wes Harper and drive them from their homes. Wes and I served together, and we always had an understanding. When one of us needs help from the other, they always get it. Period. It's the kind of promise which has to be kept." He grinned at her. " There's another thing. You saw the movie The

Godfather?" She nodded. "In that case, you heard the term 'going to the mattresses'. If things get any worse, that's what I'm going to do. It means finding an apartment or hotel room, and equipping it with mattresses, so your peoples have somewhere to sleep while they're slugging it out with the enemy. In the case of The Godfather, the enemy was a rival family. In our situation, we know exactly who the enemy is. It's MMP, Gunter and his psycho friends, and their boss, Hussein. But when I go up against them, I need to be able to surprise them, come from nowhere, as far as they're concerned. Maybe I'll need some place anonymous to stay if things get bad, but it hasn't come to that, and maybe it never will."

She jumped to her feet and gripped the neck of his dressing gown fiercely. She stared into his eyes, only inches away.

"Listen, Jack. I don't like this 'I' business. Every time you talk, it's 'me' or 'I'. We're in this together, and you'll need my help, whether it's somewhere to stay or for legal backup." She smiled broadly, "Apart from which, that attack outside the law center directly involved me. They shot at me for Christ's sake. You're fighting back, that's fine. So am I. What more can I do to convince you I'm on your side?"

He shook his head. "I know you're on my side, Kate. I know. It's just…"

"Okay, I know what you mean, but from here on in, it's 'we'. Got it?"

He nodded. "I've got it, but I have to take the car back now and get it off the street."

He left the apartment and drove back to the parking lot, where he stashed the Camaro. After he'd locked it up, he found Chuck and told him it'd be parked up for maybe a few weeks.

"You going away?" he asked him.

"Not really. It's just a special job I need to attend to. Keep your eye on it, Chuck, and if anyone comes around asking questions, give me a call on my cell."

He handed the wide-eyed attendant a twenty-dollar bill.

"Sure, sure, I'll call if anyone comes around."

He walked out to the street and hailed a cab. Twenty minutes later, he was at the local Hertz where he negotiated the hire of a suitably anonymous car. They looked at him with a deal of suspicion, but his documents and credit cards told the only story they wanted to hear, a man who was good for the hire, including the several thousand dollars he had to pay for the upfront deposit. It was no ordinary car he was taking away. He drove out in a Dodge Challenger SRT8, after admitting to himself he couldn't entirely give up on the brute power of the Camaro. With a 392 cubic inch power plant under the hood, pulling 470 brake horsepower, he was confident he had the speed to get out of trouble when he needed it. More importantly, the vehicle was finished in metallic silver, a common color that wouldn't attract too much attention; like a tree in the center of a forest. He drove back to Kate's apartment and joined her for the final part of the evening. Even though she'd loaned him the guest bedroom, she insisted he shared her bed, and again, they made love. It was slow and sensuous, and perhaps for the second time since the explosion that changed his life forever, he felt he'd regained some of what he lost. And maybe a whole lot more. The first watershed had been when he met Dr. Hermann van Rhoos and ceased being a limbless vet.

Kate Donovan was something else, an entirely different experience, but it felt no less glorious to be so close to someone so wonderful. He awoke several times during the night and had to reach for her to reassure himself she was still there, that she wasn't just an illusion. He wasn't sure when she slept, for each time he touched her, her eyes flew open, and she smiled at him, a long, lazy, warm smile of total satisfaction.

When dawn's harsh light crept over the city to begin a new day, he dressed hurriedly and went to leave.

"Where are you going?"

He turned abruptly. She'd been asleep, and he wanted to leave her.

"I have to see Hermann. One of those bullets bored through my leg, and I need to talk to him about a repair." Her eyes were narrowed, and he hastened to reassure her, "I didn't want to disturb you, otherwise I'd have told you."

"You want breakfast before you go?"

"No, you catch up on some sleep. Maybe we can grab some lunch later."

"I have to go in to work. Call me there, and we'll fix something up."

She went up to him and kissed him. It was long and passionate. "About last night..."

"What's up?"

"There'd better be a few more like it," she smiled.

He felt a joyful warmth as he looked at her tousled hair and sleepy eyes. He could smell her, the spicy musk of a healthy young woman, and he felt himself becoming aroused. She must have felt him pressed against her and chuckled, "I guess that means yes."

"It means yes," he replied solemnly. "I have to go. I'll

call you later. Be careful, I'm sure you'll be fine. The cops will be crawling all over the place, but the bad guys may try something, so keep your eyes peeled."

"I will."

He parked the Dodge several blocks away from his destination, transferring his stash to the glove compartment. If Hermann suspected he was carrying illegal drugs, the shit would truly hit the fan. He walked the short distance to reach MIT, checking the shadows as he went. He felt dual emotions; worried about enemy action that may hurt the people he was close to, yet he felt a rekindling of the excitement he'd known going into action. It had been a long time, and he never thought it would ever happen. But he felt the keen sense of rage at MMP and their murderous and violent tactics to make a fast buck.

Okay, a few million fast bucks. Someone needs to teach them a lesson in business etiquette.

He smiled as usual at the sign over Doc Hermann's door. 'Two legs good, tin legs better.'

His friend and mentor looked concerned when Taylor removed his pants, and the extent of the damage was revealed.

"Jesus Christ, Jack. What happened?"

Taylor gave him an abbreviated account of the previous day's problems. "You see Doc, these guys are picking on wounded vets, men whose lives are already in trouble, and pretty well finishing them off."

"Don't forget, Jack. You're one of those guys, or at least, you used to be."

"I'm fine now, and as long as I can get on my feet, whether they're artificial or not, I can't stand by and let this happen."

Hermann nodded absently as he exposed the sophisticated electronics and servomotors that powered the limb.

"Yes, you were lucky. The bullet clipped one of the printed circuit boards, which caused a loss of part of the control function. I can replace the circuit board, that's no problem, and it'll just need reprogramming to make you good as new. If only all bullet wounds were as easy as this one to repair."

Jack waited while he tinkered with the electronics and finally plugged in the computer interface to reprogram the control software. He turned to Hermann. "Doc, I'm grateful, that's…"

"This has to stop. Although the limbs are very strong, a bullet in the wrong place would prevent them from functioning at all." He stared into Taylor's eyes. "You know what I'm saying? If you're planning on roughhousing it with these people, a single lucky shot would leave you completely at their mercy."

Jack didn't reply for a few moments. Then he returned Hermann's gaze. "I can't let it go, Doc. These are my friends, people I've worked with. There's Wes. They killed his wife, and they're still trying to put him out of his home. There are others too, vets, people in the law center who have come up against MMP and don't have any kind of a defense. And Jerry Yates, I don't know how it happened, but he's another guy from my unit who's lying in a coma in a local hospital."

"You're telling me you can't leave it alone, is that it?"

Taylor nodded. "That's about right. I owe it to these guys, men I fought with, men who were on the same battlefields. They come home expecting so much, and all they get is shit upon by people like MMP."

Hermann nodded and began the process of uploading the new control software. Taylor waited while the final adjustments were made and for the familiar sensation that he always felt when his limbs came online, when they interfaced with his brain. It was hard to describe, a kind of tingling, not unpleasant. A feeling that he'd come alive once more, but nothing happened.

"Doc, what is it? Is there a problem?"

"No problem. I just wanted to remind you of what it would be like if they hit you somewhere vulnerable and your legs stopped working. It would feel like you're feeling now. What would you do?"

"You ever been on a battlefield?"

Van Rhoos shook his head. "I'm pleased to say I haven't."

"When the bullets are whistling overhead, bombs and missiles raining down on your position, men screaming and placing themselves in terror, sometimes you get hit. And when you get hit, it might mean you can't walk, or maybe don't have full use of your arms. Maybe blinded in one eye. You're a soldier. You keep fighting. As long as there's breath in your body and bullets in your gun, you keep going forward. That's what I do."

Hermann nodded his understanding. "I never liked that gung ho stuff, but I can see where you're coming from. Good men can't sit by and do nothing."

"Yeah, that's about it."

"I hear you, Jack, but despite the fact I have immense admiration for your abilities, and you're undoubtedly one of the best at what you do, hell you wouldn't have been a lieutenant in the Navy Seals, you have to face facts. You're up against an organization that is well armed, well funded, and prepared to go to extreme lengths to get what they want. You can't do it on your own."

Taylor was about to cut him off and argue that doing it on his own was exactly what he was prepared to do, but he bit off his words.

Doc's right. It's not a question of my ego. Am I trying to prove something? Proving that after losing my legs, I can come back and be as good or better than I ever was? Well, maybe some of that's true, but this isn't about me. It's about people like Wes Harper and the marine I met in the law center. It's about justice for Evie Harper and Jerry Yates. Going it alone means that if I get clipped, the fight will effectively end.

"You're right, but I've no idea who I could get to help out."

"What about Wes Harper? I haven't met him, but if he was a Navy Seal, he must be pretty useful in a fight."

Taylor smiled as he thought of the fights he'd been in with his old friend.

"Wes was one of the best. He saved my life on more than one occasion. When the gomers saw Wes Harper coming at them, a lot of those guys would make a run for it. He was like that, as fierce as a wounded tiger when the chips were down. But he's a broken man now, Doc. PTSD. I don't know if he'd be any help."

"I knew another broken man," Hermann replied sharply. Taylor looked up in surprise, "A man named Jack Taylor, who thought that when he lost his legs, he lost everything. And here he is, about to go back into the fight. What makes you think Wes Harper isn't able to do the same?"

"Because he hasn't got you," Taylor pointed out. "He needs someone to help him recover, someone who is the best in their field."

"I'd like to meet this Wes Harper."

"You would?"

"I would. I've invested a lot of time and research into getting you back on your feet. It seems to me you're going to need someone to watch your back. I don't want all that work being tossed away when they come a-gunning for you."

"What are you doing for lunch, Doc? There's someone I want you to meet. I'll ask Wes to come as well."

"Who is this person?"

"A friend. A lawyer."

Hermann shook his head. "A lawyer! You surprise me, Jack."

"I hope so," he smiled back.

* * *

They sat enjoying a meal in the Top of the Hub restaurant, with a view from the dining room that spanned the whole of the city. Taylor was eating from the superb menu, washing the food down with the finest of wines. He was in the company of probably the people who mattered the most to him in the world. Wes Harper, without whose tough fighting skills he would have been left bleeding and dying in some shithole in Afghanistan. Hermann van Rhoos, the genius who had given him a new life. And Kate Donovan, a girl he was still astonished at his luck in winding up with.

And sharing a bed, Jesus Christ! It doesn't get much better than that.

He could hear Hermann talking to Wes.

"I have a colleague, Wes. He's a psychologist who has done a heap of work into PTSD. He's had some good results. Why don't you talk to him?"

Wes shook his head. "It's a kind offer, Hermann. But I've had my fill of shrinks, and not one of them did me any good."

Van Rhoos nodded. "That's not an unreasonable way to see things, but I'll tell you a story, Wes. I knew a guy, and he was just like you. But his legs were blown off in Afghanistan, and the service fixed him up with a pair of legs that were about as useful as canoe paddles. When I saw him, he told me it was all a waste of time, he'd had his fill of prosthetic doctors. Yet here is, back on his feet and thinks he's like that guy from the film Die Hard. Arnold Schwarzenegger, I think it was."

They all grinned. Kate touched him on the arm in a friendly gesture. "I think you may find it was Bruce Willis, but I believe Arnie would have been at least as good if not better in the role."

He grinned. "You're probably right. I don't keep up with these things." He turned back to Wes. "Why don't you see this man, and see if it's worthwhile making one last try to put things right?"

Wes looked around at Taylor. "That was you? I didn't know, Jack. You had a hard time."

"Nah, not like you, my friend."

Doc Hermann intervened. "Listen, you pair of gung ho heroes. Don't get tied up in an argument about who was worse off. Body or mind, who can tell? But Wes, I want you to see this guy. I'm positive he'll help you."

"What's in it for you, Hermann? Why does it mean so much to you?"

"That's an easy one, my friend. I have a lot invested in Lieutenant Taylor here, and I don't want to lose it all by having a trigger-happy bunch of wackos shooting off those brand-new legs I built for him. So I need you to watch his back."

"That's it?"

Van Rhoos nodded. "That's it. He needs help, and if you can't do it, there's no one else."

Taylor stared at Wes' hard black face, and he saw more of the light returning to his eyes.

What is it? Hope, companionship, a challenge?

Whatever it was, he knew in that moment that without a single treatment from any specialist, his comrade had taken a giant leap forward in putting right so much that had been wrong inside his head.

A pity Evie's not here to see it. That it took her death to help jar Wes out of his illness and into facing the future.

"I'll do it, Doc. He can count on me. And thanks."

"No need to thank me, save it for Sol Weinberg. You can believe me, he's the best. By the way, he's calling around to see me this afternoon. We swap ideas on the psychology of wounded vets, and how to treat people like Jack here. So why don't you come on in, shall we say four o'clock? Isn't that 1600 hours in Army speak?"

"Almost. We were Navy, Doc, but what the hell, it works the same way. I guess so, yeah, I'm not doing much else. Hey, did you plan this in advance? He looked at the three of them, Jack, Hermann, and Kate. Hermann managed to look convincingly innocent.

"I don't know what you mean, Wes."

"The hell you don't, Doc, but thanks anyway. I'll be there."

"It seems to me," Hermann continued, "there's something you've missed, a step you really ought to take. You haven't contacted the police. Surely they can achieve one hell of a lot. They have huge resources to enable them to deal with these people. Legally."

Jack explained about the two cops, Wasim Malouf and Brad Stutz.

"Malouf is not in any hurry to do anything that may harm the activities of his pals at MMP, so we can only guess what kind of a kickback he's taking from Mehdi Hussein, the owner of MMP. I don't know about Stutz, but he's junior to Malouf, so I guess he just has to go along."

Van Rhoos looked thoughtful for a time. Eventually, he came to a decision.

"Those two names, Malouf and Hussein. You know they're..."

"Arab? Muslim? Yeah, we know."

Hermann nodded at Taylor. "Maybe they're related in some way. Whatever, it's something that may be worth looking at. I mean anything that connects Malouf to Hussein could be used to take to the cops. Internal Affairs, those people would certainly look into it. But whichever way it goes down, what the authorities need is evidence. Documents, contracts, bank records, stuff like that. It's more effective than using a gun."

Taylor suddenly realized van Rhoos was using the brilliant mind that had taken him to the very pinnacle of his profession to analyze their moves, and help guide them forward.

So be it, we can use all the help we can get.

"Any other ideas, Doc?"

"What about the District Attorney? I doubt that even Mehdi Hussein has him in his pocket. Or what about the press? What these people hate is to see their affairs come out in public. Yeah, a newspaper, that could be useful."

Kate cursed under her breath, "I should have thought of that. Dammit, I'm supposed to be the lawyer, and I couldn't even work out the obvious move to make. I know the DA, a little anyway. I can clear my schedule later and go see what he has to say. I'll perhaps have a go at the press again too." She glanced at Taylor. "What are you doing later?"

He reddened slightly. "I have things to do. There was some insurance on my apartment and the contents. I'll need to contact the FDNY and ask for a report, and then go see my insurance company. Some other stuff too."

She gave him a hard look, and Hermann was watching him. They knew. He felt like a deer caught in the headlights of a truck, frozen, unable to move, totally overpowered by the powerful and piercing beams. Hermann just shook his head in sorrow.

"You need to be careful, Jack. Too much of that stuff, and you'll become hopelessly addicted, if you're not already. You'll need more and more, and sooner or later it won't kill the pain. You need to be more patient."

He could feel the beads of sweat breaking out on his forehead. He was about to exclaim there was no way any of them could know what it was like, but that would be wrong. He felt certain that in Kate, he found a meeting of minds, someone who did understand what he was thinking and what he was going through. And Hermann, what he didn't know about limbless war vets was hardly worth knowing. But still, the pain. How could they know, truly, how it swept through him, scouring out his system like there were thousands of sharp blades, tearing through him, leaving him a gutted and destroyed hulk. But he couldn't talk about it. He had an urgent need.

He got to his feet and put some bills on the table.

"I have to go. I really do. Thanks, Hermann, for everything. Wes, I'll call you." He realized Kate was watching him. "I'll be fine, really. I'll come round to your place later."

She just nodded and he walked away.

It's just a bunch of nerve endings. Maybe Doc's right, I should be more patient. Fuck it! There is no pain. Yes, there is. I have to get to the Dodge. I know I left the Oxy in the glove compartment. Even though it's screwing with my mind, I don't know how else to deal with it. Not yet.

He had no business with the insurance company or the FDNY. He'd dealt with it all earlier on his cell. As he reached his car, he greedily swallowed a half-dozen Oxy tablets. Then he drove off. It was time to pay MMP another visit. The first priority of any kind of action was reconnaissance. He had a car that was both powerful and anonymous, the ideal tool for the purpose. It was time to take a look around and spy out the enemy. Then he intended to go visit Jerry in the hospital, in the hope that he may have recovered consciousness. The Oxy began to take effect, smoothing out the worst of the agony knifing through his body. By the time he drove past the offices of the property developer, his mind had cleared and he felt calmer. He pulled into the curb a block away so the Dodge was partly hidden behind a maintenance truck, and tucked the keys out of sight under the wheel arch. If things went wrong, the last thing he needed was for them to tie him to a vehicle he intended to keep anonymous. He walked along the sidewalk and found a cafe where he could sit out of sight and watch. He didn't have long to wait for something to happen. As he waited over a cup of Java, a limo pulled up, and the front seat passenger hurried around to open the door for the VIP in the back. The guy riding shotgun was Gunter. He'd have recognized him from a half mile away, preferably through the scope sight of a sniper rifle. The man he stood aside for, allowing him to exit the limo, was someone he hadn't seen before. An Arab.

It has to be Hussein. Mehdi Hussein, the owner of MMP, the man responsible for so much misery and death.

Taylor observed him carefully as he crossed the sidewalk, shadowed by his granite-like henchman. He was in his early forties, olive skinned, and with a classic, deeply hooked, Semitic nose. He was tall for an Arab, and solidly built, a man who kept himself fit. His clothes were more designer casual than corporate executive. He wore expensive jeans and a black jacket, from the cut it looked like Gucci, over a black T-shirt. His hair was coarse and dark, very shiny, and cut medium length in the kind of style that takes an hour to produce the illusion it was slightly disheveled. He wore rimless, round glasses over Obsidian eyes, jet-black and hard as steel. Cruel, Arab eyes. His shoes were polished loafers. Everything this man wore would be handmade, made to fit him perfectly. The overall impression was of power, wealth, and the kind of casual cruelty wealthy and powerful men in Arab countries often displayed. In those few seconds, he recognized a man who would without doubt be a formidable enemy. A tough, confident man who would plan his moves carefully, and execute them with ruthless efficiency. When Hussein had disappeared into the building, Taylor checked around the vicinity and found no sign of any more MMP muscle. He paid his bill and left the cafe. Alongside the office block he found a narrow alley about four feet wide, which divided it from the next building. Making sure he was unnoticed, he slipped into the alley and followed its dark length to the end, then circled around to the back of the building. The only way in or out was a door marked as a fire exit. It was locked. If he needed to get in, this would probably be the way, and he knew that if Wes were by his side, he'd open that door quicker than Taylor could open a box of chocolates. He reached for his iPhone and took some photos of the door and the area surrounding it to show Wes later. Then he decided to retrace his steps. He'd seen enough. He went back into the narrow alley and was halfway along it when he realized it was even darker than he'd remembered. He squinted ahead into the darkness. There was someone there in front of him, not just any someone. The man was huge, a mountain of muscle. Gunter Metz.

"Well, well. If it isn't the fucking Six Million Dollar Man, sneaking around Mr. Hussein's building. What's the game, cripple? You looking for employment?" he sneered. "I'm afraid Mr. Hussein doesn't employ cripples, although in your case, he may be looking for an assistant janitor. Then again, he doesn't he like people sneaking around his property."

Taylor kept calm with an effort. He could take the bastard, but he sensed, or maybe heard movement behind him. He didn't turn around, just kept his gaze fixed on

Gunter. He estimated there were another two men. It made it more difficult but not impossible. He needed to get to Gunter first, and use him as a shield in case the men behind him were carrying. He walked slowly toward the big man.

"Stop right there!" Gunter held up his hand, palm forward, like a traffic cop. "Look around, shithead. I guess you're fucked."

Taylor turned slowly. There were two men behind him, and this time they were taking no chances. They each carried an Ingram, the deadly, preferred weapon of the street drug gangs, easy to hide, and able to empty a clip of bullets into a man before he had taken more than a step. He turned back around to look at Gunter. The big man had stepped closer, and now he held a weapon in his hand. Not a handgun, it was smaller, but in these circumstances just as deadly. He squeezed the trigger of the stun gun, and the barbs buried themselves in Taylor's upper arm. The jolting electric shock almost blew his head off, and he felt as if he was dying. Even worse, he knew the voltage had done something to his legs. He tried to take a step to balance himself, so as not to topple to the ground, but his legs refused to obey his mind. He fell sprawling to the ground with a huge crash. His head hit the concrete, and as he started to black out, he heard laughter and a phrase he hadn't heard for a long time. Not since he'd been in Afghanistan. It was only a murmur, almost an afterthought, but the meaning was the same, whether in the midst of an Afghan skirmish or on a Boston backstreet.

"Allah Akbar!"

CHAPTER FIVE

He was groggy, unsure where he was, if he was even alive.
Then he opened his eyes slowly. His head hurt like hell,
like he was stuck inside the bass drum of a rock band,
and he saw his wrists and ankles were tied to the chair he
was sitting on. The only upside was that the power and
control of his limbs had returned. He breathed a mental
sigh of relief and smiled inwardly. He'd been thinking that
Doc van Rhoos would be livid if his prized patient turned
up with his hi-tech creations busted. But he had bigger
problems than Doc. It was a dark, musty room, lit only
with a single bulb on the ceiling. He could see a number
of racks fastened around the walls. They were filled with
bundles of ageing documents. It was some kind of a
storeroom, and there were no windows, so he assumed
he was in the basement of the MMP building. Of more
immediate concern were the two men who faced him.
Gunter, the muscle mountain, and one of the men he put
down when he'd visited MMP.

"He doesn't look so happy now, does he, Larry?"

Gunter said with a note of triumph.

The other man smiled as he stared at Taylor, like he was a laboratory specimen. It wasn't a pleasant stare.

"We said we'd deal with you, pal, and here at MMP we have a company policy. We always keep our promises."

He chuckled, and Gunter joined in. Larry stepped forward and slammed a fist into Taylor's jaw. He felt a tooth breaking and the metallic taste of blood in his mouth. Gunter pushed the man to one side.

"Let's have a friendly chat with our local cripple. You can deal with him later." He stared into Taylor's eyes, fixing his gaze long and hard. There was no doubt about what he had planned for him. "What's your interest in Wes Harper? Why are you so keen to get yourself killed over some lowlife nigger?"

Taylor said nothing, which seemed to enrage the big man. He slammed a fist into his guts, and it felt as if a truck had hit him. It took a huge effort to stop him from crying out, but there was no way he'd give these bastards the satisfaction.

"Not talking, eh? You will, I promise you. Once we start taking you apart piece by piece, you'll be singing like that fat cow at the opera." He looked around at Larry. "I don't have time for this, right now. See what you can get out of him. We have to know what's going on with the Harper repossession. I guess we'll have to make another visit there tonight. If we don't get Harper out, the whole scheme could go down the shitter, and if that happens, Mr. Hussein would be very unhappy. Do what you can with him, then leave him, and make sure he's well tied. I'll be back when we've decided how to dispose of him," he ended, with a smirk at Taylor. He left the room and Larry began, beating him all over his upper body, stomach, chest, arms, and head. After ten minutes, his whole body was a mass of pain.

There is no pain! It's just an illusion. A bunch of fucking nerve ends sending stupid messages to the brain. But it hurts. Forget it! I've had worse, so deal with it. There is no pain! This guy is a fucking amateur.

He tested his bonds and felt the rope tying his ankles stretch as the extraordinary power of the servomotors in his limbs applied pressure to the cords. He was aware the new legs were stronger, more powerful than they'd been before, than his real legs. But this was something else. They were so powerful, they were pressing outward, forcing against the rope, and it stretched more and more. He felt the ties holding his wrists, but there was no give there. He had to do this with his legs or he was done. He weighed the possibilities and measured the angles.

Yes, it can be done, but it'll all be in the timing.

He waited until Larry looked away from him, just for one second, checking the time on his wristwatch.

It's now or never.

He moved his legs, a massive heave, and felt the power kick in as the messages flashed down from his brain, through the synapses and into the electronic control packages to the servomotors. It was almost instantaneous, less than a millisecond. The ropes holding his ankles snapped like rotted cotton. Larry looked down, startled as he saw the movement, and his mouth dropped open in astonishment. His hand flashed to his waistband for his gun, but he was too late, too late by a mile. Taylor's right leg snapped up with immense power, and his foot connected square into the center of Larry's groin. The force was immense, enough to lift him off the ground, and leave him a candidate for singing soprano in the choir. He fell back down, to collapse in a gibbering, agonized ruin. Taylor had to follow up fast, and he used his advantage, smashing at the wood of the chair with his freed legs. The frame splintered and broke almost immediately. He was free, well almost. His wrists were still fastened to the wooden arms, and pieces of timber dangled like broken branches from his arms, but his legs were free. Larry was starting to climb to his knees, still whimpering in terrible agony. Taylor kicked him again, another well aimed blow to the groin. He smiled inwardly as he heard the breath whistle out of Larry, and then he screamed again, a high-pitched, unearthly echo of exquisite pain.

Yeah, you'll definitely be a soprano when you recover, asshole.

Now he had some movement of his wrists, it only took him a couple of minutes to untie them. He reached down and scooped up Larry's gun, then chopped him hard on the neck. He would be out for an hour or more, that was more than enough to get out. He went to the door, opened it a fraction, and looked out. When he was certain there were no other MMP employees around, he bolted it shut and left. He climbed the stairs to the first floor, and sure enough, he was just inside the rear fire exit. Instead of leaving immediately, he walked through the building until he found what he wanted, a small bathroom with a narrow window. The window was locked, but he used the butt of the gun to smash the cast metal that enclosed the tongue of the lock so it would open easily. He left the bathroom, pushed the fire escape open, and walked out into the open. When he sucked in cold air, his tooth hurt badly where it had been smashed. He made a mental note it was one thing more which MMP owed.

They're building up a huge debt, and pretty soon I'll collect on every cent, providing I'm careful. Next time I'll make sure I don't walk into an ambush like a third-rate rookie.

His rented car was still where he'd left it. He retrieved the keys, climbed in, and drove away.

When he'd cleared the area, he used his cell to call the law center. They told him Kate had left early, so he headed for her apartment, and once again parked a couple of streets away. While walking along the sidewalk, he kept a wary eye open for any sign of the enemy. MMP were prepared to stop at nothing to get what they wanted, and any illusions Taylor had that they were not as bad as he'd once thought, had disappeared for good. They were worse. He'd miscalculated badly when he'd swapped blows with them the first time in their offices. They were just street thugs, employed to coerce and threaten anyone who got in their way. He'd harbored doubts about whether they had been involved in Evie's murder. It seemed so improbable. There were the two cops to consider, Malouf and Stutz. Maybe they were on the take. They wouldn't be the first or the last to make a few bucks on the side by siding with criminals, in return for a payoff. It was too extreme to contemplate that cops could be involved in the cover-up of such a heinous crime as murder.

But what we do next? Go to the cops? Not a good idea. Maybe Kate will make some headway with the DA, which is our best hope. There's still a chance to end this without winding up on the wrong side of the law, a wanted vigilante. But there has to be justice, closure. If I have to fight for it, I will. I have a commitment, and I made promises. Promises I'll keep.

Kate opened the door, and her jaw dropped as she stared at him.

"What?" he asked her, suddenly worried, "What's the problem?"

"Jack! My God, we were worried. What the hell happened to you? Have you seen your face?"

He tried a grin through his aching lips and teeth, "You should see the other guy."

"Come on in. Wes is here with me. We thought we might need to call the cavalry to go looking for you. What happened?"

She led the way through, and he saw Wes setting on the couch. He stood up when he saw Taylor.

"Jesus, Jack!"

"Yeah, yeah, I gather I'm a bit battered." He tried to grin, but it came out lopsided, through bruised and split lips.

"A bit battered, you could say that. Who did you tangle with?"

"The enemy."

"MMP?"

"Yep, I had a run-in with Gunter and his pals."

He quickly explained. Wes was all for throwing in the towel.

"Shit, Jack. First Evie, and then they attack Kate and you on the street. Now this. I reckon it's time to call a halt. We have to give them this one. We can't fight them."

"Call a halt! The hell they've won. It's not just us, Wes. There's a long list of vets who are suffering. Anyway, since when did you ever give up? The Wes Harper I once knew would crawl through hell and back to even up the score."

He saw his friend straighten at the compliment.

"Gee, Jack, that was all a long time ago."

"Are you telling me you no longer stand up to protect your own, to fight back when the enemy is doing its best to destroy them, to get justice for Evie? Listen to me, Wesley. I'm not giving up, no fucking way. You want to, it's up to you. You need to make up your mind. Either you stay and fight these bastards, or you can find a dark hole to crawl into and pretend these bastards don't exist."

Wes reddened in shame, but Kate scowled back at him. "Jack, that's not fair. Wesley has been through a lot. Sometimes people just can't fight any more. It's time for them to take a backseat."

He gave her a sharp look. After a couple of seconds, she got it, nodded her understanding, and her lips curled up slightly. He'd issued a challenge, tried to push Wes' buttons, to pull him out of it. It worked.

"No!" Harper got to his feet and stalked around the room. It was obvious he'd been thinking hard. "You're right, I've taken enough. I won't give in to these bastards, Nossir! Jack's right. I was going to let them roll over me, and do the same to any other vets they want to kick into the shit. Enough is enough. I'm with you." He looked Jack squarely in the eye. "And in case you're wondering, I've had a gutsful of this PTSD shit. I guess it really is like falling off a horse. The only cure is to climb back on. I'm back on the horse, so what do we do now?"

Taylor nodded. His old comrade was his old self. His strength and sense of purpose, they'd flooded back in a torrent.

What I said wasn't fair. It was harsh and cruel. But

there's an old saying where I was brought up, something about being cruel to be kind. That's the way it is.

"I overheard the guys at MMP talking about going into your place tonight and clearing it out for good. I reckon we need to be there to persuade them otherwise."

Wes nodded thoughtfully. "That would be good, yeah. Except they'll be well armed."

Kate went off without a word and came back dragging two of the canvas holdalls.

"I guess we may need these." She looked at Wes and smiled. "They're not mine, by the way. I'm just holding them for Jack. I'm no GI Jane."

She bent down and unzipped the bags. Wes' eyes lit up, as he understood they would not be going into action only to be outgunned. He reverently picked up the HK 416.

"My God, I never thought I'd get my hands on one of these babies again." He looked at Kate. "It may be just an assault rifle to you, but believe me, Miss, a gun like this carried me through more than a few bad times, and never let me down."

"I'm pleased you found your favorite toy," she smiled.

"Toy!" He stared at her. "This ain't no toy. When you're fifty klicks from the nearest civilization, and half a hundred hostiles come a-gunning for you, a rifle like this that keeps on firing and taking them down, one by one, is as good as gold. Toy!" He shook his head in disgust.

"I'll take this one," Kate murmured. "The other handguns look more like cannons."

Taylor watched as Kate expertly ejected the clip, checked the load, and snapped it back in. She was a fast learner. His impulse was to object. Apart from the dustup outside the law center, he'd never been in action with a female. But one thing he couldn't argue, the bullets they fired in her direction were as real as they get.

I'll have to keep her out of the line of fire as much as I can. She's a lawyer, and these people often pack more of a punch with a couple of documents than a .50 caliber.

She looked at him, and he could have sworn she'd read his thoughts.

"Time to go kick ass, is that what they say?"

Both men glanced at her, and Wesley chuckled, "That'll do for me. Let's go see these bastards. It's time for the vigilantes to hit back."

Vigilantes. I'm sorry, Dad. It's the only way. Not so long ago, it was the American way. Maybe it's time to remember the way they did things back then, and made this country what it is, the envy of the world.

The empty house was in darkness as they drove past. The shroud of night at least hid the despair and decay, which had locked the entire street in a chokehold. He parked the Dodge fifty yards away, and Wes directed them to a rear access lane where they could approach without being seen. They crept up to the rear door of his house, and he opened it with a key. Wes went in first, dodging to one side, and Taylor went to the other. While Kate waited, covering their six, the two men went rapidly from room to room to make sure the enemy hadn't got there first. They hadn't. It was clear, and Taylor went back to call Kate inside.

"We got here first, but we need to decide how we handle this. These scumbags seem to pack a lot of clout with the local law, and I don't want any of us winding up on a murder rap."

"It won't be easy," Wes murmured. "These guys have

shown they're not afraid of gunning down anyone who stands in their way." They both noticed him wipe away a tear as he thought of his murdered wife. With an effort, he went on, "If we can't hit them hard, we'll be fighting with one arm tied behind our backs. We have to do them some heavy damage."

Taylor thought for a few moments. "I agree, but we need some insurance. This is how we'll play it. Try and aim low, and hit them in the legs, nothing that's likely to be fatal. And when we pull out of here, we'll throw the guns we've used into the Charles River. There's plenty more where they came from. That way, if the cops do try and pin anything on us, they won't find our fingerprints or DNA on any of the weapons used."

"Sounds like a plan," Wes agreed. He looked at Kate.

She darted Taylor a meaningful glance. Wes had undergone a transformation. It was as if holding the HK assault rifle had been a kind of therapy for the mentally tortured black Seal. He'd crossed the Rubicon and almost completed his journey of redemption. Holding the heavy, black weapon had empowered him. Wesley Harper was all the way back, and at that moment, Taylor knew their chances had improved dramatically.

"Okay, let's get into place. They could be here at any moment."

They staked out the house. Taylor covered the front door, Wesley the rear, and Kate went upstairs to keep a watch on the street.

It was not a long wait. The familiar minivan of MMP cruised to a halt across from the house, and four men climbed out. Taylor smiled as he recognized one of them; he had a score to settle with Gunter. His eyes narrowed as he watched them come toward the house. They approached in a finger-four formation, so it was obvious at least one of them had some military training. He cautioned himself to take that into account. They entered the front yard, and as he watched them, all four men put their hands under their coats and pulled out their weapons. Gunter and another man carried Ingrams, but the other two presented a more lethal threat.

Each carried AK-47s, the folding stock version of the famous Soviet assault rifle, as used by their paratroops and Special Forces; the infamous Spetznaz during the long years of the Cold War. Whether in the normal, wooden stock version or the folding stock, the weapons could spit out heavy caliber 7.62mm bullets at a rate fast enough to turn the tide of battle; as they had done so many times before. Like during the Vietnam War, when the volume of fire Viet Cong forces equipped with AK-47s could bring against the American forces initially left them surprised and stunned. Anyone armed with a Kalashnikov had to be treated with a deal of respect.

He called back to Wesley, "Heads up, we have incoming! Two Ingrams and two AKs."

"Shit. I'll call Kate down to cover the rear and lend you a hand. Now they're here, we don't need a lookout."

Taylor heard him run silently up the stairs, and then the two of them came back down. His comrade joined him at the front of the house.

"They haven't split up. That's one thing in our favor," Wes said. "It looks like they'll come in the front, bunched up together. Like fucking rookies."

"I don't know if they're new to this. A couple of them look like they've been in the field before. I reckon they'll keep someone out front to cover them while the main force goes in. Wes, I can cover them with the MP7. Why don't you go out the back way and circle round. I reckon you can hit them from the flank with the HK. They won't be expecting that."

"Copy that."

Wes ran toward the back of the house, and Taylor retreated so that he was at the rear of the hallway. He wasn't sure how they'd do it, but when it happened, he was almost taken by surprise. Gunter shoulder-charged the front door. One moment the hallway was empty, and the next, the big man was standing inside with the wreckage of the splintered door strewn at his feet. Two more men followed him, one with the Ingram and the other with an AK-47. Taylor pulled the trigger of his MP7 and kept the aim low. The weapon was not fitted with a suppressor, and the bellow of gunfire echoed around the confined space. He hit the guy with the Ingram in the legs and saw him spin to the floor, his pants shredded by several 4.6mm bullets that had smashed through them and torn his legs apart. The shooter with the AK-47 screamed as another bullet went through the fleshy part of his upper leg, and he limped away, cursing loudly. Gunter, the largest target, seemed to possess a charmed life. One of Taylor's rounds creased him below the knee, but it only caused him to flinch. He looked around and snapped off a burst in Taylor's direction. 9mm bullets flailed around him, like a metal hailstorm, and only the fact he was behind a heavy wooden chest prevented him from being hit. He stood up and squeezed off a short burst toward Gunter, but he was only in time to see the big man diving into the living room, out of sight.

Kate!

He leapt to his feet, and as he ran past the wounded man with the Ingram, scooped up the weapon so he wouldn't be a threat, and hurtled into the left side of the living room to distract Gunter. He rolled to the right, just as a half-dozen shots cracked out, in the direction of the clatter made by the thrown Ingram. He looked up in time to see the big man slip into the kitchen.

"Kate! Look out!"

He heard a burst of firing from Gunter's Ingram, and four shots from the 9mm Makarov that Kate held. At the same time, there was more firing from out front, so Wesley had made contact with the remaining shooter with the AK. He'd have to take care of it himself. He'd done it scores of times in the past. Kate was a civilian, and she was confronting a man who was a savage, a man who'd proved himself to be capable of the most extreme brutality. A psychopath. He checked the remaining load on his MP7, took a fraction of a second to orientate himself, and then leapt headfirst through the doorway into the kitchen. He was in time to see Gunter charge out through the rear door, and then his eyes adjusted to the light, and he saw Kate slumped on the floor in a sitting position.

Oh, God, no, no!

He crawled over to her and was relieved to hear her breathing.

"What happened?"

Her chin came up, and she gazed at him. "I'm not sure. I saw him charging toward me, so I snapped off some shots. I'm not sure how many. Then I got down here out of the line of fire. He fired back, but he missed. Then he left and ran out through the rear door."

Then they both heard the sound of the sirens in the distance. He may have bought those two detectives, but if a bunch of uniforms turned up and caught Gunter's people armed with automatic weapons, committing an obvious home invasion, they'd be in deep shit. Legally, Wes Harper was the owner of the house and entitled to use reasonable force against an attack on his domain. It was no wonder they'd run. Taylor jerked his gun around as he heard a noise behind him, but it was Wesley Harper.

"They've gone. They lit out, carrying that guy you wounded in the legs. You okay in here?"

"Sure, we're fine."

"What about the guns? They may ask some questions. I doubt the serial numbers would tie up with any legal licenses."

Taylor shook his head. "No, they wouldn't. Wes, you stay here. It's your home. I'll clear out with Kate and take the guns away. If they have any questions, you can always say you wrestled a gun from them and returned some fire."

"Yeah, I can do that," he grinned, and there was the old gleam in his eye. It wasn't just adrenaline. Wes Harper the warrior had come home. He was back.

Taylor tucked Wes' assault rifle under his coat, along with his MP7, and told Kate to put her Makarov out of sight. They left Wes to clear up the empty brass cartridge cases that would give away more than enough clues to any police crime scene investigation team. As the first of the cops was knocking on the front door, they were running out along the rear lane, making their way back to the rented Dodge. They drove back to Kate's apartment in silence. He could tell she was thoughtful. It was the second time in as many days she'd encountered deadly violence, and without doubt, she had much to think about. He turned to her as they were nearing their destination.

"We need to stash these weapons inside your place."

She looked at him, and he saw the worry in her eyes. "You think they'd come to my place?"

"I don't know. But they're desperate to do anything to level Wes Harper's house, and you're the lawyer trying to help him. Who knows what they'll do? Let me take the pistol. Your coat is long enough to hide the rifles."

She handed him the Makarov and tucked the two longer weapons under her coat. She left it unbuttoned. Fortunately it was generously cut, so it wasn't entirely obvious she was a walking arsenal. Even so, it made sense that she would walk straight into the building and not risk the open street. He stopped outside, and she got out with a quick smile and went straight in. He drove on and parked around the corner. The pain was beginning to come in jagged waves that threatened to swamp his brain.

If only I had the means to shoot up. I'll have to find that dealer again. Soon.

In the meantime, he had a few Oxy tablets. He sat in the car, took out the last of his precious stash, and swallowed six tablets. The pain relief wouldn't be great, but just the knowledge it was on the way soon dulled some of the agony. He made sure the Makarov was tucked into his waistband, hidden inside his jacket. He locked the car, and started walking to the apartment. He didn't see them waiting in the shadows.

"Well, fucking well! Look who it isn't."

He jerked around and cursed. For a moment he'd lost concentration, but began reaching for the pistol. He recognized the two faces at once, Detectives Wasim

Malouf and Brad Stutz. He waited silently.

"What are you up to, Mr. Taylor? Creeping around the neighborhood at this time of night, it doesn't look good."

He stared at Malouf. "Maybe not, but that doesn't make it illegal."

The Arab nodded and turned to his partner. "Search him, Brad, and make it thorough.

"Buddy, against the wall, feet apart. I expect you've done this before," he sneered.

They found the Makarov first.

"What the fuck is this? I take it you don't have a concealed carry permit? Do you have any kind of a permit, Taylor?"

"Say nothing, Jack," Kate came running out. She was watching carefully.

He said nothing. They were waiting, just waiting for the excuse to come down hard on him, probably wanted a chance to rough him up some. Except that Kate was there, and they knew she was a lawyer. Stutz tucked the gun in his own pocket and continued the search. Finally, he emptied Taylor's wallet and found four Oxys he'd forgotten, tucked well down behind a couple of bills.

"I guess these ain't aspirin, buddy?" Stutz asked with a grin. He inspected them with his flashlight. "Oh, yeah, this stuff sure is prescription only. You'd better show us some paper, my friend, because if these aren't legal, you're in the shit."

Still he said nothing. If they wanted their fun, so be it, but he wasn't going to help them along. They waited a minute for him to answer, and then Malouf nodded with satisfaction.

"Mister, you're under arrest. Read him his rights, Brad.

Let's take him down and book him in. Maybe a stay in one of our cells will straighten out your thinking. You're making a fucking nuisance of yourself, and I don't like that. I don't like it at all. All I want is a peaceful life, not people like you running around and upsetting our leading citizens. Let me see," he grinned, "possession of an unlicensed firearm, carrying a concealed weapon and illegal drugs. I reckon you're in for a two to five. That should keep you out of trouble."

"I'll get down there right away," Kate shouted across to him. "Don't say a word to anyone."

He felt his wrists being cuffed, and they pushed him twenty yards further along the street where they had parked their unmarked. He only had one thought uppermost in his mind.

The pain! Two to five years, the pain will kill me in two to five days. Maybe it would be just as well, more than that I can't endure. No man could. But there are other factors. Wesley, and people like him desperately need my help, and Kate who landed in my life like a star plucked out of the night sky, bright and shining. The idea my time with her may be at an end is even worse, but the pain!

He saw her looking at him.

There is no pain! It's just a bunch of fucking nerve messages jerking through my body and trying to convince me to succumb to the agony. Fuck 'em.

But even as he willed his brain to ignore the stream of negative messages pouring into it, commonsense told him it was him that was fucked.

CHAPTER SIX

He paced the cell, staring out through the bars at the occasional activity outside. Cops shuttling prisoners backward and forward, men moaning and shouting in despair and anger. The smell of human waste, urine and feces, vomit, and stale sweat mixed with the acrid tang of too much booze. He shared the cell with three other men, one black, one Latino, and a Chinese. He smiled as he thought about the racial mix in his incarceration. Almost a microcosm of modern urban America, a wide mixture of races, and surprisingly, this police cell was the melting pot. Or maybe it was no surprise. He'd heard about the behavior of long-term prisoners, where inmates formed groups aligned to their race. Black power, white power, Latino power and of course the constant threat of the Muslims, violent and angry; poised to attack the Western way of life in the name of their God. Yet here, there was none of that. They all shared the same misery; the humiliation of using a public toilet, and of being forced to wear the clothes they'd been arrested in, often torn and filthy; sometimes worse.

He wondered how long it would be before he was arraigned for a hearing. Before that happened, he needed to find a lawyer, which was something new in his life. He'd never needed one before, and for a moment couldn't think of the name of a single lawyer.

There's Kate Donovan. Will she represent me, busted for drug possession, amongst other things? I'm embarrassed I even need to ask her.

Thinking about the drugs, reminded him of the agony that was already seeping through his bones as the OxyContin worked its way out of his system. He needed something to deal with it, and fast.

What about my phone call?

He'd called out to the deputy who'd walked by earlier, but the man just laughed.

"Sure, you'll get your phone call, when we're ready for you, and not before. This ain't a five-star hotel, buddy, so just wait it out and shut up. We'll let you know."

He sat down for a few moments, and then stood again. It was getting worse, as if a thousand microorganisms were boring through his body with tiny jackhammers. He paced for a while, sat again, then got to his feet, and banged his head against the concrete wall. It hurt like hell, but at least it took his mind off the pain searing through his central nervous system, if only for a few moments. He decided to call for the deputy again. He was in serious trouble, and he knew it. When they searched him, they'd missed the fact he had artificial limbs. Normally, he'd have been content with that, but right here and now, he'd have given anything for some treatment, just a small amount of analgesics. Even aspirin, anything!

It's an illusion, just a bunch of almost invisible electrical impulses shooting through my body and telling me I'm in pain. There is no pain. I don't care what the signals are saying. It doesn't hurt. There is no pain!

As usual, the trial of strength between mind and body diverted him for a few brief, but merciful seconds, and then it came back.

There is no pain!

The door at the end of the hallway banged open, and the deputy who'd refused to help out with the phone call walked toward the cell, his eyes fixed on Taylor. His hopes soared.

Maybe this is it. I can make a phone call and try to get some help. Who will I call? I only have one chance. Kate Donovan, no, surely she will come anyway. There's Doctor Rhoos. He knows how bad my situation is without drugs to relieve the agony.

The cop unlocked the cell door.

"Come on out, Mister. It's your lucky day. Someone posted bail for you."

Bail!

It was like a miracle, an answer to his prayers. It was only with an effort that he calmed down and put aside his need to rush out and find the nearest dealer to get himself a fix. He'd be free he could arrange something within an hour, once he was out on the street. He walked out of the cellblock and saw Kate waiting for him in the lobby of the precinct. She gave him a sympathetic smile.

"You look like hell, Jack. How do you feel?"

He tried to look confident. "As well as can be expected in the Boston Hilton."

She wasn't fooled. She could probably see his skin

stretched in agony, the pain in his eyes, and the way he moved, trying to cope with the pain.

"Is it bad?"

His first instinct was to lie.

Dammit, it's my business. But what's the point? She knows the deal. We've even slept together. I have nothing to hide from this girl. Nothing.

He gave a slight nod.

She inclined her head in understanding. "You're free to go now, and I have a cab waiting outside. Perhaps it would be best to talk about it when we're out of here."

He followed her out of the precinct, and they climbed into the taxi. She looked at him.

"Where to? I mean, anywhere you want. I know what you need. You don't have to hide it. I know it's wrong, but right now you have to have something to help you cope. We'll talk about the long-term situation later."

Jesus Christ! Does she want me to check into rehab? No way. No fucking way. Not unless they have some cure for the cause of my drug taking, and that doesn't seem likely.

"Paris Street, the park."

The driver pulled away. Kate looked across at him. "What's there, at the park in Paris Street?" Her eyes widened, as she understood. "Oh! I see."

She didn't say anymore, just sat back as they drove through the busy streets of the Boston rush hour. But she held his hand, and he was grateful for the smooth warmth of her touch. It was almost like taking a couple of Oxys.

They reached the park, she paid the driver, and they stood around waiting on the sidewalk. He looked at the park in despair. Of course, at this hour most of the dealers were still in bed. And then by a miracle, he caught sight of Derek, the front man for Quint, the dealer. He was stumbling along the sidewalk. It looked as if he was heading home after a hard night, perhaps dealing, maybe even partying with his ill-gotten gains. He caught sight of Taylor and looked nervously at Kate.

"Hey, man, what are you doing here? Don't you know it's too early for business?"

"I know, but I lost my stash. I have to have some, right now."

"Who is the lady? You know what Quint's like with new faces? He sees someone he doesn't know, and he's likely to blow the motherfucker's face off."

Taylor felt like busting his teeth for the obvious threat, but he calmed down. He knew it was how the game was played, and besides, he had a more urgent need.

"She's my woman, Derek. She is also my lawyer, so I guess you should know anything we say is protected by client privilege. You're safe as Fort Knox."

The man thought about it for a few moments, and Taylor knew what was coming. It was in the eyes. Greed.

"Damn, I'd help if I could, but I'm on my way to do some important stuff. Come back tonight. Maybe we can help you then."

"Okay, I get it, how much?"

"Well, I don't know. I guess a hundred and fifty dollars would make up for messing with my arrangements."

He was about to throttle the guy, but Kate pushed him back with one hand. She rummaged in her purse and found the bills.

"I'll pay. When does he get the drugs?"

Derek's eyes lit up. "Let me see, I can be back here in

ten. How's that?"

"We'll be here," she replied, "and don't let him down. He is in terrible pain."

The drug runner gave her a strange look, "Ain't they all, lady?"

* * *

She watched as he shot up, turning away as the drug emptied from the syringe into his vein. He closed his eyes, and his entire body slumped into total relaxation as the relief seeped through every cell and fiber of his body. When he opened them, she was staring at him in fascination.

"It works fast, that stuff."

"It does, but it also wears off fast, and that's the problem which leads to addiction."

"Are you an addict, Jack?"

"I'm in pain, Kate. That's all."

They hailed another cab and gave the driver directions to where Taylor's rented car was still parked. They climbed in, and he took Kate to the law center. She said she needed to catch up with some work. He parked outside, and she turned to him.

"Listen, Jack, I'm going to look into this situation with MMP. It may be we have some legal options open to us. There's also the DA, but I don't know if he'll be prepared to help or not. My understanding is that MMP has a lot of people in their pocket, and I've no idea who's prepared to take this on and who isn't. There's also still a chance that reporter I know will become involved. I'll try to persuade him. I'll do some research and see what I can find out.

What are your plans?"

"I'm going to look around and find somewhere to stay, somewhere they don't know about."

She stared at him and frowned. "You're not staying at my place?"

"I don't know that it's safe, Kate. It could bring down a lot of trouble on your head. As soon as I have somewhere, I'll let you know." He grinned, "Maybe you can stay at my place for a while."

She smiled, relieved. "I'd like that. You will call?"

"Sure, I'll call."

She climbed out, and he drove off. He went to a part of the city he knew was cheap and anonymous, filled with empty stores and decaying buildings; and hotels which would be prepared to rent a room with no questions asked, for cash, of course. He struck lucky first time, a building of eight stories that had a certain faded grandeur, and a free wifi for the guests. The desk clerk was resplendent in a wife beater T-shirt stretched over his potbelly and last night's stubble displayed under his thinning hair. The hotel was called the Dolphin, which at least made him smile. The dolphin was the logo of the Navy Seals, and many of the guys had the tattoo on their arms, as did he. He took the key in exchange for a bundle of dollars, ignoring the ageing elevator to take the stairs to go to his room. When he opened the door, he was surprised to find it was almost a suite, with a small reception room as well as the bedroom and bathroom. It was even clean, well, relatively. The furnishings had all seen better days, but as this was purely a tactical necessity rather than a luxury vacation, he was more than content. He'd gone to the mattresses.

He spent the next couple of hours moving the canvas

holdalls from Kate's apartment to the hotel. Then he took out the weapons one by one, and stripped them, making sure they were in one hundred percent battle order. He reassembled them and packed them back into the canvas bags. The tough holdalls had padlocks to fasten them closed, and he made sure they were securely locked. The last thing he needed was an astonished room maid to discover he'd turned the room into an operations center. He knew what he had to buy next, took out his notebook, checking off the items he needed; a new laptop computer, and most important, a high-capacity USB stick. He left to go shopping, finding a local computer store that was more than happy to sell him what he needed for cash. He made sure everything was working properly before he took it away. He stopped at a military surplus store and purchased the next items on the list, dark, almost black combat fatigues, black rubber soled boots, and a ski mask. His request for an armored tactical vest raised a couple of eyebrows.

"What the fuck are you up to, Mister? Are you starting a war or something? It better not be something illegal, I don't want no part of that."

Taylor fed him a line about corporate teambuilding war games, and he accepted it with a grumble. He didn't believe it, but he was more than ready to believe the bills thrust into his outstretched paw. As far as Taylor knew, the enemy hadn't made his rental car, so he cruised past their office building once more to check for signs of increased security. But it seemed no different than when he'd seen it before. He returned to his hotel with a takeaway pizza and salad. As he was locking the car, his cell phone rang. He checked the screen. It was an unrecognized number, but he was curious and decided to answer it.

Knowledge is power, isn't it?

"It's me. Levi."

He recognized the voice instantly, Jerry Yates' son. He sounded somber.

"Yeah, what is it Levi. How's Jerry?"

There was silence on the line for several seconds, and he heard a choking sob from the other end. "He's dead, Mr. Taylor. He died an hour ago. He never regained consciousness. Jesus Christ," he wailed in anguish, "I couldn't even say goodbye. Those fuckers took that away from me."

"I'm real sorry. Your dad was one of the best, and he didn't deserve that. Levi, how can I help you? What can I do?"

"Could I call round and see you? I just need to talk to someone who knew him. I dunno. It's just you're the only thread that connects him to me. You're kind of a link. It's all I've got left."

He thought rapidly.

Is there any harm in him knowing about the hotel? What am I thinking? Levi's the son of a member of my unit, and Jerry has just been put to death by street scum.

"That would be great, Levi. I'd like to tell you about Jerry."

He gave him the address and said to meet him there any time in the next couple of hours. He went up to his room, took out his purchases, and went through them one by one. He put on the combat fatigues, the armored vest and ski mask, and pulled out the weapons he'd take with him when he went into to MMP. He'd take no chances this time. He'd decided to get inside the building, extract their confidential data files onto the USB stick, and get out. But if anyone did get in his way, they'd shown they were more than ready to use violence, to kill if necessary.

So be it, if those are the rules they want to play by, I can go along with that.

He stripped off his gear and lay on the bed to rest. It was going to be a long night. He did as he'd often done in the past when going into action, and went through the various stages of the mission. He felt a little guilty about not keeping Kate in the loop, but he knew if he told her what he was planning, she'd insist on coming along. He wanted to keep the hotel room, the operation center, separate from everything to keep her out of danger.

There was a knock on the door, and he got up to answer it. It was unlikely the enemy knew where he was this soon, but just in case picked up his P226, holding it behind his back while he opened the door. Levi.

"Hi, Mr. Taylor. Thanks for seeing me."

"Levi, you don't have to thank me. And it's Jack, you can forget the Mister." Jack rooted in the icebox and came out with a couple of sodas. He passed one to Levi. "Tell me about your father, did he go quietly?"

"Yeah, like I said when I called, he never regained consciousness. At least he didn't suffer any pain."

That's a mercy. Pain can be a descent into a dark hell, one from which it's difficult to return.

"I'm so sorry. It's a tremendous loss, to all of us. What can I do for you, Levi?"

"Tell me about him, Mr., er, Jack. I want to know everything about him, you know, his time in action with the Navy Seals."

He spent an hour recounting as much as he could of

Jerry Yates' exploits in the unit. There were times when he'd been wounded and kept on fighting, when he'd gone into the most dangerous places to rescue a comrade who was pinned down under heavy enemy fire; or to take the fight to a stubborn and brutal enemy. Jerry had been everywhere and done everything. HALO drops into hot zones. Long underwater swims, surging out onto a hostile beach, then launch a clandestine attack to devastate an astonished and terrified enemy. And finally, he told him of that day when the ambush had finally destroyed his unit as a fighting force. Jerry had suffered multiple lacerations and was carried out on a gurney, with one of his arms only connected by a few tendons and a strip of raw gristle. The battlefield medics managed to sew him together, and the hospital repaired his arm, so he was able to pick up the threads of his life, but only in a physical sense. He was finished in the service, and his mental wounds never truly healed. He didn't suffer the terrors of PTSD like Wesley Harper, but he came close, and he always found it hard to fit into civilian life.

Not that he needs to worry about that anymore, Taylor thought bitterly.

"What are you planning to do now?" Levi asked him.

"Me? I don't know. I've got one or two things to sort out, and I've got a few plans. I'm still thinking about it."

"Bullshit!"

"Excuse me?"

"I said bullshit," Levi spat out, "What kind of a fool you take me for? This place stinks of gun oil. At a guess, I'd say you have enough weapons stashed in here to start a small war. As well as that, I know your home in the North End was burned out in an attack. You're planning to hit them back."

Taylor considered what Levi had said. It went against the grain to let anyone outside your immediate circle know what you were planning.

But Christ, this is Levi Yates, a man whose father, one of my best friends, has just died.

Finally, he nodded.

"Yeah, okay, you're right. There are a few scores to settle. You know about Wes, he was in my unit too with your father?"

Levi shook his head, and Taylor quickly explained the former Seal's battle with MMP, culminating with the murder of his wife. There was also the former marine he'd overheard in Kate's law center.

"It's like this," he went on, "There are a lot of vets in this city getting shit on by a bunch of corporate thugs. It's not just the vets; these people are attacking any vulnerable people, and stripping them of their homes if they think they can turn a quick profit. I can't help all of them. It's just me on my own, so all I can do is try and help out those guys who served the same flag."

"So I guess the cops aren't any help?"

"Sure they're prepared to help, but they only help the people who can afford to pay them a kick back. Corporations, in the main."

He realized Levi was staring at him with an expression that he knew all too well.

"I guess you're wondering about my legs."

"Yeah, my father told me what happened. How did you get back on your feet? It's as if they fixed you up with a new pair of legs. How did you manage that?"

"You ever see the television program, the Six Million

Dollar Man?"

That was a bad example, for he remembered Gunter Metz's sneers.

Levi chuckled, "Yeah, of course, I've seen old re-runs. You're not serious?"

"Not exactly, but I got a pair of legs along those lines."

"So you're back to normal?"

Would you call a pain-wracked drug addict normal? I guess it depends on your point of view.

"More or less, yeah."

"That's good. Tell me, were the people behind my father's death the same as the ones who are going after Wes?"

"Indirectly, yes. They didn't actually give him the beating, but they were behind it."

"Okay then, I want to help. You can count me in."

Taylor swallowed his automatic smile.

The kid's serious but without knowing what he'll be getting into. Besides, I don't want or need any help. If anyone's going to get killed, it would be best to keep the body count low. Down to one.

"That's very brave of you, Levi, but there's nothing you can do, nothing at all."

"No? You don't think I'm serious, do you? When I was younger, Dad used to come home on leave and take me out shooting, survival training, all that unarmed combat shit. He said I was pretty damn good, about eighty percent of the combat efficiency of a Navy Seal. So don't say there's nothing I can do. I'm coming with you."

This time Jack did smile. "Coming with me? Where do you think I'm going?"

"Where? Into battle, of course, you're taking the fight

to the enemy; you're a Navy Seal. Isn't that what they do?"

"Yeah, I guess it is. Levi. It's very dangerous. You could wind up in a police cell, or even get yourself killed."

The young man adopted a fierce expression. "You think that worries me? You're wrong. There's only one thing on my mind right now, and that's to hit back at whoever is behind my father's killing. Someone has to pay. Either I go with you, or I do it on my own. Which is it, Jack?"

Taylor stood up and paced around the room, thinking. In the end, he had to factor in the best possible outcome from the available data, just as he had in the service.

On his own, Levi will be killed. I can at least try to keep him alive. And it's just possible he could help if his father trained him as well as he claims.

He turned back to Levi.

"I guess we'd better go and get you kitted out with some gear."

* * *

The break-in was easy. The window that gave access to the first floor opened easily, just as he'd planned the last time he was there. He gave the younger man a leg up, and then followed him through into the building. Working with Levi was uncanny; he was so similar to his father in every way, just a younger version. More importantly, he followed orders, which made Taylor's work that bit easier. The two armed and black clad figures, invisible at a distance of more than a few feet, moved silently through the building. They crept up the stairs. He'd loaned Levi one of the Colt 45 automatics. It wasn't such a reliable weapon as the Sig Sauer P226 he carried, but he had nothing else available, and he wasn't about to trust the new recruit with an assault rifle or a grenade launcher. Besides, if Levi opened up with the big Colt, anyone standing close by would know they were faced with someone who meant business. On the second floor, there was a reception area with a closed and locked door. It led to the data servers. Taylor snap kicked it, and it flew open. They went inside and found an array of rack mount hard drives with their CPUs. The rows of lights winked on and off as they operated, constantly chewing on the data that had been fed into them throughout the day. He knew his 32-gig USB stick wasn't large enough to swallow the entire archive; there were many terabytes of information in front of him. But he didn't want the complete records of MMP, only those that could hurt them, the protected data that was only accessible to the owner, Mehdi Hussein. He checked the file lists on a small screen built into one of the racks but found nothing. There was no way of identifying what he needed.

"We have to find his office," he murmured to Levi, "That's where we'll find what we're looking for."

The younger man nodded, and they left the room with the smashed open door as a testament to their intrusion. It was time to put the pressure on MMP, to let them know they were not invulnerable. They went on and up to the top floor where MMP had their main offices. He again kicked open the door, and they went inside. Finding their destination was easy; the door was labeled 'Managing Director, Mehdi Hussein'. Another kick, and they were in. Almost immediately they hit paydirt. He had a PC computer on his desktop left running, and Taylor shoved the USB stick into the front and began searching the hard drive. It was a Windows 7 operating system, and inside the documents folder he found an encrypted folder entitled 'Confidential and Personal'. He copied it over to his USB stick. It only took a couple of minutes, so he estimated the data it contained was probably letters, e-mails, and maybe bank records. It was what he wanted. He spoke quietly to Levi who had mounted guard on the door, holding his big Colt 45 as if he was just waiting for the chance to use it.

"That's it. We're out of here."

"They'll know someone has been here."

"That's what I'm counting on. It's a kind of psychological warfare." He grinned, "Once they think someone has been after them, they'll be shitting themselves wondering who it was. Was it the Fed's, ATF, DEA, or a rival outfit? As long as they're running around trying to find out, they'll likely take their eye off the ball. That's when we put them out of business."

Levi chuckled, "Hallelujah. I want to see these bastards burn."

They started to make their way down the stairs, but both men froze as they heard a voice from the first floor. It was a two-way radio, a burst of static, and then a distorted voice.

"You there, Joe? Any sign of intruders?"

Someone replied, someone walking up the stairs toward them, "Nothing yet, I'll check the upper floors and call you if I need backup."

"Okay. Keep your piece handy, and if you see any sign of trouble, blast it. You know Mr. Hussein. He'll go crazy if there are any security breaches."

"Don't worry, I will. If there's anyone here, it's probably some street punks ripping off the computer equipment."

Taylor recognized the voice. It was one of Gunter's people. He tried to put a face to the man coming toward them; then he had it. He'd winged one of Gunter's shooters at Wesley's place, but this was the other man.

Is it one of the men involved in Evie's murder? Maybe this is a chance for some payback for Wes, he grinned savagely.

They shrunk back into the shadows, and he noted that Levi understood his hand signals. Jerry had obviously trained him well. The beam of a flashlight played around the head of the staircase, and then a man appeared. Sure enough, the backwash of illumination showed it was Gunter's man. This was no roving security guard. He was an enforcer. The conversation was enough to demonstrate his intent to shoot first and ask questions afterward. He came closer, and Taylor waited for the opportunity to take him from behind. He would rough him up and render him unconscious, so they could get away. Then it all went wrong. Levi was good, very good for an amateur, a civilian. But he moved, only slightly, and some coins in his pocket made a faint jingling noise. It was the kind of error a Special Forces operator would never make, at least not twice; the first time was usually enough to get them killed. It wasn't his fault. The kid was doing his best. But the man, Joe, heard the tiny noise in the dark silent building and swiveled toward it. He raised his flashlight and splashed the beam over the dark figure of Levi Yates. The young man froze just for a second and then reacted, bringing his Colt 45 around to defend himself, but he was too slow, much too slow. The guard was quicker.

"What the fuck!" As he shouted, he shifted his aim and was about to fire. Taylor had no choice. He triggered his MP7 and fired a short burst, three 4.6mm shots. The echoes reverberated around the building, and the muzzle flashes lit up the man as he spun around, clutching his chest. He fell to the floor with a crash, and his pistol skidded toward Taylor. He picked it up, a Glock 17, and tucked it into the pocket of his combat fatigues. Then he rushed to check his victim, but in the spill of the beam of the fallen flashlight, he could see he was almost gone. And then he stopped breathing. Levi stared at him, his expression frozen, and Taylor knew that behind the ski mask his skin would be white and clammy from the shock and terror of seeing a man shot and killed. But he'd have to work his emotions through later.

"Let's go, let's go. If we wait around, they'll call the cops, and the shit really will hit the fan. Follow me!"

But the younger man still didn't move. He was frozen with shock. Taylor grabbed hold of the webbing fixed to his armored vest and dragged him to his feet.

"Come on, move it!"

At last he came to his senses, and Taylor heard his footsteps behind him as he followed him down the staircase. They reached the first floor, and both men could hear the commotion at the front of the building as more guards roused themselves to start checking out the building. One of them was on the phone, making a panicked call to the cops. They went away from the commotion and reached the back. Taylor intended to use the rear door, the fire exit, but since his previous visit, they'd double-locked it. He pointed his MP7 and fired a dozen shots into the two locks. The mechanisms were shredded, and the door sagged open. The echo of the shots had been very loud, and he knew they only had seconds before the guards appeared. In this situation, they only had one ally. Speed. They darted away from the building. Taylor climbed the wall of a nearby compound and found himself in the walled loading dock area of a nearby business. Levi was right behind him, and they ran through the yard and climbed a second wall to reach the outside. He pulled Levi down. They were next to the street, and a cop car was hurtling toward them, lights flashing and sirens wailing. But the cruiser drove past, heading for the MMP building.

"The car is at the back of the next block," he murmured to Levi. "We need to stay in the shadows until we reach it."

They pressed on, ducking into doorways when any traffic came near. They reached the Dodge without being seen and dived in.

"It may be an idea to take off your ski mask and the vest," Taylor said drily as they sat safe inside the car. "It gives the cops the wrong impression."

Or maybe the right one.

Levi nodded and stripped off his gear. Taylor put the giveaway items inside the trunk, started the engine, and drove away. They reached the hotel without being stopped and opened the door to Taylor's room. And he froze. His every sense signaled danger. There were lights on, and he knew he hadn't left them that way. He snatched out his Sig and rolled to one side, his eyes seeking out a target. Levi had stopped in the doorway, open-mouthed with surprise and fear. Sitting on the couch was Kate Donovan. Taylor felt his mouth drop open in astonishment.

"What the hell are you doing here?"

She didn't look too happy. "I could ask you the same question, buster. Why didn't you let me know where you were going? It took me an hour to get the name of your hotel, and I had to show the guy in the lobby some thigh to persuade him to let me into your room. It's lucky I decided to wear stockings and suspenders today, so there was something for him to ogle."

"But how did you discover the name of the hotel?"

"No, 'it's nice to see you, Kate'. This is not much of a welcome, Jack, and disappearing like that wasn't very nice. I expected more from you. It was my reporter friend, Dan Blass. He seems to know everything that goes on in this town. He found out for me."

Taylor made a mental note to chase that one down later; it was poor security. He noticed Levi Yates helping himself to a drink from a bottle of bourbon placed on the coffee table. His hands were shaking badly, and the sound of the bottle's neck rattling against the glass of the tumbler sounded like a faulty bearing in a small gas engine. He looked at Kate, trying to work out how to handle the situation. She was more than cold; she was consumed with anger that he'd done the dirty on her. He knew instinctively it was no use explaining he'd only done it to protect her. He estimated the only thing that may save him would be the truth.

"I'm sorry, truly sorry. I guess you know why I did it."

She nodded, but her face was white, bloodless with anger.

"Maybe I do, but it doesn't excuse it. I thought…"

Then she rushed toward him, just about catching him as his limbs gave way from under him.

"What is it, some kind of a technical problem, Jack?" she shouted in panic.

It was nothing of the sort. It had been like being hit with a bolt of lightning. The powerful analgesics had worn off. It was only the adrenaline reaction from the events at MMP that had kept him going and stopped the pain from resurfacing to torment him. But now it struck back, and with a vengeance. He managed to get back to his feet, shivering as the sharp daggers of agony lashed his body. She helped him to sit down on the bed. He explained the problem to her after he'd wiped the perspiration off his face.

Christ, that was a bad one!

"What you need? What can I do for you?"

"My gear, it's in the bathroom cabinet."

His eyes were closed, screwed up tight against the agony. It enclosed him, became his entire world. He heard her run into the bathroom and emerge with the wallet where he kept his drugs and equipment. He didn't know how he'd manage to inject. He couldn't focus, could hardly breathe. But Kate used the syringe to load the blessed drug; she found a suitable vein and squirted it in. Almost instantly, the terrible agony began to recede.

"How do you feel now?" Her voice was cool, soothing.

"Better. Thanks."

"Yeah, but you won't thank me for what I'm going to say now. This has to stop, Jack. You can't go on like this. There has to be an alternative."

"I don't think there is, believe me. I wish to Christ it wasn't like this all the time."

"I'm going to see Hermann. I'll bet he has some ideas about how to sort this out."

"It's a waste of time. If he knew of a way to help me, he'd have pointed me toward it."

"I doubt he knows how bad things are, but let's see what he has to say first."

She looked around at Levi, as if noticing him for the first time. He was finishing off a second slug of bourbon, and the worst of his shaking had stopped.

"What happened tonight?" she asked him.

He was about to reply when there was a quiet knock at the door. Taylor scooped up his Sig, but Kate said, "It's okay. I asked Wesley to come here."

He still wasn't taking any chances, so while she opened the door, he kept his gun held ready, but it was Wes Harper. They shook hands as his old friend came into the room.

"You'd better sit down, my friend." He pointed at the other bed in the room and looked at Kate. "Did you invite anyone else here?"

She grinned. She seemed to have regained some of the good humor she'd lost when he'd tried to shut her out, and he even dared to hope she might have forgiven him.

"No, that's everyone. Levi, you were saying?"

"Oh, yeah. You asked me about the business at MMP."

He gave them an account of what had taken place at the developer's offices. She frowned when he mentioned Taylor had to shoot one of Gunter's henchmen, but he explained there was no option. Either the guy went down, or he would have been dead.

"You forgot to mention one thing," Taylor murmured to Levi, "the USB stick. We copied Hussein's private data from his PC."

Kate eyes lit up. "Jesus! That could help. Let me have it. Do you have a PC here?"

He handed her the data and pointed to the new laptop computer sitting on a table that doubled as a desk. She booted Windows 7 and inserted the USB stick.

"Damn! I think it was all for nothing."

"What are you talking about?" Levi asked her. "We almost got killed getting that out."

"It's encrypted, Levi," she replied gently. "I don't think this information will be of any use to anyone, except the person with the key to open it."

Levi laughed, "Are you serious? We used to break those encryption keys for kicks when I was in school. Give me ten minutes, and I guarantee I'll have it open."

She looked doubtful, but she passed the laptop across to him and left him to it.

"How are things with you?" Taylor asked Wes, who sat patiently in silence, waiting for them to explain. His old buddy carried himself now with the bearing and confidence of a professional soldier, or more accurately, a Special Forces operator. Wes was back. Harper gave him a fierce glance.

"Inside, man, I'm burning up. I feel as if I've wasted the last year sitting around waiting for someone to help, but I reckon I'm gonna be okay now. I saw the shrink your guy found for me, and he made a lot of sense. But what it comes down to, is no one can help me, except myself."

"And your friends," Taylor pointed out firmly.

"Yeah, that too. That's what the shrink told me. And I came to realize, if you want to get on with your life, to get justice, you gotta go out and get it yourself. That's why I'm here, Jack. This thing you started, I want to see it through."

Jack closed his eyes, wondering what kind of a road he was going down. They could fight together for justice, but it could easily put them into a full confrontation with the law, as well as Hussein's bunch of murderous thugs. He had little doubt Hussein would increase his security, probably by a factor of five or ten.

It's going to be tough from here on in, real tough. He smiled, what was that song? 'When the going gets tough, the tough get going.'

Yeah, that's it. These people, Kate Donovan, Wes Harper, and Jerry Yates, they're behind me all the way in their determination to see some kind of justice done. Well, that's fine by me, except I don't want to see any more people close to me hurt or killed. What can I do? The best I can. That's the only answer. Wes' wife has already paid the ultimate price, and Jerry Yates too. So yeah, it's too late to pull back. People are already dying. All I can do, am honor bound to do, is to put every ounce of effort into ending the toll companies like MMP are having on vulnerable vets.

He could see Kate watching him carefully, weighing him up, and waiting for his response to Wes Harper's outburst. He looked back at her, then at Levi, Wes, and finally to Kate. Before he could speak, Levi cried out.

"I've got it! I've opened the data. Jesus Christ!"

They crowded around the small screen while Levi scrolled through an email the Arab had sent that morning. They read it with growing astonishment. It was a message to detective Wasim Malouf, thanking him for his help with the company's recent security problems. It promised him a position as security director on the board of the new company that would own and run the new mall on the site of the homes in Wes Harper's neighborhood. On the surface, there was nothing they could use, not directly. It could be argued there was a degree of corruption, maybe, Hussein talking to a policeman about an offer of a plum job after he'd just done them a favor. But a clever lawyer would argue that Malouf was simply lining up a new job after taking early retirement from the Boston Police Department.

"That bastard cop," Wes snarled, "it's no wonder he wouldn't help us. Him and that sidekick of his, they're on the damned take, just as we thought."

"It's not enough for us to take him down," Taylor cautioned. "Neither does it say anything about the partner, Brad Stutz. I'm not sure he agrees with everything his superior Malouf does." He turned to Levi. "Can you keep going with the data and see what you can uncover?"

"Sure, I can take it home if you like. I could work on it there and let you know what I find."

Taylor shook his head. "No, that data stick stays here. When they know what we've taken, and they will know soon if they don't already, they'll scour this city with a fine toothcomb to locate it and get it back. We don't know what else is on it, but my guess is there's enough on there to do Hussein a deal of hurt."

"In that case, I can upload it to the web, to a secure storage location where we can access it from anywhere. It will mean that retrieving the data stick won't do them a bit of good."

"Do it. That information has to be protected at all costs."

While Levi continued checking out the data, he poured them each a slug of bourbon. They sipped their drinks in silence. Kate was sitting next to him, and she took his hand as if for reassurance he wasn't going to get away from her, not again. Finally, Wesley put his glass down and broke the silence.

"Jack, we need to know where we go from here."

Taylor stared at him. There was no point in trying to sweeten the medicine. He had to spell it out for them. After all, they'd be putting everything they had on the line, their lives.

"So far, we've given them a bloody nose, and got possession of data which could be used as evidence to do them a lot of harm. But now it could get real messy, tougher than you would believe. People are likely to die." He watched their grim faces as he spoke, catching their eyes, and none of them flinched. "My guess is they'll come gunning for us with everything they have. The bottom line is this. We're at war, and isn't going to end until one side wins."

CHAPTER SEVEN

Levi and Wes left the hotel to go home. They arranged to return in the morning to prepare for the next stage of the operation. Taylor didn't offer to fill them in on the details, for the simple reason he hadn't a clue how they were going to handle the mission to bring down MMP. A lot depended on what Levi found hidden amongst Hussein's data, and there was the question of what moves the developers decided to make when they realized the extent of their data loss. Taylor hated being on the defensive again, but right now, he didn't have too many choices. After they left, he turned to Kate.

"Any observations? I feel I've let them down. They needed to go off with something more positive than 'I'll let you know'."

"You haven't let anyone down, Jack. You have problems of your own, and yet you're trying to help these people to deal with the biggest threat they've ever faced in their lives. How's the pain, by the way?"

"I'm okay. Thanks for that shot earlier."

"Yeah, I could get ten years doing that. I'll talk to Doc Hermann tomorrow. There has to be another way. I doubt he realizes how serious it's become. It isn't until you spend a lot of time with someone, intimate time," she smiled shyly, "that the extent of it becomes clear."

"I'll manage," he shrugged gruffly.

"Cut the fucking macho crap! You can't manage, and you know it. You're a fine man Jack, and as far as I'm concerned, the issue with your legs is pure bullshit. It's sorted. All you need is to get over this pain problem, and I'll bet you could win the Boston Marathon."

"This year or next?" he grinned.

"Whatever. One more thing, you haven't invited me."

"Invited you to what?"

"To stay here with you, at least for tonight."

They lay naked together on the bed. He marveled at the touch of her firm, smooth skin as he inhaled the erotic musky scent of her. She ran her hands down his back, and then down his legs, past the join where his new legs began, and down past the exposed knee joints. And then she moved her hand and ran it up the inside of his leg and cupped his penis. He shivered at her touch, and buried his head in her sweet, shampoo-fragranced hair. The shot had started to wear off, and the pain was back. The jagged barbs that were the first indication lanced through him. But it wasn't so bad, as if he'd had another small hit, and the pain receded as he devoted himself, mind and body, to this girl who lay in his arms.

If this is one way to deal with it, I'm good.

When they could wait no longer, and the foreplay had brought both of them to the point of a climax, he entered her, and the lovemaking became more intense.

Both their bodies were slippery with perspiration, and it added to their sense of enjoyment, their pleasure in each other. They reached the end together, and Kate couldn't stop herself, she screamed out loud and long, filled with the most exquisite ecstasy. Afterward, they lay on the bed, silent. No words were needed. Until Kate's cellphone rang.

"Donovan. Who is it?"

She put her phone on speaker so he could hear. It was her reporter friend, Dan Blass.

"Hi Kate, it's me, Dan. Listen, I found some dirt on that guy you were asking about. You know, Mehdi Hussein, the Arab who owns MMP."

"That's great news, Dan. Well done."

He seemed to sense that her mind wasn't totally on the conversation. "Hey, I haven't called at a bad time, have I?"

"No, it's fine, of course it is. When can we see what you have?"

"I can meet you in the morning, say eleven o'clock. How about the Clarion Diner? Do you know where that is?"

"Yes, of course. We'll see you there then."

She ended the call. "What do you think? This could be what we need, someone who's prepared to blow the lid of Hussein's scam."

"Can we trust him?"

She nodded slowly, thoughtfully. "I think so. Yes, I'm sure we can. After all, he's a journalist. His job is rooting out corruption and stuff like that. It'll be fine. Let's go see what he has."

* * *

The Clarion Diner was an obvious place to meet; the building had once housed a local newssheet called the Patriot Clarion. These days, its claim to fame its fresh brewed coffee, which many patrons claimed was the best in the city. They approached the building from across the street, keeping an eye out for any signs of enemy action. Despite her confidence, Taylor still harbored a nagging doubt about the journalist. The diner came into view, about sixty yards away, and as they drew near, they saw Dan Blass walking toward the diner from the opposite direction. He constantly checked his surroundings, looking from side to side; his face wore a worried expression, which in view of the propensity of MMP to use extreme violence was unsurprising. It looked as like he may have been genuinely on their side, until another man came into sight, shadowing Blass at a distance of about ten yards. He was huge, dwarfing the other pedestrians around him. His face carried a look of savage intent, and when he looked across the street and spied Taylor and Kate, his smile was colder than the chill of an Arctic winter. Gunter Metz. They stopped, and Taylor looked around for the obvious trap. Sure enough, two men were watching them from a car parked a few yards behind them, Gunter's men.

"Kate, we need to get out of here, fast!"

"But…"

"Just move, let's go!"

One of the men in the car leaned out the window, and Taylor saw he was holding an AK-47S with the stock folded. It was probably the only thing that saved them. Without the stock tucked into the shoulder, it was virtually impossible to aim the weapon accurately. He fired off a quick burst, half a dozen shots that whistled overhead and missed them by a couple of feet. In the distance, they heard a cry, and Taylor saw Blass thrown to the ground. Two of the rounds meant for them had gone past and hit him. It looked to Taylor as if the wound was fatal, two 7.62mm bullets at such short range would hit a body like an express train. He dragged Kate into a narrow alleyway and started to run. He could hear the other men pounding along behind them, and he risked a quick glance behind. Both men were fit, probably former Special Forces, and behind them Gunter was doing his best to keep up. Taylor's tin legs bore him swiftly along, but he was worried about Kate. She wasn't trained to carry out the kinds of lightning fast maneuvers that were necessary for urban escape and evasion.

He briefly considered splitting up and drawing the men away from her. But if they saw the move, at least one of them would go after her. He had to get her away. He kept moving, using every trick of cover and angles to try and throw off their pursuers, but the men were still close behind. In desperation, he guided her into a narrow alley; a sign indicated it led to a large department store. But almost as soon as they'd rounded the corner, he saw his mistake. It was a delivery entrance, and all the doors were locked. He turned around, but it was useless, the men were almost on them.

"We'll keep going to the end of the alley and hold them off from there."

She ran on gamely until they reached the end of the narrow lane, and then they stopped. There were some garbage bins pushed against the building, and he tucked her down to hide behind them, but it was a futile gesture. AK-47 bullets would go through the bins as if they were no more than paper bags. Their pursuers slowed as they realized they had their quarry cornered, and then Gunter appeared. He walked along the alley and stopped halfway.

"You may as well give it up, Taylor. If you're lucky, I might let the girl go."

Taylor was still working out his options. He knew if he put down his pistol, the men would shoot both of them down like dogs. He had only one card left to play, and that was time; time, in the desperate hope that someone may happen by and called the cops. He tried to sound confident.

"It doesn't work like that. If you try and take us, I'll kill at least one of you before you get to me, maybe two. Which of you men wants to die first?" They looked at each other, and it was obvious he'd hit home. "If you let the girl go, I'll surrender."

He could see Gunter thinking furiously how he could twist the arrangement so as to allow him to get both of them, without losing any men.

"Okay, but you'll have to put the gun down first."

Taylor laughed, "What are you, some kind of an amateur? You know it doesn't work like that. She clears the area before I drop the weapon."

Gunter went up to his two shooters and talked to them briefly. Then he turned back to Taylor. "We got a deal, cripple. She can walk out of here, and when she's gone, you put down the gun."

Do these guys think I'm some kind of a half-wit?

"No deal, Gunter. The only way this will happen is if we all holster our weapons, and stand well clear while she walks out of this lane. Once she's gone, I'll hand you my weapon."

"No, Jack, no! They'll kill you."

"They'll try to kill me," he murmured. "Trust me, a lot of people have tried to kill me in the past, and I'm still alive. We have to do it this way."

"No, we don't." Her purse was slung on her shoulder; she reached into it, took out the Makarov and held it ready. He'd forgotten about it and he cursed. The last thing he wanted was for her to be caught in the crossfire of a gun battle. The other men watched carefully, but if they were concerned that both Taylor and Kate were now armed, they didn't show it. Perhaps they had little reason to worry; the two AK-47s and Gunter's pistol were more than a match for two handguns.

They stood in silence, confronting each other like it was an old-time Wild West gunfight. Even though a shootout would likely result in their deaths, he couldn't help but think of the old Gary Cooper movie, High Noon. All they were missing was the music.

I seem to remember Gary Cooper survived that one.

"Do not forsake me, oh, my darling."

She looked at him curiously. "What? What was that?"

He realized he'd spoken out loud. "Nothing. As soon as the shooting starts, get behind cover and keep your head down."

They waited, and the men facing them waited, each for the best possible moment for a chance to gun down the opposition before they had a chance to return fire. Neither side blinked. Then one of the shooters raised the barrel of his weapon as he prepared to deliver a burst from his AK-47. Jack aimed back at him, and his finger tightened on the trigger. And he stopped when he saw them.

"Hold it right there, motherfuckers!"

He looked up; two men had entered the narrow lane, two familiar faces. Wesley Harper, who carried Taylor's own MP 7, and Levi Yates, with the big Colt 45. Gunter and his men looked around uneasily. Even with the two assault rifles, they were sandwiched between four hostiles armed with three handguns and a modern assault rifle. They could still do wicked damage, but now the odds had changed. They were outnumbered four to three, and chances were they could all die. Wes followed up on the shock of his arrival, advancing slowly toward them, and keeping them covered with the wicked-looking MP7.

"Get out of here, or I'll empty the whole clip into you, and don't think those fucking commie popguns frighten me. I used to eat those fuckers for breakfast back out in the field. Now move your sorry asses!"

They looked at each other, and one of them licked his lips. Gunter knew it was the end. He nodded, and they backed away out the end of the narrow lane. They all heard his shout just before he disappeared.

"Don't think this is over. You're fucking dead, all of you. Dead!"

Taylor and Kate ran to join the two men.

"Wes, Levi, how the hell did you find us?"

He explained they'd returning to the hotel and seen them leave for the meeting with Blass. Levi followed them while Wes went to the hotel room and retrieved their weapons. He hid them under his coat and called Levi, who guided him to their position with his cellphone.

"Thank Christ," Taylor smiled grimly. "You got us out of one nasty situation." He stopped, as he thought about the enemy they faced and came to a decision. "It's time to stop these bastards back footing us. If we don't take the initiative now, we could find ourselves losing the war. So far, it's only been a couple of minor skirmishes. Let's make sure the next battle is one we're going to win."

Kate glanced at him. "How do we do that?"

"We take the fight to the enemy, that's how. We go right to the center of their stinking black heart and cut it out."

"Fucking A," Wes exclaimed. "It's about time."

"Right. The center of this thing is Hussein. I suggest we head back to the hotel, and get ourselves ready to go visiting."

They called a cab and returned to his room. Kate disappeared into the bathroom to wash away the sweat and grime of their encounter. When she reappeared, she'd remade her face, done her hair, and looked as fresh and beautiful as if she'd done nothing more strenuous than dinner with her lawyer friends. She stood outside the bathroom as they stared at her.

"What?"

"I guess we're all thinking the same thing," Wes replied. "You sure are a sight for sore eyes, Kate."

She went bright scarlet, mumbling her thanks for the compliment. Then her eyes found Taylor. "What's the next move?"

"We've been talking about that. It's time to pay him a visit, a home visit this time. Can you discover where he lives?"

She nodded. "It's no trouble. I'll get my clerk at the law center to look up the city records. Give me five minutes. It shouldn't take any longer."

While she was working the phone, he pulled weapons out of the canvas bags. Wes took the HK 416, and tucked a spare Colt 45 into his belt. Taylor wasn't comfortable with giving Levi anything more lethal than a handgun, and he handed him another Colt 45. But his father had trained him well on a variety of ordnance, and he eyed the M203 launcher hungrily.

"I put in a lot of time with one of those. My father brought home a box of practice grenades for me. We took it out into the woods and took down more than a few trees."

"You think you can handle it?"

"Like riding a bike."

He nodded. They could need the kind of heavy firepower the launcher would bring to their small band. Kate still had the Makarov. She seemed to be growing familiar with it, and as she was the only one of them with no training of any kind, it was enough for her to handle. Besides, it was a simple, tough weapon, as she had already demonstrated. He took some spare clips for his MP7 and the Sig Sauer P226, and after a moment's thought, dragged out a couple of innocent-looking rectangular, green metal cans from the bottom of one of the bags. Kate finished talking on her cell and went over to look at them.

"What are those?"

"Claymore mines. Just in case we need to get out of trouble in a hurry."

"What do they do?" she murmured, picking one up to inspect it, and grunted in surprise at the heavy weight.

"The M18A1 Claymore, this little tin can, is an anti-personnel mine. The name was taken from a large Scottish sword, by the way. Unlike a conventional land mine, the Claymore is command-detonated and directional, meaning it's fired by a remote command, shooting a pattern of metal projectiles into the kill zone like a shotgun. It fires these steel balls out to a range of about one hundred yards or so, in a tight, 60° arc directly in front of the device. We use them in ambushes, and as an anti-infiltration device against enemy infantry. They're also good against unarmored vehicles, like jeeps and trucks."

She swiftly handed the Claymore back to him. "It sounds horrible."

"It is. It's intended to be, but it's not as horrible as being chased by an angry horde of hostiles, and having no way to stop them hacking you to pieces. There are only four of us going in there, and we have no way of knowing what kind of opposition we may face." He smiled, "Just think of the Claymores as life insurance in case things start to look bad."

She shook her head, unimpressed. "Let's hope it doesn't come to that. Jack, you're not planning to kill Wasim Hussein? Because if you are, it makes this an assassination mission, and you can stop right now."

He took her by the shoulders and stared into her eyes. "Don't you know me better than that? We're trying to put a stop to this craziness, and every time we get near them, they start shooting at us. They do that, and we have no choice but to shoot back. But what we need is to grab the guy at the top, Hussein, and use our leverage to force him to stop."

"What leverage?"

"Oh, yeah, I forgot. You haven't done this before. It's quite simple; once we have him, he has a choice. Either put an end to this or we kill him. Easy. That's the leverage, his life."

"But you just said…"

"I know what I just said. It's a threat, that's all. He won't know that we won't go as far as killing him. The object is to make him believe we will."

"So promise me, you're not going in there to assassinate him."

"No way. Unless…"

She looked at him, her eyebrows raised.

"Unless he's trying to kill you. If that happens, he goes down."

* * *

It was a huge, old mansion on the outskirts of the city, illuminated by the rays of a moon that was almost full. The night was clear and cloudless, and Taylor cursed their luck. What they really needed was darkness to hide their approach and gusting winds to cover any sound they made. He put the thought aside. Luck was something you made, not a gift from the Gods. Accidents of weather and climate they just had to deal with. But the light of the moon sure showed the mansion at its most striking. Apparently, crime paid. Probably built by a 19th century wealthy shipping magnate, it was almost a fairytale castle. The building, tucked away behind a screen of tall trees, was constructed of pale gray, almost white stone with a dark gray, slated roof. Taylor counted at least eight large windows on the first floor, the same on the second floor, and several gabled windows set into the roof. At either side of the graceful structure was a round, turret-like extension that seemed to be tacked on at either end to the main house. Each of these turrets had a high, pointed roof, so the overall effect was like something from an old Hollywood movie set, or a medieval French chateau. Taylor had given his people instructions on how to follow signed orders so there would be no need for verbal commands that could be overheard. Wes had no problem with the arrangement, and Levi had learned much from his father. It was new to Kate, but she nodded her understanding. Besides, he arranged it so she would backstop him, and Levi would go with Wes. Taylor took a last look around. It seemed to be quiet.

He murmured, "Okay, let's move in. We'll keep it silent from here on in, so try and use hand signals where possible. Wes, you and Levi follow the line of trees to the right of the chateau and check out the rear. Kate, follow me. We'll skirt to the left, approach the front, and make entry by forcing one of the ground floor windows. We'll meet up in the hallway, and split up to search the house. I don't think there is anyone there. It's so quiet, but if any of you run into the enemy, you know what to do."

He ignored Kate's frown.

We have a job to do, and these scumbags drew first blood. They reaped the wind, and it's time they felt the chilly blast in return.

There was no problem reaching the house, and Taylor crouched next to one of the decorative windows with Kate right behind him. Everything was securely locked, so he had no alternative. He smashed the window with the butt of his MP7 and waited to see if the sound of breaking glass would draw attention from anyone inside.

"I don't think..."

Something. A sound!

He flashed a hand signal, but she looked blank.

"Quiet!" he hissed.

She fell silent, and he listened again. He was sure he'd

heard something, a faint noise, but he couldn't place it. It was like a squeak, something blowing in the wind, or maybe a small animal, that was possible. The noise didn't come again, so he unlatched the window, and they climbed inside. They were in an ornate hallway, and for a few moments they could only stare in silence at the opulent surroundings. The walls were clad from top to bottom in ornate marble; there were rich Persian rugs scattered at intervals over the marble floor. On one wall, there was a huge mirror with an intricate, thick gilded frame. Other walls carried a selection of paintings in similarly decorated frames. Taylor doubted any of them were reproductions.

"His business is sure making a bundle," Kate muttered, still wide-eyed.

He put a finger to his lips to silence her, and listened again. He was sure he'd heard that faint whine again, but when he concentrated, there was nothing. He jerked his gun around, hearing a noise from the back, but it was only Wes and Levi. He nodded to them, indicating they would start searching the first floor. Kate started to walk toward the staircase. A sixth sense told him what would happen almost before he took note of the security system that guarded it.

"Stop!"

It was too late. She put one foot on the first step and all hell broke loose. Whatever Hussein was trying to protect, or hide, it was clearly on the upper floors. No doubt the alarm was set on the staircase as a convenience, to keep the upper floors alarmed, and yet allow free access to his guests in the reception areas. Kate had broken some invisible beam, and the house echoed to alarm sirens, wailing both inside and out. The noise was deafening, and in addition, floodlights switched on outside to illuminate the grounds. It was surreal, an abrupt transition from the night's silence to the total chaos of the security systems. He heard the noise again, but this time there was no mistake. The whine was rising to a howling crescendo, and then the loud barking started, the deep throated, angry snarl of big mastiffs. Now he understood, they'd been stationed in some room, ready to be let loose when the alarm system automatically opened their cage door.

"Dogs! They'll be on us in a few seconds, Get moving, form a defensive perimeter."

"But, Jack, they're just dogs," Kate objected.

And then she gasped as the pack swarmed down the staircase, and the first two animals came into view. Taylor squeezed off a half dozen shots, and they went down, tumbling lifeless to the floor. One of the shots hit a dog behind, and it whined in agony but came on. Behind him, Levi cried out.

"Jesus, I know those bastards. They're Presa Canarios. Their bred for fighting, and when they get their teeth into someone, they won't let go. They're killers."

Taylor had read about them too. The Presa Canario hailed from the Spanish Canary Islands where the formidable animals were trained for hunting, and for war. During the 18th century, English merchants came to the Canary Islands, bringing with them their working and gladiator dogs, notably Mastiffs and Bulldogs. They also brought with them their traditions of pit fighting, for which their breeds and the island dogs were inevitably mixed and eventually bred to produce the ultimate fighter. The breed came to be used for guarding and driving cattle, but they were the same killing machines as when they first entered the fighting arena. Wesley opened fire as the rest of the pack came into view; single shots that slammed into the brutal animals and knocked them down before they could reach them. Except one, it came on; it seem to have a charmed life as it charged toward them without being struck by any of their bullets. It launched into the air, diving unerringly toward Kate Donovan's neck. She saw it coming and froze, and then there was the blast of a heavy handgun. Levi's .45 caliber bullet smashed into the animal, and the power of the heavy round knocked it away from its intended attack path. It was already dead when it landed on a ten thousand dollar antique Persian rug.

"Nice shooting, Levi," Taylor gave him an approving nod. "I can't see any more yet, but we need to keep our guard up. I guess those alarms will bring a posse of security men inside of about ten minutes. That's all the time we have. If we're not out of here by then, we won't get out."

"Those dogs were guarding the upper floors," Kate shouted. "We're on limited time, so we should search up there, and see if we can find anything we can use against Hussein. It's obvious he's not here, so we may as well make the best of it, and try and to take out something worthwhile. It could be we'll find documents to support that data you brought out from his office. Maybe even enough to bring him down."

Taylor nodded. "It doesn't make up for missing Hussein. We need to confront that bastard on our terms, but it's better than nothing. Levi, you go with her and see what you can find. Wes and I will set up a defense here, in case anyone turns up before we can get out. You'd better hurry it up. We're down to about nine minutes. You know what you're looking for, any kind of documents and photographs that could link him to illegal activities."

They ran up the stairs, and Wes went to the front of the house to check for signs of a response to the alarms. Taylor went to the rear and opened the door to check outside. He immediately slammed it shut and ran back to find Wes, but Harper was already running toward him.

"Jesus Christ, you see what I see?"

"Yeah, there must be twenty or thirty of them running around outside, the same breed of dog. The security system released them into the grounds. I guess the idea is to hold any intruders here until the guards or cops arrive; or rip them to shreds, so they never get out."

"How do we get out of here?" Wes asked. "We can take those brutes down, sure, but it'll take time. Hunting them down could take an hour, and we don't have an hour."

"You're right. We don't have an hour, so start picking them off. I'll go check on Kate and Levi. I guess that ten minutes is going to seem like a pretty long time. At least we're safe enough inside here."

He turned to start up the stairs but stopped when Wes shouted.

"They're inside the house!"

Fuck!

He'd forgotten the open window he'd used to force an entry. Already, he could see the first two dogs were sprinting towards them, and a whole pack of them howling and barking at the window as they competed to squeeze through the narrow opening.

"Fall back to the staircase! We'll try and hold them there."

The staircase was wider than he would have liked for defense against a howling pack of killer dogs, but they didn't have a choice. They stood shoulder to shoulder halfway up to the first landing, and shot the first two dogs as they tried to come at them, their slavering mouths open, teeth bared to savage.

"Kate!" he shouted up the stairs. "We got problems. You need to hurry up."

He heard her voice shouting back to him. "We need more time, Jack. There's a treasure trove of stuff up here. Documents, contracts, photographs, everything we need to link Hussein to local politicians and officials he must have bribed to obtain permissions to demolish whole streets of people's homes. But it's taking time to sort through them and find what we need. We can't leave now. We've hit the mother lode."

"Okay, we'll try and hold them off, but for Christ's sake, hurry!"

For some reason the dogs had stopped their direct attack and were pacing around in circles in the hallway, growling and snarling, as if they were psyching themselves up for the next attack.

Is that possible? Do dogs do that?

"Jack!" Levi called down from the second floor. "A heap of guys have turned up outside, and they don't look too friendly. The guy in charge is an Arab, looks like it's our guy."

Hussein! So that's why the dogs stopped. He used a whistle or electronic device to hold them back until he was ready.

He turned to Wes, standing beside him on the staircase. "They'll come at us soon, probably use the dogs to hit us first, then come in shooting behind them."

"Use the HK on full auto if they come at us. I'm going

to deploy a Claymore."

He planted the green metal landmine, digging the spikes into the woodwork, and went to the bottom of the staircase and into the hallway, to peer out of the big window at the end of the room. He could see them, a group of armed men. Guards, mercenaries, call them what you like, their intention was the same, to kill them for daring to intrude on their master's privacy. In front of them he recognized a familiar figure. Mehdi Hussein stood separately from them; out in front, a determined, vengeful warlord ready to kill to defend his turf. Taylor ducked back to rejoin Wes, and they waited for the attack.

"They'll unleash the dogs first. There are about ten guards out there and Hussein. They're coming to kill us, so when that Claymore detonates, give 'em hell!"

They waited as the seconds ticked past.

"What do you think?" Wes muttered. "I don't like this. It's too quiet."

"I'll go back down and check."

Taylor stepped back down the stairs and peered out. It was about to begin.

CHAPTER EIGHT

He watched Hussein wave to his men, and they began deploying in a semicircle. It was obvious their intention was to flank the front of the house. When they were in position, they waited motionless. The Arab took a small electronic device out of his pocket and pressed the button, simultaneously pointing at the house. Immediately, the huge, slavery mastiffs bounded forward, barking and snarling, intent on only one thing, to savage, maul, and kill. He ran back and joined Wes on the staircase.

"Fall back!" he shouted. "And keep your head down. I'm about to detonate the mine. The dogs are on the way."

They crouched on the landing of the second floor and looked down the stairs. The first of the dogs raced into view, growling and snarling, panting in their furious thirst for the kill. The rest of the pack was hard on their heels. It was time. He pressed the remote trigger and suddenly everything changed. It was if the dogs had hit a wall, but this was no ordinary wall. It was a living, lethal, murderous barrage of metal fragments, propelled by the force of the explosive charge. It tore through flesh and bone, killing some of the dogs outright. A few were left shrieking and dying on the expensive carpet that covered the floor of the hallway. Taylor snapped off a few well-aimed shots and finished off the wounded animals. And then Hussein came into view in the hallway. The Arab jumped back behind cover. His expression had been of stunned disbelief. Then they heard his voice. "Kill them! Kill them all!"

They hunched lower as a hurricane of gunfire splintered the walls. Hussein's gracious mansion was quickly becoming a ruin as the storm of bullets smashed around them. Now the Arab stood out in the open, watching and directing his men. Taylor fired off a couple of shots toward him when the incoming fire slackened momentarily, but the Arab was obviously wearing an expensive armored vest, and he only staggered slightly as the shots impacted on the heavy Kevlar plate. Now he was aware of the danger, and he shouted an order as he threw himself out of the line of fire. He shouted another order, and the firing intensified. Taylor was about to call to Kate and Levi when a burst ripped chips of wood from the balustrade next to where he crouched. The shots were loud, too loud. They were closer, much closer than he'd realized. He fired off a quick return burst, then shouted at Wes. He saw Levi had joined him with his big Colt, and they were firing single shots down the staircase and along the hallway to deter Hussein's men from coming any nearer.

"Move up to the second floor landing! We'll regroup and defend the staircase from there."

They raced up, and Taylor flinched as more shots whistled around them. Their situation had deteriorated badly. He'd hoped to hold them off until Kate had what she needed, and then slip out into the darkness after they'd killed the power to the exterior lights. But the main power switch was on the first floor, so his plan was completely fucked. He cursed himself for even considering they could get away with anything so simple. It was Hussein's house, so he would have thought to keep them away from the switches that controlled the security lights. They were on his turf.

"We're in trouble," he heard Wes murmur.

He smiled, something of his old friend's humor had returned.

"Maybe."

Levi looked alarmed. "Does that mean we're not getting out of this?"

"We're not finished yet, my friend. It's just that Wes is a natural pessimist."

"I wonder why that is," Wes added.

They turned as Kate hurried toward them. "I think I have everything. Two backup hard drives, a bunch of original legal documents and contracts, and a small notebook, which I think lists his offshore bank accounts. If this isn't enough to bring him down, we may as well give up. If he's doing what I think he's doing, at least from a quick read of some of this stuff, a lot of people are going to be very interested in having a chat with him. I'd hazard a guess he's into money laundering, tax evasion, fraud at just about every level, extortion, and plenty of other dirty little schemes we don't even know about yet. If we can…"

They all ducked as a renewed and sustained burst of gunfire chewed into the walls and woodwork all around them.

"He's brought his whole team inside," Taylor muttered.

"It's what I was hoping for. I guess it's time to leave."

"It's what you were hoping for?" Kate exclaimed. "I would have thought it was the last thing we needed."

He thrust her head down as the enemy opened fire again. Short, three round bursts, and then someone emptied an entire clip at them. She looked at him.

"Thanks. But how is any of this good?"

"If they're inside the house," he explained, "they're not outside the house."

"It still sounds bad."

"No, it means we can hightail it out of here."

"How do we get to ground level? You want us to jump out the window or something?"

"Or something. Don't worry; it's taken care of. Just take care of those documents. I'll worry about getting us out of here."

He rummaged in his pack and took out a reel of fine line.

"Wes, you know what to do. Use one of the windows at the rear of the house. Secure the line, but don't drop it outside until the lights go out."

He nodded and dashed away.

"Uh, do you know something I don't?" Levi asked him. "I mean, the switch for those security lights is sure to be downstairs, maybe even in the basement. It sure as hell isn't up here on the second floor."

"Don't worry about that. It's taken care of."

Taylor dragged out the second Claymore mine and began setting it on the landing. He noticed an ornate, inlaid console table topped with a vase of fresh flowers, midway along. He positioned the Claymore between the legs of the table, out of sight. As directed, he made certain to correctly position it to 'face the enemy'.

The firing from downstairs began to slacken, so they were up to something. Wes came back and nodded to indicate the rope was in place. Taylor ordered Levi to check the front windows to see if any of the hostiles were outside. He raced away, and Taylor turned to Wes.

"Did you see the overhead power line connecting the electricity to the house at the rear?"

"Sure, I wondered if we'd have to take care of that," he smiled, lifting his rifle. "You want it cut?"

Taylor shook his head. "Not yet, I want it to be a surprise for our friendly local Arab and his friends. Locate a window as close as you can get to the cable, and be ready to shoot it out. I'm guessing your HK 416 will make a useful set of wire cutters."

"Should do it," Wes nodded, and he went off to locate the overhead cable.

Taylor looked around; satisfying himself they were in the best possible position to make an effective exit. Levi returned and announced that the grounds to the front of the house were clear. It looked good, and he was about to shout for Wes to shoot out the line when a renewed burst of firing made them duck down. They heard the sound of many heavy footsteps charging up the staircase; a new attack had begun. The firing became intense, as Hussein's men pointed their guns around the corner at the top of the staircase, firing along the landing close to where Taylor's group waited. Levi screamed as a bullet sliced a piece of bloody skin from the side of his neck. Taylor nodded to Kate.

"Deal with it. It's just a flesh wound, but you must stop the bleeding. Levi, give me that launcher."

He passed over the M203 he'd been holding and a bag of grenades. Taylor checked the number of rounds while Kate fastened a dressing over the wound on Levi's neck.

There are enough. More than enough to give Hussein's people a bad day.

He flinched as he felt something slam into him. When he looked down, he saw that again he'd taken a round through one of his artificial legs.

These 'tin legs' are maybe more of an advantage than I realized, in a hot situation at least.

It was the second time he'd taken bullets through Doc Hermann's creations. And then he remembered the previous damage to his legs, which had threatened to stop him dead. He got to his feet, staying clear of the stray rounds ricocheting up and down the long landing. He tried walking and was brought up short. The damage was more serious than he expected. His right leg, the one that had taken the bullet, had stopped functioning.

"Is it bad?" He whipped around to see Kate crouched down next to him. He shook his head. "I'll be fine, just as soon as we get out of here. Is Levi okay?"

"The bleeding has stopped. But I need to know if you can walk, Jack. The truth."

"I can walk!" He regretted his savage rejoinder even as he spat the words out, and he saw the look of anguish in her eyes.

At least it's not pity.

He got to his feet and pulled her up and away from the swirling ricochets and chips of stone and plaster whistling around them. But he moved with difficulty, for his right leg was locked. All he could do was use it as a support while he dragged himself forward with the left leg. His irritation rose as he saw her watching him like a concerned mother hen.

"Look, I can make it! I've been in action with guys who've lost the use of both their legs, and they've still managed to crawl away. I can do it."

"Right." She shifted her gaze to a spot behind him as he heard a thump on the floor. "What's that?"

He whipped his head around, shoved off with his left leg, catapulting them away to land flat on the floor.

"Grenade! Get your heads down."

Kate gaped in astonishment, and then he slammed her face down hard into the thick rug that covered the floor. Levi had recovered fast, and he dived through a doorway into one of the bedrooms. The blast lifted them off the floor. He felt the air sucked out of his lungs, but mercifully none of them were hit with the metal fragments. He could hear Hussein on the first floor, shouting at his men to stop throwing grenades because they were damaging his antiques.

Jesus? Forget the human beings; just mind the furniture. A bit late for that, you fucker, he smiled.

"It's time to get out. Wes, cut the line."

"You got it, Boss."

They all heard the shout from downstairs.

"Taylor!"

Wes came back. "What do you want me to do?"

"Go to the window and standby to blast it, but wait for my order."

The former Seal loped off, and Taylor decided to give Hussein a chance to speak.

Does he know what we're planning? Probably not, so it'll come as a surprise when the place is plunged into darkness. It sure is nice to have something up your sleeve. Whatever the wily Arab intends, the power going out will certainly screw his plans.

"What is it, Hussein?"

"This has gone far enough. If you and your people put down their weapons, I'll let you go without anyone being hurt."

"Is that right? What guarantees do we get that you won't shoot us down like dogs?"

"You have my word. Look, I'm at the foot of the staircase, and I have put down my weapon to speak to you. Surely that is enough to persuade you of my honest intentions."

Like fuck it is!

Taylor put down the launcher and wormed his way forward, conscious that it was difficult belly crawling with only one good leg. He peered around the edge of the staircase and sure enough, the Arab stood at the bottom of the steps, with both hands held out in the open.

Should I take the shot? One bullet through the bastard's brain and it'll all be over. To hell with any notions of playing fair! I have the lives of three other people in my hands.

He eased his MP7 forward and sighted along the barrel. And as he did so, another fusillade of shots smashed around him. One pierced his upper arm, and he crawled back out of range, cursing himself for falling for Hussein's trap. The pain and numbness of the wound reminded him of the old pain, the agony that had dogged him ever since he regained consciousness in the hospital bed to find he'd lost both his legs. It was one hell of a place to realize he needed a hit of Oxy. A jet of agony ripped through him,

ERIC MEYER

and he closed his eyes to try and conquer the pain. When he opened them, he saw his hands were shaking badly.

"Jack! What's wrong? Is it very bad?" Kate blurted out, her face screwed up in fear.

"Gimme the launcher."

"What?"

"The fucking launcher," he snarled, "give it to me, now!"

She hurriedly snatched it off the floor and handed it to him. "You don't have to be nasty."

"Yes I fucking do. Gimme that bag of grenades, move it!"

She picked it up and gave it to him without another word. There was a grenade already loaded in the M203. He pointed it down the staircase and fired. The missile smacked into the woodwork near the bottom, ricocheting off the surrounding walls in the hall. It detonated with a satisfying roar, and he heard the screams from below. The blast radius had caught some of the enemy, possibly even Hussein, except he knew bastards like that were too clever to be caught so easily. They paid other people to take the hard blows. Wes watched him closely and waited. Taylor turned to him.

"We're getting out, cut the line."

He heard the chatter of the HK 416 as his friend emptied the clip into the overhead power line. There was a flash like a lightning strike outside, and then everything went dark, inside and outside the house. He looked at Kate and Levi, who watched and waited for his orders. He smiled inwardly.

At least she's worked out the heat of battle is no place for a debate.

"Okay, join Wes. He'll be waiting with the rope. We're leaving."

A half-dozen automatic weapons opened up, and the bullets ricocheted around them as the attackers tried to hit them with random strikes from ricochets, but they kept low as they crawled toward the bedroom where Wes waited. Taylor brought up the rear, for the simple reason that every movement was agonizing, like death by a thousand cuts.

"All of you get moving down the rope. Watch out for any signs of enemy activity down there, but I think they're all inside the house."

"What about you, Boss?" Wes asked, reverting to the old way he used to speak to his platoon leader.

"I'll wait until they come, and then I can detonate the Claymore. As soon as it detonates, I'll join you."

The three of them stared at him. They knew the truth. Knew he'd intended to hide it from them. He knew in his heart he was finished. It was only by using every last ounce of his iron will that he'd been able to keep going at all. The agony of his amputated limbs was tearing him apart. It was like being eaten up by a machine, hard, cold, and relentless. If he hadn't lost the use of one leg, maybe he could have tried to ignore it and keep going. But the adrenaline of action that had sustained him thus far was used up. Every last cell in his body screeched in unbearable pain. Each movement was like the torture of an inquisitor, designed to torment, to reduce him to a gibbering wreck that would do anything, say anything, and then welcome death just for an end to the pain.

"No, I'll cover our six," Wes said quietly. "You go ahead down the rope."

"I'm staying, Wes. I gave you an order. You have to get them out of here." The two men stared at each other for long moments until finally Taylor explained. "I can't go on, Wes. It's the end of the line. Everything's fucked up inside. You're the only one who can get them out of here."

His old partner sighed, "Yeah, I guess it's hard, but you remember how it used to be in the platoon? No one gets left behind. No one. Nothing's changed. We go out together, or not at all."

He shook his head. "It isn't going to happen. I mean it. I'm finished. My body is closing down on me, and that busted up leg is just about the end. I'll stay here and hold them off while you get out."

"And then what? You know what'll happen. They'll kill you. Is that what you want?"

Taylor shook his head, but even that was now an effort. Every movement resulted in more jagged shards of pain tearing at his weakened flesh.

"What I want has nothing to do with it. One way or the other, I'm finished, Wes. I can go out with a bang, with honor, protecting the people I love. Or I can hold you up, and make your escape all but impossible." He stared into Wes' dark eyes. "You can't carry a cripple out of here. Your only hope is to make a fast exit while I hold them back. You know that decisions sometimes have to be made for the good of the majority. Sometimes a life has end to enable three good people to live."

He sensed his vision starting to fade as the agony tearing through him began to shut his body down. Blood was oozing out of the wound in his arm, adding to the already impeded circulation from his double amputation. The shot that pierced his leg must have upset the data transmission lines, causing him to lose the muscle coordination to his other extremities, his arms and his hands. The signals to his brain, both his own and electronic, had gone crazy. He was a human being stretched beyond any reasonable hope of survival. He knew he was close to death.

"Bullshit!" Wes spat out. "There's no way! No way! Where's the detonator for that Claymore?"

Unable to resist, Taylor slowly opened his hand, and his friend took the remote.

* * *

Wes turned to Kate and Levi. Both of them were looking at Taylor in sorrow and disbelief.

"Get him up on the window ledge," Wes ordered them. "As soon as I give the order, Levi, get down to the ground as quick as you can. Kate, when he's down there, pull the line back and tie it around Jack. I'll lower him down. First, it's time to deal with those bastards."

His voice had become an angry growl. He picked up the launcher and the bag of grenades, snapped a new clip into his HK, and marched onto the landing. He could hear the sounds of Hussein's men as they inched slowly up the staircase, ready to renew their attack. He needed to hit them with one huge blow that would smash their morale, a blow so massive it would hold them back long enough to make an escape. And he knew exactly how to do it. Just as Taylor had done earlier, he bounced a grenade from the launcher down to the first floor. Before it exploded in the hall, he put another grenade in the air, then a third, and a fourth. He could visualize the entire hallway alive with lethal shards of shrapnel, as blast after blast shook the house. The men on the stairs had only one option; he'd effectively shepherded them with the grenades. They ran forward, away from the terrible shards of hot metal. They came onto the landing in a rush, filled with anger and terror in equal parts, determined to destroy, to gut, and to smash into broken fragments this hated enemy, who had caused so many of their comrades to fall injured and dead. Wes could see them now, without exposing himself to the gunfire. There was a mirror opposite the doorway where he crouched. It was smashed and cracked into many pieces, but enough glass remained for him to watch Hussein's men charging toward him until they were almost adjacent with the ornate, inlaid wood console table. Its vase of fresh flowers lay broken on the floor, several feet away. Wes hit the detonator, and everything changed in an instant. If Hussein thought the charge was about to bring his troubles to an end, he was wrong. The Claymore exploded in a thunderous roar, and seven hundred one eighth inch steel balls, propelled by a pound and a half of high explosive, hammered into the charging group of men. Most were killed outright, their bodies turned to bloody gristle, smeared over the walls and ceiling. None escaped the blast. Only a few, maybe three or four men were left alive. Perhaps for them it would have been better if they'd been killed outright. The cloud of hot steel had shredded their bodies, and they lay in a bloody heap. Incredibly, another man came forward, a man who'd been prudent enough to stay out of the line of fire until the others had prepared the way with their broken flesh. As Wes gazed at the carnage the Claymore had wrought, Hussein stepped onto the landing. He carried an AKM, the carbine length Russian assault rifle, and he leveled it at Wes and pulled the trigger. Wes felt the heavy bullets punch into his vest. He was thrown back, bounced off the doorframe, falling breathlessly on the floor in full view of the Arab. Hussein walked forward slowly, picking his way over the torn and broken bodies of his men.

"I think it is time you paid the price for interfering in my affairs, and for the damage you have done to my home," he said quietly to Wes.

"Yeah? You got a lot to learn, Hussein. People are a damn sight more important than a bunch of fucking paintings. Maybe when you learn that lesson, you can join the human race."

Hussein nodded coldly. "Sadly, my friend, you are about to leave the human race, so it is unlikely you will ever see that happen. I suggest you say your prayers."

His face twisted into an expression of fury as his finger tightened on the trigger, but the bullet that cracked out did not come from his gun. It was a 9mm bullet, one that sliced a chunk from the Arab's ankle. He jerked away and screamed in agony, loosing off a half-dozen shots into the already torn and broken plaster of his home. He took shelter around the bend of the staircase, peering back to see the cause of his pain. Taylor had used the last reserves of his strength to crawl forward, and though his vision was heavily fogged by agony and blood loss, had managed to loose off a single shot. He'd been unable to find the strength to raise his Sig Sauer above ground level, but it was enough. Hussein limped away down the stairs, blood streaming from his ankle. Wes turned around and saw his old platoon commander hovering between consciousness and unconsciousness.

"That was a motherfucker of a shot, Boss," he

murmured, still shocked from the bullets that had impacted his vest. "I thought my number was up."

Taylor dimly heard him through the thick soup that seemed to surround his body. The pain had changed to a different level, a kind of confusing, surreal experience.

It no longer hurts. That's strange. Everything's spinning. I know where I am, but why? I know it's a mission. It has to be completed. The Grim Reaper is reaching out his hand and beckoning, inviting me to join him.

It was his last recollection before he blacked out.

* * *

Kate Donovan looked at him in dismay. Taylor was clearly out of it. Levi had finally succumbed to blood loss and was slumped on the floor. Wes was groaning out on the landing. The bullets that impacted his vest seemed to have sent him into a state of shock. She had no idea how many survivors there were from Hussein's force, only that the Arab was still alive. She'd heard him shouting and then screaming when Taylor's last bullet hit him in the leg. She knew she had to get them out; somehow she had to force them to move. She went out to the landing and knelt down to talk to Wes.

"Does it hurt?"

"Is the Pope a Catholic?"

If he's able to make a joke, maybe there's a chance.

"Wes, I need you. Taylor is unconscious, and I think he may be dying. Levi's wound means he can't do much to help, so it's just you and me. We have to get out of here, and that means lowering Taylor down on the rope. It's the only way. Hussein is still down there somewhere with a machine gun. If we go down the staircase, he'll finish us. It has to be the rope."

He nodded, getting painfully to his feet. She steadied him as he stumbled, trying to get his balance, but he removed her hand.

"I can make it," he smiled. "I guess I just have a couple of bruised ribs, but it's nothing worse than that." He walked across to Levi. "Get out! We're going."

The young man looked up at him, and Kate gasped as she saw his face, pinched and strained.

"I can't, Wes. I feel dizzy. I need to rest."

"Fuck getting any rest!" he shouted. "Get up! Get your ass of the floor, soldier. Taylor is badly wounded, and if we don't get him out of here right now, he'll die."

"But…"

"Look, Levi," Wes said in a voice that was gentler, "you can do it. I've seen men in far worse condition than you run a mile to escape a screwed up mission. What are you, anyway, a fucking pansy? What would your dad think? That you're too weak and useless to hack it? Is that he'd expect from you?"

Levi shook his head, and Kate watched in amazement as Wes' macho challenge had its desired effect. He dragged himself up and stood there swaying.

"What do you want?"

"We have to get Taylor to the window and lower him down. He's a big guy. It'll take three of us to do it without killing him."

They dragged him to the window. Wes expertly tied the rope around him, and they used almost the last of their reserves of strength to bundle him out and lower him to the ground. Wes ordered Levi to climb down the rope next, and after a moment's hesitation, he obeyed, even though his movements were zombie-like. He almost made it, but eight feet above the ground the blood loss took its toll, his hands opened, and he dropped the final few feet to the ground where he landed like a sack of potatoes. Mercifully, he didn't fall on top of Taylor. Instead, he lay close by, obviously stunned. Wes nodded to Kate.

"You're next. Make sure you hold onto the rope until you reach the ground."

She climbed out of the window and slid down. As she put her feet on the grass, Wes came hurtling down to land beside her. She stared at him. He was festooned with weapons. As well as his HK 416, he carried the Levi's M203 grenade launcher and Taylor's MP7.

"Wes, we don't need all of those. It'll just be a burden. What's important is to get away from here and deliver Jack to the ER room."

"And when the cops arrive? If we leave our weapons here, covered in our own fingerprints, they'll be after us like we were Bonnie and Clyde. We have to take them with us. We can explain away so much, but the guns, no way."

"Hussein may not call the cops," she replied. "He has a lot to explain here, and I'm not entirely sure he'll want to spit it all out to the authorities."

"Maybe you're right, but I'm not taking any chances. I'm taking the guns. Let's go."

She never knew how they made it, but it was all down to Wes. Somehow, they were able to drag Taylor across the dark grounds to the edge of the property and reach the vehicle they'd parked hidden inside a small copse. She drove; Wes was all in after using the last reserves of his enormous strength to drag them away from the house.

She marveled at the change in the man. It was part physical and part mental, but one thing was for sure, he wasn't the same person she'd visited in his squalid house. Whatever had happened to him while he was serving overseas had changed him from a man with infinite strength and resources, a good man, even a great man, to the shadow that she first met. And now that man was back. Strong, granite-like, virtually indestructible. Would there be a return to the bad times after this series of setbacks? He hadn't been too badly wounded, but she wondered if it would be enough to send him back into the depths of despair and depression from which he'd emerged. She doubted it, for Taylor had that effect on people. He possessed an enormous inner strength. It was more than physical strength. He had that rare quality within men that inspired others around him to follow him, and to emulate him. To overcome any obstacle. She looked at Jack. He was lying across the back seat with Levi pushed into the corner. She knew he might die. The combination of the previous wounds, together with the terrible beating and the blood loss he'd sustained, could just tip him over the edge. And yet Jack Taylor was not the kind of man to just roll over and die. Not until he decided it was time. She suspected he'd fight until the very end to stay alive. Probably not for himself, but because he felt he owed it to his people to keep drawing breath to take care of them.

"He can't die." She surprised herself for speaking out loud.

"He won't die," Wes muttered. "It'd take more than some two-bit fucking camel jockey to finish him off."

She was grateful for Wes' confidence.

"We have two take him to the Emergency Room, Wes.

We'll go straight ahead to Boston General."

"That's a negative. You take him there, and the cops will be all over him. We're heading for Southie."

"Where?"

"South Boston, it's what the locals call it."

"Is there a hospital there?"

"There's somewhere for us to hide out while we work out our next move. And as soon as we arrive, I'll call Doc Hermann. He'll fix him up. He won't let Jack die."

I hope not, more than anything else in the world, I don't want the man I love to die.

* * *

"Where am I?"

He could see their shapes around him, and he recognized Wes' voice. And then Kate spoke. She said something he couldn't quite make out. There was someone else in the room, a man, and then his eyes focused. It was a stranger, no, he'd seen him somewhere before. He just couldn't remember where.

"You're in South Boston, Jack. You're safe."

He looked at Kate, then down at the mass of dressings covering his body, and the drip bags that hung from portable stands. But it wasn't a hospital. It was a bedroom. Whose?

"Boss," Wes murmured quietly, "this is Lincoln, Lincoln Moss. We're in his house."

Kate's face swam into his focus. "Lincoln is one of my clients at the law center, Jack. I believe you may have seen him there when you came to visit about Wes' problems."

I remember him now. The former marine, he was with

his wife, and they were trying to avoid a foreclosure on their house. It must be this house.

He nodded to the stranger.

"Thanks, Lincoln. It's appreciated."

Moss nodded. "It's no problem. Anything I can do, just say the word."

He looked at the former marine. Moss had skin that was a few shades darker than white, but he was paler than Wes. He'd once been good looking. His big marine's physique was still in evidence, and despite his years, he looked tough, like aged oak; a man who hadn't forgotten everything he'd learned in the Corps. His hair, like the Marines, was a buzz cut. Dark, almost black, short enough for the skin of his scalp to show through.

Taylor looked at Kate again. "How did you fix me up? This setup looks pretty professional."

"I called Doc Hermann. He came here and fixed you up. He cleaned your wounds, Levi's too. Levi is in the next room, and he fixed him up pretty good. Hermann said he's repaired the worst of the damage to your leg, and when you recover your strength, you'll be as good as new. He wants you to go see him as soon as possible. He has some kind of an upgrade he wants to install."

"He always has a new upgrade," Taylor smiled, and then winced.

The pain, it's coming back, maybe not as bad still. It was worth getting beat up.

"It doesn't hurt too much." He hadn't meant to say it aloud. He hated admitting he had a problem, that he was anything other than as fit and able as the next man. But it was too late.

"That's the drugs," Kate replied quietly.

"Right. Are you telling me Doc Hermann prescribed IV painkillers? That's not like him. Jesus, I must have been bad."

"Yes, we thought you were going to die. Hermann hasn't changed his mind about anything. I got you the drugs."

"You mean…"

"Yeah, I found a dealer on a street corner and bought what you needed."

He couldn't bring himself to reply. He knew what she would have felt, the same emotion he felt every single time. Sick disgust that things had got so low it was necessary to deal with lowlife scumbags. But there was something else. His appreciation of her soared to new heights, that she'd been prepared to do that for him, to go against everything she believed in.

"Thanks. I owe you for that one."

"Don't be stupid, Jack. You don't owe me anything."

He nodded dumbly. What she'd done represented something that was worth much more than money.

"Did Hermann say how long before I'm back to normal?"

"About a week. He wants you to talk to a psychologist when you're recovered, about weaning yourself off the drugs."

Taylor feared little, but he lived in terror of losing his supply and having to endure the resulting agony. A psych would want that.

No way.

"Fair enough," he lied. "I want to thank you all. You did a fantastic job, getting me out of there. Is there any noise from the cops?"

Wes stared at him, and Taylor could see his lips moving

as he muttered in anger. "What are you talking about, 'got you out of there'?" He blazed. "You got us out of there, Boss. If you hadn't done what you did, we'd have been dead. All we did was walk away after you'd ripped Hussein's shooters into little pieces. The cops were all over the house afterward. I don't know who called them, but there was so much noise from the gunfire and explosions that people would have called it in. They couldn't have missed it. I'll bet they heard it from the Top of the Hub. The sky was crowded with news helicopters too, but none of them have the full story."

"Are we wanted for what happened there?"

"The cops called around to my office. They want to talk to you," Kate said quietly. "I would guess Hussein has cooked up some story. He must be terrified of you, the way you've gone after him with all guns blazing."

"Good."

"Good? It's not good. It's not good at all," she said angrily. "The moment you appear in public, they'll be all over you to drag your sorry ass downtown and beat the truth out of you." He saw her expression change. "There's another thing. I got an unofficial message; one of the MMP people came into the law center, Grant Williams, the manager. He says Hussein is prepared to end it now, if we stop the war. He'll forget what happened, leave us alone, and won't even press charges. He's frightened of the documents we took from his house, of course. That's why he's making the offer. I'm still looking through them, but I suspect there'll be enough in there to make life very difficult for him."

"That's good news."

"So this violence can end?" she replied hopefully.

"I meant it's good that Hussein is frightened I won't stop until I screw him into the ground."

"I don't understand. We've lost, Jack. Sure, we can cause more damage and upset, but he'll put it all right in the blink of an eye. He'll screw the money out of his business interests and won't even notice it's gone. As for his men, I would guess all it means is now most of those guards are dead he won't need to pay them. There's nothing more we can do. That guy Williams said he's brought in new men; many more than he had before. I believe there are around fifty of them to protect his interests. He's better protected than the President. You can't go anywhere near him. He's surrounded by a ring of steel."

He saw Wes and Lincoln watching him. He knew they didn't see things quite the way Kate saw them, any more than he did.

"Nuts."

She looked puzzled. Wes and Lincoln both smiled. "Nuts?"

"Wes, tell her."

"Sure. Kate, did you learn about the Battle of the Bulge when you were in school?"

She looked uncertain. "Wasn't that the war in Europe?"

"Yeah. General McAuliffe was the divisional commander of the 101st Airborne Division, the Screaming Eagles. They were defending Bastogne, in Belgium, during the Battle of the Bulge, in the Ardennes Forest. The Germans surrounded him, and told him to surrender, or they'd open fire and wipe out his force."

"Did he surrender?"

Wes shook his head. "Did he hell. He sent back a one-word reply. Nuts!"

Her face paled, and she looked at Taylor. "You don't mean…"

"I mean that no lowlife Arab scumbag tells me when I can lay down my guns and hightail it out of town. What was it Hermann said? A week before I'm out of here?"

She whispered a reply, "Yes, at least. Please, you need to take it easy."

"Wes, Lincoln, I'll get a night's sleep. Tomorrow I'll get dressed, and we'll resupply everything we need from the store in my parking garage. Then we hit him."

"Hit him? You must be mad? Hit him where? Kate asked.

"When Gen McAuliffe was surrounded at Bastogne, I believe he said for the first time it gave him a unique advantage. No matter which direction he went in, he'd be able to engage and destroy the enemy. I'm sorry Kate, but this has to end, and on our terms. Hussein's going down, and anyone who stands with him."

"Hooyah!" Wes shouted, the former seal.

"Oorah!" Lincoln shouted, the ex-marine.

Kate shook her head. "You stupid, macho bastards. You're mad."

"So you'll stay clear of this?" Taylor asked anxiously.

She gave him a grim smile. "Not in a million years. I've had enough of trying to patch together the wreckage of his victims' lives. I'm in."

She turned as a familiar figure hobbled in through the door, covered in bandages. It was Levi.

"You can count me in. Dad would turn in his grave if he thought I was backing out now."

Kate shook her head. "If Hussein could see us now, I doubt if he'd be too worried."

"I can promise you this," Taylor said quietly. "That guy has a helluva lot to worry about. More than he could ever imagine."

Wes nodded. "Amen to that."

CHAPTER NINE

His sleep was not peaceful. The drugs Kate had introduced into the drip that fed into his veins were not enough to satisfy his urgent need. Every cell in his body cried out for relief. And yet in his mind, there was an emotion screaming even louder. He reflected on the formidable Arab he had set out to destroy, a man who had built his fortune on other people's poverty, misery, and death. He left a long trail of ruined victims in his wake, from the war vets whose lives he destroyed by conning them out of their homes, to his employees, the men he was prepared to throw away like chaff to defend his illicit fortune. There was no doubt the man had to be dealt with. This had to end. He thought about the problem of Wasim Malouf, the cop who'd thrown in his lot with Hussein. All he could do was sidestep him, and hope that sooner or later the police department would catch on to the evil he'd perpetrated on the very people he was paid to defend. Taylor could see dawn peering through the drapes, and in the chill, grey light, he saw Kate Donovan, asleep in an armchair close to his bed.

So she's been keeping watch on me, he smiled.

In slumber she looked if anything more beautiful and more exotic than when she was awake. Her face was completely relaxed, and her hair had flopped down over one eye, giving her a tousled, faintly erotic appearance. He jumped as her eye opened. She grinned at him.

"Jack Taylor, you were watching me. I was supposed to be watching over you. I must have fallen asleep for a few moments. How do you feel?"

He hurriedly checked his watch.

Jesus Christ, it's already 0900! Today I planned to get dressed and put into action the plan I've been working on ever since I woke in Lincoln's house.

"I'm okay, but it's late. I need to get dressed. Where are my clothes?"

"I put them..."

It was as far as she got. The bedroom door burst open as if hit by a hurricane, and a man forced his way inside. He carried a typical doctor's bag.

"Doc!"

Hermann van Rhoos nodded. "Yeah, I'm a doctor, and that means you're going nowhere, pal. I have to check you over. Sol, come on in and take a look at the kind of problems I have with this guy." Another man came into the bedroom. "This is my colleague from MIT. Sol Weinberg, meet Jack Taylor, my prize patient and the source of a good few headaches."

The new arrival walked forward, smiled, and offered his hand to Taylor. Tall, thin, neat to the point of fastidious, with a bow tie and custom-made suit with contrasting woolen vest. His face was pale; this was a man whose career obviously kept him indoors. His piercing blue eyes gave the impression they saw everything, and understood even more. Yet they also carried a look of compassion and warmth, which made Taylor feel here was a man to like. His hair was a rich blonde, beginning to turn grey in places, and he wore a small pointed moustache. The impression he formed impressed him. Sol Weinberg looked like a man who could stare deep into the human psyche, find the cracks and strains, and instinctively repair them with the deft touch of a highly trained surgeon.

Maybe he can help, maybe not, but the timing couldn't have been worse.

"Doc," he said to van Rhoos, "I appreciate what you're trying to do for me, but right now I have some important stuff to deal with. I'll give Dr. Weinberg a call when I'm finished, and we can fix up to get together."

The psychologist smiled gently, but van Rhoos shook his head. "Not a chance! You know as well as I do the problems you're experiencing with pain. Sure, I know some of it is physiological, but a good deal is psychological. A few sessions with Sol, and you'll feel a lot better believe me. Besides, you can't go anywhere right now. You've had one hell of a battering, and if you try moving around before you're fully recovered, you'll undo all the good work I've done putting you back together." He stared hard at Taylor, trying to impress upon him the importance of what he was saying. His expression softened. "Just a week, Jack. Just seven days, maybe even five if you make good progress. And during that time, you can have a couple of sessions with Sol."

They argued, and Taylor knew he was in for a fight. If there was one man in this world who he respected more than any other, it was the one who had given him back his life. But it was no go.

"Doc, there are people in trouble, people who depend on me. If I don't get back out there and finish the job I started, a whole lot of crap is going to fall on their heads. It's something I have to do." Something occurred to him, an argument he could use with Hermann that he may listen to. "You haven't fixed me up just to put a coward back on the streets, have you?"

Hermann stared at him long and hard. Finally, he grimaced and turned to his colleague. "What do you think, Sol? Is there any way I can persuade this stubborn bastard to follow his doctor's orders?"

Weinberg wrinkled his brow in thought and shook his head. "I doubt it. In my experience, a man with that kind of motivation is like one of those supertankers that sail the seas loaded with oil. Once they've started, there's no stopping them. I'd suggest giving him what help he needs, and attaching a couple of conditions."

Hermann nodded thoughtfully, but Taylor snapped out, "What conditions?"

"That you come to my rehab clinic as soon as you're done, and make time for your appointments with Hermann of course. It's nothing you can't manage, just turning up to see your physician. And if we physicians think patients are putting themselves at risk, the law allows us to compel them to be detained." His smile was back, but behind it Taylor could see there was an iron will that matched his own. He nodded.

"Agreed, I'll be there. I reckon we'll need two or three days to finish this business. One way or the other."

He chatted to Sol while Hermann gave him a quick

physical. Eventually, the two doctors left, and only Taylor's 'squad' was left in the room. Wes, recovered from his PTSD, managing to cope with the discomfort of a couple of cracked ribs; he was rock solid and as tough as the hide of a buffalo, so he'd be fine. Lincoln, the ex-marine, older but still in good shape, and like Wes, threatened with the loss of his home; so he was determined to put his old military skills to the test once more. Levi, he looked pale. He'd been hit hard, but while Taylor was unconscious, Doc Hermann had given him a transfusion of a couple of pints of blood to help him recover what he'd lost from his wound. And Kate. Beautiful, clever and full of grit, a girl without whom he'd undoubtedly be dead by now. He was loath to put her in the path of danger because of his strong feelings for her. Feelings he knew could go nowhere. They'd grown close, but it was no good. He couldn't burden her with a crippled vet, no matter how good his prosthetic limbs. She was entitled to her own life, a good life, with a man who was strong and whole. Yet he knew dissuading her from this fight was a waste of time. In the short time he'd known her, he'd seen at first hand the single-minded determination that marked her out as someone special. There'd be no stopping her, so all he could do was take every precaution to ensure nothing bad happened to her. He could see they were watching him carefully. Waiting. Finally, he smiled.

"Okay people, let's get this moving. We need a car. We can't go back for the rented Dodge. We have to pick up the weapons and equipment I have stashed in the underground locker at my parking garage. We'll need to replace the stuff we lost at the mansion, and maybe grab a couple of items to give us an edge when we next meet

Mehdi Hussein and his friends."

"I have a car. It's not much, but you're welcome to it."

He nodded at Lincoln. "That's great, anything that runs will be fine. What vehicle is it?"

Lincoln Moss grinned. "Why, it's a Lincoln of course. She's an old 1990 town car. She has a good few thousand miles on the clock and a few holes in the bodywork, but I keep the mechanics in trim, and she runs pretty sweetly."

"That'll give us plenty of room for our equipment," Taylor replied, with a nod of thanks. "I need to get dressed, if you guys could give me some space."

"You want me to lend a hand?" Kate asked him.

"I thought you'd never ask."

It may have been old, but Lincoln's Lincoln was a classic, in a rich maroon finish with sumptuous dark gray upholstery. The paintwork was dotted with rust in places, and the leather was cracked and slightly torn, but as Kate drove away, the huge V-8 engine that still beat healthily under the hood gave a low-throated gurgle. He looked at the rich walnut control panel and couldn't help but admire the finish of this beautiful piece of machinery.

A few hundred dollars, well, maybe a few thousand, and several weekends' work, and she'd look like new.

He was nervous about the materials they'd taken from Hussein's house because she'd decided to keep them with her, and because of their importance. They were on the back seat in a briefcase Lincoln had given them.

"It'd be better if we left them here," he'd tried to dissuade her.

"No, Jack. This stuff was taken illegally. If the cops found out about Lincoln, they could bust in here and have all the evidence they'd need to pin that business at

Hussein's place on him. I'll find somewhere better to keep them."

They reached his parking garage, and Chuck regarded his new conveyance with astonishment.

"Hi, Mr. Taylor. Wow, that's really something, but it doesn't look like your usual wheels."

"It's a project, Chuck. The Camaro looked worse than this when I bought it. She just needs some love and attention, and she'll be one beautiful piece of machinery."

"I guess you're right," the attendant nodded doubtfully. "Good luck with it, but I reckon it'll be more than a few weeks before it's done."

"It's the journey I enjoy, my friend. Arriving is just the icing on the cake."

Chuck nodded again as he raised the barrier and allowed Kate to drive inside.

The parking bay next to his Camaro was empty, so she slid in adjacent to Taylor's gleaming red muscle car. He handed her the keys, and she backed up the Chevy enough to gain access to the underground store. She opened the high security locks holding the steel hatch in place, and Taylor helped her lift the heavy cover. He carefully made his way down the steps, grunting in pain from his injuries, and surveyed his store of ordnance. She watched him with concern.

"You're in no shape to go up against Hussein and his goons, Jack. Doc Hermann is right. You need more time to recover."

He shook his head. "It's now or never. I learned in the service that when you start putting pressure on the enemy, you keep hitting them. You never let up."

"I think they've been putting pressure on you, on us.

229

That's the problem."

He looked up at her. "Maybe you're right. In which case, it's time for the winds of change to blow through that greasy bastard's company."

He picked out two more Claymore mines. They'd saved their asses during the attack at the mansion, and maybe they'd come in useful again. Then he bent down, feeling every muscle strain with the effort of moving, and dragged a wooden case from the floor and passed it up to Kate.

"Be careful. This baby is heavy."

"What's inside the box?"

"Russian-made RPG. It's the shoulder-launched weapon that's the terrorist's choice of killing machine, after the Kalashnikov AK-47, of course. It'll give us the ability to standoff and hit them from a distance. Kind of like artillery," he grinned.

Her eyes narrowed, but she made no comment. He filled a canvas bag with more grenades for the M203 launcher and stuffed in boxes and clips of ammunition for their personal weapons, the HK 416, his MP7, and the different calibers for their pistols.

Levi's heavy Colt packed a .45 caliber round, while his Sig Sauer a 9mm bullet. Wes' HK 416 used a 5.56mm NATO cartridge, and his MP7 the tiny but incredibly powerful 4.6mm ammo. A lot of different calibers, not normally good military practice, but for Special Forces, it was not unusual. Whichever weapon the job needed was the one you carried.

"You still packing that Makarov?" he asked Kate.

She nodded. "I doubt any girl in your company would be well-dressed without it."

He looked at her, she wore the beginning of a smile, but

there was a grim message there. This wasn't her scene, and the sooner it was all over, the better. She was more used to using a lawyer's briefcase to fight back against crooks, than a gun. Even so, she understood what they were up against. Probably, Mehdi Hussein had learned the art of running a business in his brutal homeland, some Arab shithole, wherever that was. He didn't yet realize that in the United States, people were different. Most, though not all, people had standards, and in general treated each other with a degree of humanity. A humanity that was often absent in the lands ruled over by the fanatic Islamic warlords. As far as Taylor was concerned, by declaring war on wounded vets, Hussein had declared war on every decent American, those who cared for the people who suffered and died for the freedom of their homeland.

Someone has to stand up and be counted, that's for sure. People have to draw a line in the sand. What was it that a philosopher had once said?

'All that is necessary for evil to flourish is for good men to do nothing.'

Yeah, it was some Brit, Edmund Burke, from a book I read long, long ago. So bring it on, Hussein. The good men are not going to do nothing. They're sick to their fucking back teeth with the shit you've been dishing out. Now you're going to get some of it pushed back in your face.

He gathered together several blocks of C4 plastique that were long past their sell-by date, together with their detonators, and passed them up for Kate to load in the trunk.

She helped him load the rest of the ordnance into the huge trunk of the Lincoln. It was just as well Lincoln Moss hadn't owned a Japanese compact. It would have made their mission almost impossible. Even so, Taylor had to force the lid down hard to close it. She took the wheel and drove away. Taylor waved to Chuck as they went under the barrier.

"You won't recognize this car when we come back, my friend. Just wait and see."

"You betcha, Mr. Taylor. You go for it."

He brought the barrier down, and Kate drove out of the garage and onto the street. She got ten yards before a car swerved across their front, forcing her brake to a halt, an unmarked car with a strobe light flashing inside the windshield.

"Cops."

"Yep," Taylor agreed, "but I only see one. That's strange. If this was a bust, there'd be more of them."

He recognized the guy who stepped out of the car and approached the Lincoln. Detective Brad Stutz. They both climbed out and waited for him to come up to them. They eyed each other in silence for a few moments. In Stutz's case, it was more of a glare. Finally, he spoke.

"Do you people mind telling me what's going on? You, Taylor, you're nothing but trouble. Wherever you go, I see chaos and destruction. But you, Counselor," he said, looking at Kate, "I would have thought you'd have better things to do than chase around Boston helping this guy make a mess of our fair city."

She wasn't fazed. "Where's your friend, that other cop, Wasim Malouf? Has he gone to visit his good friend Mehdi Hussein to collect the payoff?"

The young detective flushed bright red. "I don't know a damn thing about any payoff. If there's something you know, and you're not telling me, maybe you should come clean. If a cop is bent, the Department can't do anything about it if they don't know. Are you saying Detective Malouf is on the take?"

They both laughed. "We don't have any evidence," Taylor explained. "But there's a long list of people, many of them wounded war vets, who your friend is helping Hussein to put them out of their homes so he can redevelop. Maybe you think he's doing it for free? How about a favor to a friend from the local mosque, is that what it is?"

Stutz sighed and shook his head. He stared back at Taylor. "I honestly don't know. I've had suspicions for some time about him, but he's the senior man, and I don't have a lot of choice but to follow his orders. Internal Affairs contacted me yesterday. Malouf is under suspicion. They didn't tell me what it was for, but it doesn't take a genius to work it out if what you say is true. By the way, you didn't hear that from me. It's confidential."

He stared at them for a few seconds, waiting for a reaction. When he realized it wasn't coming, he pressed on.

"You know about that business at Mehdi Hussein's house? Someone went there and shot the place to pieces. I've been out to look at the crime scene, and it's like downtown Baghdad after the Second Gulf War. The place was strewn with bodies, and smashed up furniture and artworks. We understand most, if not all of the victims were mercenaries. Ex-military people." He looked hard at Taylor. "So I assume it would need someone with military training to take down people like that. I checked your records, Mr. Taylor. You were a Navy Seal." Taylor didn't confirm or deny anything. He just waited. "It would need someone from an elite unit to wipe out a bunch of mercs. Do you know anything about it?"

Taylor considered his reply. He knew they were treading a fine line. They had a trunk full of weapons and equipment, and if he gave Stutz the excuse, the guy could impound the car and obtain a search warrant to open it up. He had to say something, just as long as it didn't incriminate anyone. Especially Kate. She was a practicing lawyer, and the last thing she needed was a brush with the law that would wind up with her disbarred as a convicted felon.

"Where are you going with this, Stutz? What do you want from us?"

"The truth. A lot of things are going wrong in this town, and now my boss is under investigation. It looks to me as if Hussein and Detective Malouf are linked, and something happened at that mansion as a result. I'm looking for some answers."

I have to give him something. After all, he's a cop, so he won't just give up.

"On or off the record? And I would remind you," he said with a grin, "I have my lawyer with me."

"Yeah, I see that. You can have it any way you like. I'll take it off the record for now if you want. It may change later."

"I can't give you names, but everything I tell you is documented and true."

He nodded his understanding. "Could you provide evidence of that? Witnesses, documents and so on?"

Taylor nodded. "Yeah, we can. Enough to put those bastards away for life."

"Okay then, let's hear it."

Taylor sketched out the story from when he'd first encountered Hussein's muscle hammering in the foreclosure sign outside the home of Wes Harper. He told him about Jerry Yates, and the street gangs who were responsible for his death. Street gangs working with Hussein to tear up the lives of local people and drive them from their homes. He told him, without giving any name, of the former marine who'd gone to the law center after Hussein's MMP began to target his home. Stutz looked at Kate with his eyebrows raised, and she inclined her head that it was true.

He nodded. "Okay, I think I got it. If this deal is as big as you say, it's a conspiracy that must involve a lot of people. I mean; you can't get away with something that big without inside help from the Department. Someone had to make the complaints go away."

"Not someone, Detective. Wasim Malouf."

He looked at her. "Maybe you're right. What about the fight at the mansion?"

"I'll tell you what I heard," Taylor said with a straight face.

"Whatever. Give me what you got."

He gave a brief outline of the battle at Hussein's mansion.

"Why would those people have gone in there, what were you," he stopped, and smiled, "I mean, what were they after?"

"Documents, hard drives, data records, you name it. I think it's what you cops call evidence. What you're paid to go looking for."

Stutz flushed. "Okay, okay, maybe we fell down on this

one. Did these people find the evidence they were looking for?"

"I believe they did, yes."

He was thoughtful for a few moments. He looked up and down the street, as if to make sure they weren't being spied on.

"Okay, I need to know what these people took out of Hussein's place."

"I'll get in touch with them," Kate replied. "I'll let you know."

He nodded. "Make it quick. This investigation is starting to move, and those documents could make the difference between a conviction and allowing a dirty cop to go free. Believe me, most of us want this cleared up pretty soon. If Detective Malouf is on the take, he can rot in hell as far as we're concerned."

Taylor nodded uncertainly. "You'll understand when I say it's hard to believe that, Detective Stutz."

He flushed. "Nonetheless, it's true. I know we're not perfect, but give us some credit, for Christ's sake."

They agreed to contact him the following day to arrange a handover of any material they could obtain from the 'unknown people' who'd invaded Hussein's house. Finally, he nodded he was satisfied.

"Okay, but make sure you call me the second you know anything. If this gets screwed up, I'll spend the rest of my career giving out traffic tickets."

As they drove away, Kate glanced across at Taylor.

"Do you trust him?"

"I don't know. But we need him, someone on the inside. He seems on the level, so we'll cooperate for now, but we also have to make certain we cover your back."

"Me? But why?"

"Because you're a lawyer. The last thing you need is to tangle with the cops and maybe get disbarred."

"And you? You think if they locked you up, you'd be okay?"

He knew what she meant. He'd almost been climbing the walls when she got him out of the cell. He shrugged. "I guess I'd manage."

She gave him a pointed look, and he looked away. The damage his body had sustained during the attack on Hussein's mansion was still not healed. There was no way he could listen to Doc Hermann's advice and rest for a few days. What he told them was true, once a mission began it was essential to keep the pressure on, to attempt to keep the enemy back footed. He was about to say something more, but he winced. The old agony was returning, starting to build in the familiar vicious waves. Lashing attacks that tortured every fiber of his being. He saw his face in the vanity mirror; his skin was pale, clammy, and wan. His face seemed to dissolve into a thousand fine wrinkles, and his eyes half closed as he attempted to contain what was eating him up inside.

"You're not managing now, are you?"

He said nothing. If he told the truth, he would have to tell her he wanted to shout a long scream of agony as he pounded his head against the windshield, in a forlorn attempt to take his mind off the pain. He knew it wouldn't work. It never did, just as he knew there was only one way out of the horror that his world had descended into.

She turned to look at him. Her face was unreadable. "I know you need a fix. You want me to drive there now?"

His reply was a single word, almost inaudible, a word

murmured out of shame and despair. "Yes."

She made an illegal U-turn and headed toward Paris Street.

The sense of relief that it would end soon lightened his mood. "It's come to something when your girlfriend knows the route to your dealer," he joked, trying to be light-hearted, about a subject that was anything but.

"That's the first time."

"Excuse me?"

"It's the first time you called me your girlfriend."

He shrugged. "I guess it's just a figure of speech. After all, we slept together. That must mean something."

"That's it? We slept together, so it must mean something?"

"I guess," he mumbled. "No, I don't know."

Dear Christ, why am I saying the wrong things? Stupid things. This girl deserves so much more than that, than me.

He knew he'd screwed up. She wanted a different answer from him, and more from their relationship. But what she wanted was more than he could give her.

Christ, I'd burn to share my life with this amazing girl who seems to surprise me at every turn. It's just…wrong. She has to understand it's out of the question.

She was silent as she drove to Paris Street. She put on the parking brake and told him to wait in the car. She attended to the whole thing herself, and to his surprise Quint was in the park.

The man himself; maybe he's short of staff. Could be his runners have been scooped up in some bust.

The drug lord was massive, a hugely muscled black man who resembled Mike Tyson with a few extra steroids.

He had a reputation for ruling his crime kingdom through a combination of threats of extreme violence, and occasionally carrying out those threats. The cops were convinced he had a string of murders to his name, and it was an open secret they'd pay dearly to find out where the bodies were buried. But he was protected by his reputation, which he worked hard to maintain. Everyone knew that dropping the dime on Quint was tantamount to begging for a death sentence. Whether people were clients or employees, it made no difference. They were either loyal or they weren't. And if they weren't, their life expectancy could be measured in days, if not hours. Taylor watched carefully, his hand on the butt of his Sig Sauer, as Kate bought the drugs. To his surprise, the big black man treated her with an amicable courtesy. When she climbed back into the car, he asked her if Quint had charged a premium for dealing with a new face. She turned to him with a surprised glance.

"No, certainly not. I didn't even need to discuss price. He told me what you've been paying over the past few months and said he would keep the price the same. Why? Did you think he'd try to gouge me?"

"Oh, no, he's a perfect gentleman," he smiled. "I'm sure he's a pillar of the Boston business establishment."

"Oh, I doubt that," He smiled as she missed his sarcastic comment completely, "but I told him I was your lawyer, so he's probably careful not to screw you, in case you decide to sue him."

"Are you serious…" He stopped, as he saw the broad smile on her face. She'd turned the tables, and the joke was on him. He stared at her, and she stared back with a gaze that was bold and brazen, honest and open, with eyes that were filled with warmth, and something else.

I don't want to go there. She needs more, so much more.

"We need to find a motel," she said abruptly. "You're all in, so don't argue. After you've shot up, you must rest for a few hours, and get over the worst of the pain that I know you're feeling. Don't argue, I know a nice place just outside town, and I'm driving there now."

"But..."

"I said don't argue. Besides, I have the drugs in my pocket. Another word from you, and I'll toss them in the Charles River. So shut up."

He shut up.

* * *

He lay on the bed in the motel room, feeling the blessed relief as the intravenous injection seeped through his body, and the agony swiftly drained away. He looked around. It was like motel rooms everywhere, soulless, shabby, and dismal. But it was private and anonymous.

"You want something else to ease the pain?"

He stared at her. "Like what?"

"Like this."

She undressed, taking off each garment slowly and carefully, until she stood naked in front of him. It was one of the most erotic displays he'd seen, and would surely put a professional stripper to shame. He could feel the heat in his groin and knew he was rock hard.

"Your turn to strip. Now just relax and let me do everything."

"Yes, Ma'am," he smiled. "A guy could get used to this."

"That's what I'm counting on."

He made no reply. He didn't want to spoil the moment. She gently removed his garments, one by one, until he lay naked. He didn't want to look down at his body, at the stumps that connected to his prosthetic limbs, with the exposed titanium knee joints. Didn't want her to wonder at the cables and caps protecting the interface to the miracle of electronic wizardry that had given him his life back. But he needn't have worried. She instinctively sensed his need.

"This is my show, Jack Taylor, so close your eyes and let me get to work."

So he did, and she did. He felt her tongue licking him, his face, his body, and his arms, even the tops of his legs. And finally her hot mouth closed over his throbbing penis, and he almost exploded. She pulled back.

"Whoa, cowboy. You're pretty keen, but I need you to hang in there a while longer."

She lay beside him. He touched her firm young breasts, hearing her moan as he gently brushed her nipples, and he traced his hand down her flat, smooth stomach and to her vagina. She moaned again as he lightly touched her clitoris, and then began sighing in ecstasy as he applied soft pressure to just where she liked it. Soon, she removed his hand and climbed on top of him, guiding his prick into her hot, soaking wet vagina. They made love slowly; so slowly. Each sensed what the other needed, and they held back until it was impossible to wait longer, prolonging the moment so that the orgasm when it came swept over them both. They were transported to an erotic heaven that blocked out their thoughts and their worries. They were together, and right then their whole world was just that room. There was nowhere else.

"I love you."

He looked up at her face. It wasn't a surprise she'd said that. He felt the same way, an emotion more powerful then he'd ever felt before in his life.

What do they call it? A cul-de-sac, yeah, that's it. A road you travel, and yet there's no way through. It's strictly shut ended.

He could feel her hurt when didn't respond. It was that tender, post-coital moment when lovers murmur things to each other, things they want each other to hear.

I can't burden her, no way.

He felt the reaction dragged out of him, and knew as he finally spoke it was wrong.

"Yeah."

"That's it? Yeah?"

Her hurt began turning to anger, and he tried to head it off, that she'd listen to reason? He stroked her hair and looked into her eyes, seeing the mixture of love and hurt that seemed to set them ablaze.

"I'm damaged goods, Kate. Just a broken squid that spends his life worrying about where to get the next fix."

"Squid?"

He grinned. "It's a nickname for a Navy Seal. You have to know that I feel something so powerful for you it almost hurts. No, that's wrong, it does hurt. But you deserve a whole man, not some pain addled, washed-up addict."

He felt her relax. Maybe she had listened to him and understood his explanation.

"That's okay, Jack, we'll work on it. As long as I'm not a 'wham, bam, thank you, Ma'am' kind of one night stand."

"Never. Not as long as I draw breath, I'll always be

there for you. Always."

They lay for a while longer, in that private world that is the dwelling place of lovers. She explained to him how the worst night of her life was at Hussein's mansion, not because of the violence and death that was all around them. It was because she thought he might die, and she'd lose him. She finally made him promise to listen to what she was about to say.

"As for that washed-up addict crap, you're the bravest, toughest man I've ever known. You have more to offer a girl than any of the men I've met before, much more. Listen to me, Jack. Those guys we're working with, Wes, Levi, and Lincoln, they'd die for you. Do you know that? And I'll tell you why. You inspire that kind of loyalty in a man because they know that you'd do the same for them, and go a few miles beyond if necessary. If you think I'm going to just let you get away because of some feeble excuse, think again, buddy. You've got a lot to learn about Kate Donovan."

He was tempted to let his guard down. He'd need to think on what she'd said. There was a lot to consider. They dressed and prepared to leave the warmth and security they'd known so briefly, to once more go out and prepare to face the enemy. He was about to ask her about the Makarov pistol when there was a knock at the door.

"I'll get it."

He walked toward the door, happy that he really could walk without feeling the agony that so often engulfed him.

"Who is it?"

"It's the manager. It's about your car."

Oh, fuck! The trunk's full of weapons. What could be the problem?

He opened the door and knew instantly he'd made a fatal mistake. Gunter Metz stood there staring at him, a sneer on his thick lips. Next to him was the Arab, Mehdi Hussein, flanked by a couple of hard-faced bodyguards, each with a hand inside their coat. They didn't need to tell him that if he made a false move, those hands would come out fast out holding pistols, and he'd go down in a hail of bullets; and so would Kate. They wouldn't leave a witness alive, especially her. He kept his hands in view.

"What do you fuckers want?"

Metz sneered even wider, and the two guards laughed. Hussein fixed a smile on his face that was a long way south of being genuine.

"Why, Mr. Taylor, I want to talk to you, just a little chat. May we come in?"

Gunter put a hand the size of a dinner plate on his chest and pushed hard. Taylor went back, cursing as his artificial leg betrayed him. He stumbled and fell to the floor. At the back of his mind, he made a note to explain the technical glitch to Hermann, and then he smiled inwardly.

The chances of getting out of this alive are not good, so maybe the Doc will have to look for another guinea pig to use for his experiments with the miracles of neurobiological technology.

The men stormed into the motel room, and one of the bodyguards closed the door. He ignored the hand Kate offered him and got to his feet. Hussein regarded him with an expression of fake sympathy.

"Yes, of course, the man with artificial legs; pity about that. I wanted to…"

"The girl hasn't got anything to do with this, Hussein," he interrupted. "If you want me, that's fine, but let her go."

"I think she should stay. We've been to a lot of trouble locating you, Mr. Taylor. I'm rather tired of your efforts to damage my business interests, so I've decided to put an end to it."

So this is it, it's the end. No way am I going easily.

He began moving his hand toward the pistol under his coat, but three guns barrels whipped up and pointed at Kate.

"No, I wouldn't advise it. My men have instructions to shoot the girl if you try anything stupid. I suspect you have some foolish affection for her, and so would hate to see your girlfriend riddled with bullets. Put down your gun, Mr. Taylor. Use the left hand! That's it, slowly, and give it to Gunter."

He did as he was ordered and handed over the Sig Sauer. Hussein nodded with satisfaction.

"Excellent. Now, you're wondering why I'm here, I imagine." Taylor said nothing, and the Arab smiled and continued. "I'm not here to kill you." He saw Taylor's skeptical expression. "No, no. I don't wish to do anything illegal." His smile broadened. "I've done what any good citizen would do, you see. I called the police." He looked at his wristwatch in satisfaction. "I imagine Detective Malouf will arrive shortly, about ten minutes should do it, and he'll put both of you under arrest. I understand he's bringing the Boston PD SWAT team along, just in case you get any ideas of doing anything stupid, like trying to escape. Try that, and they'll shoot you. You see; several witnesses have come forward who will testify to the murders of a number of my employees at my private residence." He looked at Metz. "What is the punishment in Massachusetts for multiple murder, Gunter?"

"Life imprisonment, without parole," the gorilla replied.

"Just so. That should keep both of you out of my hair, and everything is nice and legal. Of course, should you care to return the items you stole from my house, it is entirely possible these witnesses may suddenly change their mind about what they saw."

"Fuck you, Hussein."

His eyes blazed for a moment, and Taylor had a glimpse of the intense cruelty that lay barely concealed beneath the surface.

"I see. It doesn't matter. After your arrest, Detective Malouf will arrange to have your homes, places of work, and vehicles searched, as well as those of every person you have come into contact with." He looked thoughtful, and turned to the guard at the door. "Go check inside their car, and see what's there." He looked back at Taylor. "By the time the cops have finished, they will have retrieved my property, and I'll make sure they find enough solid evidence that will guarantee your conviction for murder when you come to trial."

Taylor felt the raging frustration of being unable to move. Hussein had a pistol on him, but that was no problem. The guns pointed at Kate were impossible to circumvent without her being killed. He felt the despair of failure creep over him like a thick fog. For himself he cared little, but for her, and his old comrades, he knew he'd effectively lost every chance of helping them achieve some kind of a life.

"Nothing to say?" Hussein smiled. "It's too bad. If you'd let things alone and not try to interfere, you could have enjoyed your life without having to face spending the rest of it in prison. Even so, you should consider yourself lucky. In my country, you would have been slaughtered out of hand long ago."

"Which particular shithole do you come from?" Taylor asked him. He was racking his brains trying to think of any way out, but so far there was nothing. He had the satisfaction of seeing Hussein's flush of intense anger.

"I am Syrian, and I can assure you that my country has a long and proud history."

This time Taylor laughed out loud. "Syria! That's a dump where the shithole Arab states toss their garbage. I've heard it called the Devil's asshole."

Hussein lost it then, stepped forward, and slashed across with his pistol. Taylor took the blow on his face, and felt the iron foresight cut the skin of his cheek. But he made no move to prevent it. He was too conscious of the hairsbreadth that separated Kate from death. Gunter gripped Kate's arm so fiercely she let out a tiny squeal of pain. As Taylor wiped the blood from his face, he looked around the room to see if there was any possible opening he could take, any way he could get the drop on these guys. He briefly considered needling Mehdi Hussein some more, and when he came close to hit him again, grab him and used him as a shield. But the equation came back to Kate Donovan.

They'd simply threaten to kill her, and I'd have no choice but to back down.

Hussein checked his wristwatch, nodded, and smiled.

"It shouldn't be long now. Enjoy your last moments of freedom, Taylor. And your lawyer friend, she'll take the fall with you." He looked across at Kate. "Unless you do a deal with the DA. I imagine if you testify against this man, it could shorten your sentence. Who knows, you may even escape with a suspended sentence? Of course, you'll lose your lawyer's license, but that will serve as a lesson for you to be more careful when you try and cross powerful people."

She looked back at him, and even Taylor cringed at her eloquent expression. Without saying a single word, she managed to convey her opinion of the Arab with her eyes. And the opinion was straightforward. 'You stink worse than a piece of dog shit that's been on the sidewalk in the midday sun.'

"Hey, Mr. Hussein, lookie here. I found it on the seat of that Lincoln outside. I think it's the stuff you were looking for."

He handed the case to Hussein, who looked inside with a smile that grew broader when he realized he'd got it all back. Kate darted a glance at Taylor as if to say, 'I'm sorry, I screwed up.' He shook his head imperceptibly, 'it's okay.' But they both knew it wasn't. Under the guns of Hussein and his people, with the cops arriving soon, and the evidence they'd fought so hard to obtain, all gone. Hussein snapped the case shut.

"I think that changes things. You know, I had thought about having you both killed. Just after you're released on bail would have been a good time. You could just disappear, and they'd assumed you'd fled, but now it's not even worth the trouble. You've got nothing, except a long prison sentence hanging over you."

Taylor returned his glance. "It isn't going to be like that, Hussein. You think this is ended? You're finished! You know that. You're scum, a dog turd you'd pick up on your shoe on the sidewalk on a hot day, rank and stinking. I'll be seeing you, Hussein, and next time, it'll be different."

The Arab flushed crimson, as crimson as a person with his Mid East tan could flush. Taylor smiled and glanced around at his men. They kept their faces straight, except for one of the bodyguards whose mouth twitched a little, as much as he would dare.

He probably served in Iraq or maybe Afghanistan, Taylor reflected.

Gunter kept a straight, stony face, the perfect muscle, a robot that could be programmed to destroy at his master's command. They faced each other. It was a tense moment. Taylor wondered if he'd gone too far, but they were interrupted by a knock on the door.

"That must be Detective Malouf. Time to get you out of my hair."

One of the bodyguards opened the door and stepped back, allowing a detective who held up his shield to enter. Hussein wore a look of surprise on his face. It wasn't Wasim Malouf. It was his partner, Brad Stutz. He recovered quickly.

"Detective Stutz, thank you for coming so fast. These are the people I want you to arrest."

Stutz gave him a cold glance. "I don't know what gives you the idea you can dictate to the Boston PD who we arrest, Mister. I'll decide how this works. Clear?"

Hussein nodded quickly. "Of course, of course. But I made a complaint to your department. I assume you came to investigate."

"I do have some questions for these people. But first, I suggest you and your people go home. If I have any questions for you, I know where you are."

Hussein's jaw dropped. "But, you will arrest them?"

"I already told you how it works, Mister. Now get out of here. This is police business."

The bodyguards looked at their boss, clearly unsure of how he wanted to play it. Gunter still held onto Kate, but Hussein gave him a nod. He released her, and they walked out the door. Hussein was last to leave. He glared at Stutz for a few moments, then left, slamming the door behind him.

They looked at each other for several seconds.

"Care to explain, Stutz?" Taylor asked.

The detective nodded. "I can tell you some of it but not all. We managed to delay Detective Malouf so I could get to you first, but he'll be along soon with the SWAT guys, so we need to get out of here."

"We?"

"Yeah, you know that Internal Affairs is investigating Malouf for possible links to that guy Hussein. When I found out what Malouf had planned, I contacted IA, and they told me to come and get you away before Malouf arrives."

"What about you? I thought you were his partner."

"That's true, but he's involved with some pretty bad people in this town, your friend Mehdi Hussein chief amongst them. I may not be the best cop in the city, but I think I'm above that kind of shit."

Taylor stared at him. "Yeah, I reckon you are, Stutz. Thanks for the help. What happens now?"

"We still need more evidence to bring him down. As soon as we have what we need, IA will take it to the DA, and hopefully Detective Malouf will be off the streets for a very long time. But it's important he doesn't know about this, so I want you out fast."

"What about you? He'll go crazy when he arrives and discovers you've let us go."

"I'll concoct a story to explain it. Don't worry about me. Just get yourselves go somewhere he can't find you. Between him and that Arab, I wouldn't rate your chances if he comes gunning for you."

Taylor nodded. He looked at Kate. "You ready to go?"

"I was ready twenty minutes ago."

He smiled and let her out the door. The Lincoln was still parked where he'd left it. The window in the rear door was smashed where Hussein's man had busted it open, probably with the butt of his gun, to grab the case. He cleared away the worst of the broken glass. Kate unlocked the front doors, and they climbed in. She looked across at him.

"Which direction are we heading in?"

"We'd better go to Lincoln's place. We need to talk to them and get ready to start."

"Start what?"

"A war."

252

CHAPTER TEN

Kate drove in silence. There was still traffic on the city streets at this time of night, but it was very light and not enough to slow them. She insisted once again on going with them. Lincoln, Levi, and Wes were sitting on the back seat, fingering their weapons, silent, grim-faced, and determined. Taylor remembered her expression, and he loved her even more for it, just as much as he was terrified for her safety.

"I'm coming, so you guys better get used to it. If this is the end of Hussein, I want to be in at the finish. It's no good arguing, Jack. Besides," she grinned, "I'm driving, and I have the car keys. Stop wasting time. I want to pay the bastard a visit, one he'll never forget."

He could see her hands, white on the steering wheel as they gripped it hard with the tension she must be feeling. She was a lawyer, not a soldier. The three of them, himself, Wes, and Lincoln, had all seen action in battle. His father, Jerry Yates, had trained Levi in the use of weapons. The young man had learned survival, as well as simple battle tactics during their war games.

Kate acquitted herself well in the attacks on Hussein's empire, yet is that enough? I know damn well it isn't, not by a mile.

He closed his eyes and made yet another prayer, that she wouldn't be hurt. It was a soldier's prayer, as soldiers the world over prayed for the welfare of their families, their bodies, and their very souls.

We have to end it, and wipe this plague off the city streets for good. And end it without Kate being hurt, or any of the others. I started this, so I'll deal with what comes my way. If it means I don't survive, so be it.

Even as the thoughts streamed through his mind, he recognized them for what they were, death thoughts. So far, they'd sustained a heap of injuries but no fatalities. Hussein was no fool. He'd be gathering more forces, more mercs ready to defend his business. Once he knew they'd escaped Malouf's net, he would prepare for the attack he had to know was coming. They had to hit him where he least expected it, and take him and his empire down for good. If they failed, he would strike back with a gang of armed thugs, many of them men with military training. And he had the support of Malouf, the corrupt Boston detective who still hunted them and would be determined to smash Taylor before he was brought down himself.

He felt the agony starting to course through his system, tapping out the little messages to his brain, insisting he get a fix, and fast. He ignored them. The only chance of succeeding in this mission would be if he kept his mind focused and sharp, and any kind of powerful analgesics would have the opposite effect. He smiled, thinking of the call he'd had on his cell from Detective Brad Stutz, just a couple of hours after they left the motel.

"I thought you might want to know that Mehdi Hussein has moved out of his mansion. I guess someone destroyed it for him, and it'll take a long time to rebuild it the way it was."

Taylor was puzzled. "Why should I give a fuck about that bastard and his mansion?"

Stutz had chuckled. "No reason. Except, I thought you might want to know he has a small apartment at the rear of his offices on the sixth floor of his building. He's there right now, with a bunch of guards."

His hopes soared. They'd been discussing how next to hit the bastard. It had to be at night, which meant they had to find out where he was staying after the debacle at the mansion. Until they knew the address, they were stymied. Now they knew.

"I appreciate it, Stutz."

"Yeah. You understand I'm telling you this because I don't want you going anywhere near that address. In fact, I'm giving you a direct instruction to stay away from Mr. Mehdi Hussein until our investigation of Detective Malouf is complete, assuming we ever get enough evidence."

"Is there a problem?"

"Could be. We had collected a bundle of stuff ready to use against him, but the box that contained everything disappeared, along with the Internal Affairs cop who was carrying it. My guess is the case has gone into a furnace, and the officer is at the bottom of the Charles River."

"I'm sorry."

"Yeah, I knew the guy. We were at the academy together. He's got a wife, couple of kids."

Taylor said nothing at first. It was cop business, and

Malouf was sure piling up the enemies.

"I'll deal with Hussein. What's happening with Malouf?"

"He called in sick and disappeared, just dropped off the radar. You'd better keep your eyes peeled. He's a bad man to cross."

Taylor nodded. "Yeah, so am I. And thanks for the help."

"Remember, I told you to keep away from Mr. Hussein. Don't go anywhere near his building."

Taylor clicked off. They were in Lincoln's house, and the others were watching him, as they tried to work out how to locate and destroy the enemy. They'd only heard part of the conversation.

"What is it?" Wes asked him. He sensed something was up.

"We know where he is. The office building."

* * *

Kate drew up two blocks away from the target. Taylor opened the trunk and sorted through the commo equipment. He handed them a radio headset each and gave abbreviated instructions in its use.

"This stuff is full duplex, and it uses a digital frequency agile band, so we don't need to worry about eavesdroppers."

Kate gave him a puzzled glance as she clipped on the earpiece and bent the microphone boom so it matched his.

"Frequency agile? Is that good?"

He smiled. "Just technical garbage, nothing to worry about. All you need to know is we'll be in contact with each other the whole time. Levi, you see that cellphone tower on the building across the street?"

"Yeah, sure, can't miss it."

"Once we take out the landlines, Hussein could use that to call in more shooters, or the cops."

Disrupt and destroy the enemy's communications. One of the first lessons any Special Forces operator learned, or indeed, any military man.

He nodded his understanding. "Give me a few minutes. I'll deal with it."

He disappeared into the darkness of the Boston night. They caught glimpses of a dark, shadowy figure ascending the fire escape. He was as good as invisible. Taylor took out his cellphone and watched the signal strength indicator. After less than five minutes, he smiled as it dropped to 'no signal'.

"He's done it. Let's get moving before they send a maintenance man out to repair the tower. Wes, you worked on communications systems in the Navy before you came into the Seals, yeah?"

"Sure, I did a couple of courses. Never amounted to much."

"It doesn't need to amount to much. Look across at MMP's building. You see the overhead phone lines?"

He smiled. "I'm on it."

He drew his long, heavy combat knife and walked quickly along the sidewalk. He held the knife low in his right hand, and it was almost invisible with the blackened blade and black hilt. He looked back at them for a moment, and they saw his white teeth smiling at them. He located a suitable place to reach the cables, and as they watched, he disappeared into the gap between Hussein's building and the next block. Taylor checked his watch, and it only took

Wes two minutes to slash through the lines. Unless he had a satphone, which seemed unlikely in the center of the city of Boston, Hussein had just lost all his communications with the outside world.

"That's it, lock and load. It's time to move in."

Kate insisted she needed nothing more than the Makarov. Wes took the M203 launcher, slung it over his shoulder with a bag of grenades, and picked up and HK 416 with plenty of spare clips. Levi reappeared and selected an AK-47S, the short, folding stock version of the iconic AK-47 to supplement his heavy Colt pistol. Lincoln took a Colt 45. "Damn, I had one of these during my time with the Marines. Not the most accurate gun in the world, but when all else fails, you can beat the enemy over the head with it."

"Yeah, that oughta do the trick," Wes smiled.

Taylor picked up the mention of accuracy. As far as he knew, the Colt was a good gun. "How's your eyesight, Lincoln? Not as good as it used to be?"

The former marine shook his head ruefully. "I guess not, but I'll make out."

"Sure you will, but why not make it easy on yourself? You need more than the Colt, why not try the Mossberg?"

He took the Mossberg 500, a pump action, 12 gauge shotgun from the trunk and handed it to Lincoln.

"That's the 14 inch short barrel version. It carries five shells, and you can load more on the fly. Just point and shoot. You're sure to hit something," he grinned.

Lincoln was sold. "Yeah, that sounds like my kind of gun. I'll take it."

"Just be careful with that scattergun, my friend. Remember, when you get into a firefight, it can get pretty confusing."

"Don't worry about me, just point me at the enemy. As you say, I'm sure to hit something. What about you? You carrying the MP7?"

"Not this time. I'll stuff a few spare mags for the Sig Sauer in my pockets, and I'll take two of these babies."

Their eyes widened as he picked up the two Russian manufactured RPG portable rocket launchers and slung them on his back. He saw their expressions and grinned.

"If we run into any trouble, I want to have something that'll pack a punch."

Wes nodded sagely. "Yeah, the RPG should do it, Boss."

Taylor took a last look through the gloom at the target building. It all looked quiet enough. Lights were blazing on the sixth floor.

Good. Hello, Mr. Hussein.

He turned back to his team and pressed the transmit button.

"Commo check, is everyone strength five?"

The replies came in, and he was satisfied. "One thing more. Wes, there's a box of demolition explosives in the trunk with detonators. Can you handle it?"

Wes nodded and rummaged in the trunk, pulling out the box of C4 plastique and detonators. Taylor took a last look around.

We're ready, as ready as we ever will be. I've got qualms, sure, reservations by the score, but who ever thinks going into battle is a pushover?

"Okay, move in."

They walked casually along the sidewalk, keeping to the shadows, ducked into the alleyway at the side of MMP, and stopped short of the rear. Taylor indicated they should wait while he crept toward the corner to check for the guard he was certain would be on duty. He started as Wes touched him on the shoulder, and pointed at his black combat knife. Taylor nodded his agreement, and Wes took over the point. He reached the last corner of the building where they were only yards from the rear door, when both men smelled the cigarette smoke. He flashed a hand signal at Taylor, who nodded and raised his Sig to cover him. Wes went forward in almost total silence until he was only a couple of feet behind the guard. The man had a pistol in a shoulder holster outside of his combat jacket, ready for immediate use, but stupid. Any cop on patrol seeing the holstered weapon would be sure to run him straight in. He was enjoying a cigarette, humming a tune softly to himself between puffs of smoke. At the last moment, he heard something and began to turn, but Wes' huge black hand clamped around his mouth, the other hand with the knife slashed across his throat. Wes stepped aside to avoid the sudden spurt of arterial blood, lowered the body to the ground, and nodded to Taylor. He ran forward and searched the body. Sure enough, the guard had a bunch of keys in one of his pockets. Seconds later, Taylor was unlocking the rear door. He touched the microphone button.

"We're in. I want everybody inside and out of sight, so make it quick and keep it quiet."

When his team was inside, he closed the door but left it unlocked in case they needed a fast exit. He told them to wait while he crept forward to the foyer, but the security desk was empty.

I don't like this. It's too easy, much too easy.

He started back to the rear but stopped at the foot of

the staircase. Keeping completely still, he strained his ears to listen. Within seconds, he heard it, the soft rustle of pants' fabric, maybe the tiny squeak from the rubber sole of a boot. He'd heard enough, and he rejoined the team at the rear.

"They're playing it pretty cagey. It looks like they're expecting trouble, and they've mounted an ambush somewhere between the first and second floors. It's clever. Even if we take out the shooters waiting for us, the noise will alert the rest of the guards that we're here. It's going to make it difficult to press on up the staircase."

"What's our alternative?" Kate asked him.

"There isn't one. It's quite simple. They're standing between Hussein and us. To reach him, we have to take them out. Wes, you ready with that launcher?"

"Just say the word, Boss."

"Head to the foot of the staircase and fire two grenades up to the second floor. As soon as the second one explodes, we go up fast. Stay right behind me, and if anything moves, shoot it. Lincoln, you're number two. I reckon that scatter gun is going to see some action."

He could see Lincoln Moss, the grizzled ex-marine, was nervous. He was older and hadn't seen action for a long time, but he was no less determined.

"You show me the target, and I'll do the rest."

He nodded at Wes. "Do it."

They waited while he got in position at the foot of the staircase and took aim. The noise as he fired off each grenade was like a hammer blow, which echoed inside the formerly dark and silent building. But as each grenade exploded, it was like the vengeful wrath of Thor, the mythical god of thunder. The first massive roar as the small bomb detonated rocked the entire edifice, and the second grenade was no less awe-inspiring. As the echoes of the twin blasts reverberated around the six stories, they heard the start of the screams. Taylor estimated there were four men on that landing, four shooters lying in wait for them, ready to riddle them with bullets as soon as they appeared. The screams of the wounded were terrible, piteous even. But they only had two choices, either the enemy went down or they did. A no brainer.

"Move now! Before they recover." They raced up the stairs after him, and even Taylor, after so many long and bitter fights during his career with the Navy Seals, was astonished at the amount of destruction they'd caused. Human destruction, the four guards were lying broken and bloody on the landing. Two were dead, one was clearly dying, and the fourth only lightly wounded.

"Help me, please!"

Kate automatically went to minister to the wounded man. She didn't see the pistol he held in his right hand, nor did she see his eyes move as he prepared to make a grab for her and use her as a human shield.

"Not this time, buddy!" Taylor murmured, pointed his Sig at the man's head, and pulled the trigger twice. His brains flew out, plastering the carpet and walls around him. Kate leapt up, her face furious.

"Jack, for Christ's sake! He was wounded."

By way of a reply, Taylor knelt down and showed her the man's hand, still holding the pistol, a Glock 17. "He was about to use this on you."

She gulped. "My God, I didn't realize."

"No, you're new to this. Stay behind me if you want to live."

She nodded dumbly and waited behind him. Her protests about killing a wounded man had stopped, as she began to understand the terrible realities of asymmetric warfare. He looked around for Wes.

"One down, five to go. You all set for the next one?"

"Roger that, loaded and ready."

"We'll play it differently. They know how we did this, so this time, they'll be behind cover, waiting for the grenades to explode. Fire the two grenades, same as last time. I want all of you to blaze away and shout as if we're charging up the stairs like a herd of spooked buffalo. That's your cue, Wes. They'll come out ready to hit us, and you let them have it with the next two grenades."

Kate was beginning to look more than pale. Even in the dim emergency lighting, her horror at the carnage was obvious, her eyes screwed up, her face tense and lined.

Maybe I should have warned her that the bloody violence we encountered at the mansion is not unusual for this kind of work, but things could get a lot worse. Right now, there's no other way to stop Mehdi Hussein other than going head to head with his goons. Otherwise, he'll keep right on destroying people's lives, committing murder and mayhem on the streets of Boston to further build his evil empire. He has a choice, to conduct his business honestly, or otherwise. He's chosen otherwise. He drew first blood in killing Evie Harper, setting all this in motion.

Even as he thought about it, Taylor cautioned himself not to be too optimistic. They had a long way to go, four floors to be accurate. And if there were guards stationed on each floor, which he had every reason to assume there were, they'd have to wade through a whole lot of blood to reach the man who'd caused it all.

Wes fired two grenades, and they crouched out of blast area of the searing steel fragments as they waited. The noise of the explosions died away. Taylor jumped up and started firing, shouting. They joined him, firing burst after burst up the staircase, bellowing orders and encouragement to each other. Wes timed it perfectly. Just as the first of the return fire hammered around them, two more grenades flew out of the barrel of his launcher in quick succession and exploded on the landing of the third floor. The return fire stopped immediately, replaced by the screams and howls of agony of the wounded defenders. They'd caught them out in the open.

"Let's go."

They ran at a furious pace up to the third floor, once again they came across the bloody carnage that Wes's grenades had caused. All four guards were down. This time one was dead, two lay dying. Another was unhurt, recovering from the shock of the pressure waves that had shocked him with their ferocity. He was a hard-bitten, angry man; obviously furious that what he'd assumed were a band of amateurs had bested him. He swept up his rifle, an M-16 A2. Taylor shot him in the head before he was able to pull the trigger. Astoundingly, one of the others, a man who was clearly dying, was still determined to fight. Perhaps he didn't understand the extent of his injuries as he tried to level the barrel of his M-16. Lincoln pulled the trigger, and the boom of the Mossberg 12 gauge cartridge echoed around the office space. The other wounded man miscalculated and thought they'd turn the situation around. He'd lost his assault rifle in the blast but ripped out a Glock from his bloody uniform. The Mossberg roared again, and he slumped back down with half his head blown off. Lincoln saw Kate's agonized glance.

"I'm sorry, Ma'am, but if he shot you, I'd never forgive myself."

She nodded her appreciation, even though the horror in her eyes eloquent testimony to her shock at the slaughter. Taylor ran to the staircase leading up to the fourth floor. Lincoln ran behind him, and Kate and Wes followed. Maybe the old marine's eyes weren't as good as they used to be, but there was nothing wrong with his hearing. He heard the clatter of the metal objects before anyone else.

"Grenades! They're throwing them down the stairwell! Back!"

Wes automatically grabbed Kate and threw her behind a filing cabinet. He dived after her. Taylor flattened himself behind a Xerox machine, Levi shrank back into the stairwell they'd just emerged from, and the grenades went off. Four, five, six massive explosions. When the noise died away, he tried to look through the dust and gloom to make out how his people had fared. It was like a thick fog. He keyed his mic.

"Kate, are you okay? Wes, is anyone hurt?"

"I don't think so. Kate's fine," Harper replied. "Where's Levi?"

"I'm here."

He crawled around the head of the staircase and joined them. He looked around.

"Where's Lincoln?"

"Lincoln?" Taylor whispered into the mic. "Where are you?" Nothing, just silence. "Spread out and try to find Lincoln. He was just…"

And then he came across him. At the foot of the staircase, a body lay slumped. He ran over and knelt down next to the shattered and torn remains of Lincoln Moss. His mind ran through an entire gamut of emotions within a single second.

This man served his country proudly, comes home, and has to fight for his very right to keep his home against the man waiting for us at the top of this building. Perched in his web like a bloated spider, pulling unfortunates like Lincoln and other vets into his web, holding out the prospect of the dream of owning their own home, until it suits him to snatch it back from them on some trumped up pretext to make even more money!

Taylor's thoughts were a kaleidoscope of rage, anger, and his own personal nemesis, agony. Since he'd decided not to self medicate in order to keep his mind clear, he was paying the price. He could sense the insidious fingers of pain creeping through his body, searching out the cracks in his nervous system and starting to tap out the messages to his brain. Urgent messages, telling him to pull out, locate his dealer, and inject the blessed drug that would give him relief for just a few God-given hours.

Fuck 'em.

"Jack?" He looked up and saw Kate standing beside him. "Is he dead?"

He nodded. "The poor bastard didn't stand a chance. Maybe this was all stupid. I shouldn't have asked any of you to come. Hussein has everything on his side. I feel like we're a kind of David, going up against the might of Goliath."

"You didn't ask any of us to come," she pointed out. "We volunteered. Besides, I believe David won that one."

"Yeah, but we're fresh out of miracles, as well as a slingshot and stones. We've taken on too much. We should consider getting out now before I get anyone else killed."

"You didn't get anyone killed. Hussein did. Jack, we need to press forward and deal with him. If we pull out now, he's won. "

He looked back at her. Her face had changed, as if Lincoln's death had turned a switch. The shock and horror were fading, to be replaced by another expression entirely. What she wanted now was revenge.

"Did you hear what I said? We came here with five of us. Now there are only four. How many do I have to lose before we give up?"

His mind was a turmoil of conflicting emotions.

I've never given up a fight, not once. But neither have I ever faced such overwhelming odds, with only a washed-up Seal suffering from PTSD, two civilians, including Kate, and myself. For Christ's sake, no matter what Doc Hermann's done, I'm still a limbless vet. I have to make a decision, one way or the other. To get out, or to press on, and I have to make it now, or the enemy will realize they have us beat and launch a counterattack.

He vaguely heard Kate speaking.

"What? What did you say?"

"I said get up!"

"But…"

"You need to get back on your feet, whether you're going to continue what you started, or run away and find a dealer to sell you your next fix. What's it going to be, Jack? Before you make up your mind, I may as well tell you, I'm going all the way to the sixth floor. That fucker is going down, and if I have to pull the trigger myself, that's fine."

Wes and Levi stood close by.

"I'm going on," Wes said. There was nothing of the

man he'd seen a couple of days before, trembling with the symptoms of PTSD. He stood tall and proud as if one of his ancestors had been a Zulu war chief.

"Me too," Levi intoned solemnly. "They killed my dad. The only way I can honor his memory is to deal with Hussein. I'm going on."

Taylor suddenly understood the extraordinary caliber of people with him on this mission. Civilians, a vet with PTSD, but it made no difference. They has the kind of fighting spirit that would have carried them over the cliffs of Omaha beach during World War Two, blasting every Nazi who stood before them.

He felt different, as if he'd just taken a hit of painkillers, yet without the usual floating, euphoric feeling. He felt charged and more alive. Proud to be with these people, no matter what happened. They were staring at him, waiting, waiting for him.

"I reckon Hussein has just chalked up another reason for us to get him." He looked down at the body of Lincoln Moss. "My friend, this one's for you." He looked up. "Let's do it."

They waited, sheltered away from the blast area of further grenades they may toss down from the fourth floor. Taylor outlined their next move.

"We stopped to finish off these guys," he nodded at the bodies of the defenders they'd killed when they reached the third floor, a few feet away. "Big mistake. It gave them a chance to hit us from the next floor. This time, we're going all the way. The men on the fourth and fifth floors may think they've finished us with those grenades, so I doubt they'll be expecting our next move."

He outlined their strategy for storming the intervening

two floors to reach the sixth floor, and their target, Mehdi Hussein. Wes loaded the launcher, aimed at the staircase to the fourth floor, fired a grenade, reloaded and fired again. The moment the second missile was on its way, they went to their positions and waited. After a few seconds, the defenders did as expected, and tossed down grenades, three in all. Kate, Levi, and Wes began their performance, the performance of their lives, or possibly the performance to save their lives. Tucked into his position, Taylor smiled to himself as they shrieked and moaned in pretended agony. After a few seconds, the shrieks died down. He heard Kate sobbing, calling, "Help me, I'm dying." It was Oscar material.

He heard shouts of exultation. Hussein's men were calling to the defenders above them on the fifth and sixth floors. It was all over! All they needed was to go and check the bodies, and then they could go drink a few beers and celebrate. He heard the guttural tones of Gunter Metz congratulating the men. They walked down from the higher levels to join in the fun. Taylor estimated a dozen men, whooping and shouting excitedly as they hurried to gloat over the bodies of their victims. He was hidden in a utility closet next to the base of the stairwell. Some of the grenade fragments had sliced through the door, and he knew he'd taken a couple of hits to his legs. He also had a nick in his hand, but the wounds were incidental. He had business to attend to. He'd made an appointment, and he intended to keep it. The voices and backslapping came nearer, and he opened the door a fraction as a crowd of armed men came into view only ten yards from his position. The launcher was armed and ready; he simply aimed and pulled the trigger. The missile struck the wall at the head of the staircase as it detonated. Hussein's men were literally shredded by a massive blast and a hurricane of metal fragments. One moment they were an armed band, happy, exultant even, about to celebrate the fruits of their victory. The next moment, they were an almost unrecognizable bundle of broken, bleeding flesh and torn clothing.

He shouted to his people, "Go, go!"

He could have saved his breath. They were already moving, and as he raced up the staircase, were only feet behind him. They had to pick their way over the charnel house that was all that was left of the opposition before they reached the fifth floor, which was empty. Taylor looked up at their final destination, Hussein's personal domain; the nerve center where he controlled his personal fiefdom of violence and extortion. It was a tough call, to go on, and maybe walk into an ambush. Or wait, and throw away the advantage of surprise. But he had to know what they still faced. He called a halt.

Will they be waiting for us, Gunter Metz, Mehdi Hussein?

They were waiting for them.

"Very clever, Mr. Taylor." Hussein stepped out in plain view with Gunter at his shoulder. "It seems I underestimated you. You are a man of infinite resources. A pity you don't work for me."

Taylor swallowed his amazement.

What's the guy up to?

Even in the semidarkness, there was illumination from the emergency lighting. Enough for the Arab to see he carried another RPG launcher on his back.

"It all over, Hussein. You only have one chance, and

270

that's to give it up now."

"What do I get in return?" he called back. Taylor was alerted. Hussein's voice was almost calm. No way was it the voice of someone who'd just seen his men obliterated, his headquarters building half destroyed, and was facing the ruin of his business empire. He looked around. The other three members of his team were standing close by.

"Get back," he murmured. "He's up to something. Get behind some cover before he takes action."

"But he's beaten," Kate objected. "Surely, he'd give anything just to get out of here alive."

"No. He's planning to hit us. I just don't know how, but he's playing for time. Move it, all of you. Get away from here."

He made them take cover out of sight of the staircase. They didn't have long to wait before they found out what Hussein had planned.

"I smell smoke," Levi said.

"And gasoline," Wes added.

"Bastard!" Taylor ranted. "He must have another way out of here, probably a fire escape. He's planning to burn down the building with us inside it. We have to get out right now, before we're trapped."

He led them back to the stairs. They were about to charge back down to the first floor and out of the building when he looked up. A long, thin stream of gasoline was trickling down the staircase, with a tongue of flame racing along it as it came nearer.

"Forget the stairs," he shouted. "We have to find another way out of here."

He raced into the huge, open plan office, threaded his way past desks and partitions until he reached the wall furthest from the burning staircase. The fire was taking hold, and when they looked back, the entire stairwell was a sea of flames. Taylor reached a window and attempted to open it, but like most windows in modern office buildings, it was sealed shut.

A fire escape! Where the hell is it?

He shouted at them to begin searching. It shouldn't be hard to find it. The emergency lighting would be designed to point people toward it in case of fire.

"Over here!" Wes shouted. Levi was with him. They were standing by the door with the familiar crash bar fitted to all fire exits. But when they pushed hard, nothing happened. They pushed harder, but it was solid.

"Fuck it!" Wes shouted. "It's locked. Stand back, all of you. I'll hit it with the grenade. That should open it."

He retreated from the door, loaded the launcher, took aim, and fired. The grenade spat out of the launcher, rebounded a couple of feet, and then exploded. They ran forward and looked out through the shattered remains of the fire door, onto empty space, and a long, long drop.

"The fucking bastard!" Wes snarled. "He's taken away the fire escape. No wonder the door is locked. Why the hell would someone do that?"

"He's a paranoid Arab from a land where they spend half their lives watching for the knife in the back. He has a virtual fortress on the sixth floor, so the last thing he'd want would be a way for his enemies to get to him," Taylor explained.

"How are we going to get out?"

He opened his mouth to reply to Kate but stopped. They heard the roar of the engine as it started spooling up. The sound was unmistakable to anyone who'd spent much of his career in Special Forces. Taylor and Wes exchanged glances.

"Helo!" Wes shouted.

Taylor nodded ruefully. "Of course, I should have worked out where all that gasoline came from. He'd have to have a means of making a fast exit. I guess he has something on the roof, a small helo like one of those Robinson R44s, and a few drums of fuel. Damn, he's getting away, and there's not a thing we can do about it."

He stared out the gap where the fire door had been, as if somehow he could make the missing fire escape appear. He knew that in a short time the aero engine would roar to a crescendo as the pilot lifted off, and they would see the helo soaring away across the rooftops of Boston. Hussein would congratulate himself on disposing of his enemies, and no doubt the destruction of his office building by fire would be the subject of a massive insurance claim, so he'd more than cover his losses. He'd probably make a profit. Whatever wages or bounty he was paying the men who'd guarded him, now lying dead in the flaming stairwell, would never be paid. And he'd blame it all on Taylor, and put the cops onto him and the people with him. It was all very, very clever. Except that Hussein hadn't won yet. He turned to them.

"Search this floor. There has to be something we can use to get us down to the ground level. A rope, some drapes or blinds to tie together, a fire hose, anything. See what you can find."

They started checking out closets and storerooms, but there were no drapes to knot together, nothing useful. It was an office building, not a hotel.

"Shit, at least one of these people must have had a

hobby. Mountaineering, shark fishing, there has to be something, some line, something," Wes grunted.

Levi shouted across, "It's not much use to us, but someone working here is a scuba diver. His equipment is stored in an aluminum case next to this desk. I recognize the brand, US Divers. I did some scuba myself once in the..."

Taylor's mind was racing.

If I can make it through the smoke and flames to the roof, maybe I'd be in time to prevent Hussein's helicopter from leaving. I could use the air bottles to breathe, and cover myself with wet coats or towels to prevent the fire from burning me to a crisp.

"That's how I'll stop him. Get those bottles out and make sure they're full. I need a bottle with a harness. Fix a regulator to it, and find a mask. That should do it, but hurry it up, that helo could lift off at any time."

He explained what he was about to do. He could see Kate thinking furiously, trying to work out how she could stop him. She tried to talk to him, but he ignored her.

Hussein has to be taken down. Otherwise all of it, the deaths and the bloodshed, was for nothing.

He suddenly had an idea to get them out, and he called Wes over.

"Find cable to make a rope. Rip out the cables that run to the electrical outlets, and if you think they're not strong enough, double or triple them up. On a floor this size, there has to be hundreds of yards of cable. You should be able to make a rope long enough."

Wes nodded. "We'll get right on it, but it's a long way down."

"I know, but you don't have any other choices."

"I can come up there with you. I want to see that bastard die."

He smiled at his friend, the traumatized Seal who'd recovered to become the formidable fighting man he'd once known. "Thanks, but you're needed here, Wes. If anyone can get these people out, it's you. It has to be this way."

Wes left him and began ripping out every piece of cable he could find. Levi arrived and handed Taylor the diving equipment.

"I checked the tank. It's full."

Taylor nodded as he put down the remaining rocket launcher and strapped the harness on his back. He put the launcher on one shoulder, grunting as he felt the additional weight. Levi passed him the mouthpiece from the regulator. He tested it by sucking in air and then pulled down the mask over his eyes. Kate appeared with a half dozen coats and jackets she'd found hung around the office, and had drenched them in water. She arranged them around him, and he almost staggered as he felt the additional weight of the sodden garments. She draped a last wet coat to cover his head, fixing it like a hood so he was able to see. He stared around at them for a few brief seconds, peering through the glass lens of the mask, realizing it could be the very last time. Without a word, he started for the staircase. There was no time for goodbyes, for sentiment. Through the mass of sodden garments, he heard Kate say something, but he ignored her as he reached the flames licking around the staircase. They were already spreading into the open office area. Taking a firm grip on his Sig, he started to run up the flaming stairs.

At first, the fire and smoke were the problem. He

could feel the burning heat as his clothes dried and began to smoke, but he had to ignore it and press on. The big problem was the colossal weight he carried, the launcher, the air bottle, his weapons, and the wet garments protecting him from the flames. He stood before the site of the final part of his odyssey. Ahead of him, the sixth floor was only yards away, and up there was his formidable adversary, the man with such a callous disregard for life, a man who was prepared to sacrifice anything and anyone in the name of profit. He looked down. His pants were hot and smoking, and as he watched, flames began licking around his ankles. Yet he felt no pain, and he smiled.

If there ever was a time to be grateful for prosthetic legs, it's now.

He ran, hurtling up the staircase like a sprinter, ignoring the weight of everything he carried, and fighting his way through the smoke and flames. When he reached the landing of the sixth floor, it was empty. Of course, Hussein and Gunter would be on the roof, preparing to board the helicopter and escape. He threw off the coats that covered him. They were already dry and starting to catch fire. He unstrapped the air bottle and mask, and unslung the launcher. Holding it on his shoulder, with his pistol in the other hand, he headed through the empty office. He pushed open the door and found himself in Hussein's private apartment, furnished with thick carpets and priceless works of art. It was like a miniature version of his mansion. Ahead of him, a folding staircase reached up to the roof. He ran to the base and started to climb. The engine of the helo had settled into a regular beat, so it was warmed up and ready to take off. He climbed the last few steps, balancing the launcher on his shoulder, and walked out onto the roof. Fifteen yards in front of him, the helo was revving up as the pilot prepared to engage the collective and take off. Hussein and Gunter stared out at him through the Perspex windows, their faces white with shock that he'd made it so far. The aircraft started to vibrate as it reached full power, and Taylor raised the RPG and took aim. He saw Hussein speak quickly to Gunter, the engine revs died away to a steady tickover, and the door opened. The big man leapt back down to the ground, carrying an M-16. He strode across the roof, pointed the assault rifle at him, and sneered.

"If you fire that rocket at the helicopter, you'll kill us all. Do you want to die?" he shouted above the roar of the wind and the steady beat of the engine.

He's right. The explosion when the rocket hits the helo will ignite the fuel tanks, and the entire roof will become a fireball.

"Tell the pilot to switch off the engine, and we'll talk," he shouted back.

Gunter edged back and spoke to Hussein. After a few moments, he turned back and stared at Taylor. "First, we put down the weapons. Mr. Hussein said nothing happens as long as you threaten him with that fucking thing."

He gestured at the rocket launcher. Taylor nodded, tucked the Sig into his waistband, and slowly lowered the RPG to the ground, as Gunter did the same with his M-16.

The engine shut down, and the rooftop fell almost silent, only punctuated by the sound of the wind as it occasionally gusted and swirled around them. The big man glared at him. "Now what? What you want?"

"Your boss has to answer for the murder of my friends, and for stealing the homes from their families."

"They were only minnows," a new voice shouted. He looked past Gunter. Hussein had stepped down and stood on the rooftop. He cradled a small submachine gun. Taylor recognized the Mac 10.

"They were people, Hussein," he shouted back. "They were my friends. You have to pay. You're not leaving this roof."

But Hussein only smiled in return and leveled the wicked little submachine gun at his belly. "I don't think so, my friend. Back away. Gunter, pickup the RPG and toss it off the roof."

The big man sneered and started to move, but Taylor grabbed for his Sig and shouted, "Touch that and you die, Gunter!"

The sneer on his face died away, and he looked back at his boss for instructions. Hussein's finger tightened on the trigger, and Taylor catapulted out of the line of fire as a deadly hail of 9mm bullets peppered the concrete around him. There was a steel and concrete air vent nearby, and he rolled across the concrete rooftop to hide behind it. Another dozen rounds dented the air vent, and then he ran out of ammunition. Taylor looked around the side of the vent, but Gunter had his M-16 and was ready for him. Unlike Hussein, he knew his business, and he opened fire with tight, disciplined three shot bursts. Taylor managed to snap off two shots from the Sig, and Gunter ran back to the helo, crouching down next to his boss. The launcher lay where he'd dropped it. It was the equalizer. He could see the two men talking, pointing at the launcher and at him. They were conjuring up a way to kill him, to stop him using it. They took the only sensible option. Gunter ran one way and Hussein the other. They were heading for the elevator shaft, which would give them enough cover to hide behind and hit him with gunfire. He measured the angles. There was only one place for him to hide on the rooftop. Then he ran. The Robinson R44 waited silently on the helipad. He ran around to the pilot, wrenched open his door, and gestured with the Sig.

"Get out and lie face down on the roof. Do it now, or I'll toss you off the edge."

The pilot's face whitened. He was dressed in the uniform of a charter pilot, dark blue pants and matching windcheater with gold epaulettes over a white pilot shirt. On his head, he wore a headset, which he removed before he jumped to the ground. He lay prone. Taylor frisked him, but he was unarmed. A couple of shots whistled overhead. He ignored them, knowing they wouldn't risk destroying the helo. It was a standoff, and a sudden gust of smoke and flame from inside the building reminded him that time had become a very precious commodity for all of them. Gunter and Hussein stood staring at him, uncertain. They couldn't go forward, nor could they could go back. Taylor was out of options as well. He could fly the helo, but knew the moment he attempted to take off, the two men would rake it with gunfire. And then his mind cleared, and he knew what to do. His entire life had come down to this one moment.

I'm going to die. It's the only way to defeat this evil bastard who came to America to gouge a fortune out of the weak and the sick. My biggest regret is I won't see Kate again. I can see a kaleidoscope of images of her, her face when she's happy, when she's angry, and when we made love. And there's the pain. It's a pity. Doc Hermann has done so much for me, and he almost got there, but the pain is formidable, and I couldn't get past it.

A cloud of dark smoke roiled out from below onto the roof and was whisked away by the wind. The building was now fully ablaze. There was little time to wait. He debated the best way to go.

Whichever I choose, a bullet in the head, a leap off the roof, I have to make sure these two men are dead. Once I'm certain of that, I can go in peace.

He checked the load on his Sig and prepared for the final confrontation with Hussein and Metz.

CHAPTER ELEVEN

"Jack! You there?"

It was Kate's voice, shouting in his earpiece. They hadn't used the commo, there'd been no need, and he'd even forgotten he had it plugged into his ear. He cursed.

Is she still in the building, or is she outside? Christ, I thought they were all long gone.

"Kate? What gives?"

"I wanted to let you know about Wes. Levi found another set of scuba gear, and he's coming up to see if you need any help."

"Christ, no! Wes, if you can hear me get out! Kate, tell me you're outside on the ground."

"Sorry, Jack. You know the way it works. We leave when you leave. There's enough cable to reach ground level, and we've made it into a rope, but we won't use it until we all go out together. "

Damn! As if I don't have enough problems. Everything's starting to go wrong. If they don't get out, they'll die in the fire.

He was about to insist she got out when he looked in astonishment at Wes. He'd came charging out of the roof hatch, his clothes on fire, like a smoking demon risen from the depths of hell. He was clutching the grenade launcher, which poked out from underneath the damp and smoking garments that protected him from the fire.

"Wes," he shouted urgently. "Get over here, behind the helo."

Hussein and Gunter tracked off a few shots in his direction, and he saw Wes stagger as one of the rounds found its target. Then he flung himself down on the ground behind the aircraft. He grinned at Taylor as he removed the damp coats.

"Damn, that was hot work. It looks like we were right. You do need help."

"You should have left. Are you okay? It looked like one of those rounds clipped you."

"Nah, just a scratch, it caught me in the side. It's no problem."

Taylor sighed and checked the wound. There was little blood, so it was nothing they needed to worry about. He raised his eyes to the heavens.

I had it all worked out, but I shouldn't have expected them to tamely abandon me in the burning building.

"There's nothing you can do here, Wes. It's a Mexican standoff. They can't take off without me shooting them out of the sky with the RPG. I can't leave because they'd hightail it in the Robinson. It's a miracle you made it across the roof, but getting back will be impossible. It's directly in their line of fire. I guess what saved you is your somewhat unexpected appearance."

His friend was quiet for a few moments, pondering

their situation, and then he looked around at Taylor.

"This was a shut end mission for you, wasn't it, coming up here? You weren't coming back!"

Taylor looked back at him. He didn't reply, but he knew Wes could read him. They heard the sound of sirens in the distance.

"If the fire department gets here, they'll rescue Hussein," Wes pointed out. "Is that what you want?"

Taylor shook his head. He knew he'd miscalculated badly.

Wes put a hand on his arm. "You know I trained as a demolitions specialist in the Service?"

Taylor nodded absently.

"How about I fix up a little surprise inside the helo? I can modify a couple of these grenades, enough to do the trick."

He considered for a few moments. "They'll search the ship before they take off. They're sure to suspect something."

"There's an inspection hatch at the rear," Wes persisted. "Underneath the tail rotor assembly. It's to service the gearbox assembly. If something goes inside there, they'll never find it. I guarantee it."

Taylor mulled it over. It was a chance, maybe their only one. A possibility to get out alive and still end the career of Mehdi Hussein. He turned to Wes with a cold smile. "Set the charge. When you're done, I'll see if Hussein goes for it."

It was only a matter of minutes later when he shouted over to the two men.

"Look, Hussein, there's no need for us all to die here. I've got a deal that can save us all."

A pause. "What do you want?"

The man's Middle Eastern accent was thicker now that he faced the possibility of perishing in the burning building.

"We go out the way we came in, down the stairs, and you can leave in the helicopter. There are two of us here now. Things have changed. I don't want my friend to get hurt."

"So you're beginning to see sense at last. What about my pilot?"

Taylor glanced to where the man still lay prone on the rooftop.

"He's here, and he's alive. We haven't touched him."

Another pause. "Very well, I agree. You can get out."

" Were coming out now. Keep your weapons pointed away from us. My friend here has a grenade launcher. It's armed and ready to fire. One shot from either of you, he puts a grenade into the Robinson, and we all die."

"Agreed. You can come out now."

They fastened the air tanks on their backs, and put the still damp but smoking garments over them. It was their only chance, and not a particularly good one. For a few moments, Taylor debated taking the time to wet everything down again, but decided against it. If they didn't leave then, it would be too late. They started toward the roof hatch. Wes walked backward and kept the launcher targeted on the helo. Taylor covered the two hostiles with his Sig. He could see the RPG several yards away, but he knew if he tried to scoop it up, they'd open fire. Everything depended on Wes' improvised demolition charge.

They started down the folding stairs that led to Hussein's apartment when abruptly a barrage of shots cracked out all around them. Hussein and Gunter had decided to finish them off before they left. Wes was thrown to the floor as at least two rounds caught him in the body. Taylor felt the impact of a bullet take him low in the side, and he knew it was going to be one hell of a painful wound, either close to or in the kidney. It could be enough to kill him if he bled out. Then he laughed out loud as he had a thought.

We're trapped in a burning building with flames roaring in front of us, and a pair of psychotic killers behind us. Sure, I might die, but not from this wound.

He dragged Wes out of sight of the roof hatch and examined where the bullets had hit him. Blood was dripping onto the floor. It was impossible to locate the source, hidden under the damp coats and clothing. He used his knife to slice two chunks of material off the jacket that covered his head, and stuffed them into the general area of the bullet wounds. It was the best he could do. If they didn't get out fast, he'd die in the flames anyway. He stared at Wes. His friend's face had the drawn, haggard look he'd seen so many times before.

He's in trouble if I don't get help real soon.

"Is it bad?"

His eyes were tight shut with the pain, but he opened them to mere slits.

"I gotta be honest with you, Boss, I've felt better."

"Can you walk?"

"Are the Navy Seals the finest bunch of fighting men in the world? Course I can walk. I can carry you with me if I have to."

He smiled. If there ever was a time when Wes's macho toughness was needed, it was right then. Taylor got to his feet, wincing as the pain of his own wounds lanced through him. Nothing else mattered other than getting his friend out, nothing at all. Above them, he could hear the helo spooling up. The fate of Hussein depended on the munitions hidden inside the tail rotor casing. It would work, or it wouldn't. In the meantime, he set to work. He considered the equipment he carried. The air bottle and regulator, the mask, his Sig, and the mass of damp garments seemed to weigh a ton. He was aware he was losing blood from the wounds he'd taken to his hand and body, but he forced himself to ignore them.

There'll be time to worry about them later, if there ever is a later.

The fire seemed even fiercer, and the thought of having to fight their way down the blazing staircase was daunting, but it had to be done. There was no other way. He looked around at Wes.

"It's time to go. Are you set?"

Wes had put his mask and mouthpiece back in place, and some of the damp coats to protect him. But he was swaying on his feet, and Taylor could see blood had pooled on the floor where it was leaking from his wounds. He looked into Wes' eyes.

"We have to go, buddy. You have to walk down."

Wes shook his head. "I was premature with that macho bullshit," he murmured, his voice distorted through the mouthpiece. He spat it out. "I can't make it, Boss. This is one time when you gotta believe me. There'd be no point anyway. I'm shot full of holes, and I doubt I'd even make it to the emergency room if we did get out of here. There's only one way to do this. Get yourself down that staircase and out of the building. Make a life for yourself and Kate. I've seen you two together. You were made for each other."

Taylor shook his head. "No, that ain't gonna happen, Wes. It's…"

"You gonna leave that poor girl all on her lonesome? Get out of here, and leave me. Maybe there'll be some kind of an afterlife, and I can join Evie, so we can have some of the happiness that was taken from us in this life. Don't argue, get…"

Those were the last words he said before he pitched forward, overcome by blood loss and lapsed into unconsciousness. Taylor caught him and held him upright. He knew what he had to do and had no idea whether he could manage it, even get halfway. But he had to try. He bent his knees, folded Wes' huge body over his shoulder, and stood up. He grunted with the chilling weight of the big man, encumbered with a second set of air tanks and wet coats. The tremendous weight on his body caused his wounds to bleed even more. He knew he had a very limited timeframe before he followed Wes into oblivion. He looked at the flame-engulfed staircase, sucked in a huge breath through the mouthpiece, and started forward; first one foot and then the other. Every muscle, every bone, every fiber, and every nerve ending screamed at him to stop.

Now I understand a new truth. The pain of lost limbs is as nothing compared to this.

Although he had some protection from the flames, the pain of the enormous weight and his wounds made his body feel as if he was already standing inside the fire, naked and burning. He took another step, and another. Each time he moved, he screamed. The sound was muted through the mouthpiece, yet it was a kind of release. He took two more steps, and two more. Then he lost his balance as his body gave way, and he tumbled forward down to the landing of the fifth floor. He must have blacked out for a few moments because when he came to, he was in a haze of confusion before realizing where he was. He held Wes steady on his shoulder with one hand, gripped the stair rail with his wounded hand, and used it to pull himself upright again. He couldn't prevent another muffled scream, and another and another.

I'm burning! Dear God, I'm burning up inside, and burning up outside. Just let me die, anything to get me out of this pain.

He heard a groan as Wes stirred on his shoulder.

"What, what gives?" he mumbled.

Then he fell unconscious again. Taylor sucked in more air. A half dozen gulps, more, a dozen breaths, until his lungs were full. He forced himself to concentrate his mind on anything except the terrible task he faced.

I could die. I was prepared to end it up on that roof, but the others don't want to die, not Kate, Levi, and Wes. I have to keep going. I have to make it. Keep going, Taylor. What am I, a sniveling drug addict? Fuck that, there is no pain, none! It's a bunch of fucking nerve ends, that all. This time, they're not going to beat me. No fucking way!

He started down again, one step, two, three. Screaming, weeping, ignoring the terrible damage he knew he was doing to his body.

Too bad, I'm still breathing. Hang in there, Wes, old buddy.

He had to stop. His brain began to swim, and he knew his body was collapsing with the impossible burden he carried. It nagged him to stop, to give up the impossible task. He ignored it, and yet again worked through the angles, the options. Yet there was only one, to keep moving. Staying there meant the flames would incinerate them both. The jacket on Wes' head burst into flame, and he threw it off, and adjusted the rest of the damp clothing to keep his friend's head away from the inferno. Then he started down again. A few more steps, and he realized his pants were on fire, which meant his legs were burning. He could smell the stench of burning plastics as the polymer of his prosthetic limbs began to burn and melt.

Maybe it's one advantage of losing your legs. If you get caught in a fire, the artificial replacements can catch fire and be replaced afterward. If you get out!

Two more steps, and he staggered when his muscles betrayed him, and he almost dropped Wes. With an effort of will, he locked his body to hold it upright. He was using the stair rail, holding on to it with one hand as he carried on. But when he reached the bend in the staircase, the rail had disappeared. Probably it was destroyed when they fought their way up through the building, a victim of one of the grenades that had been thrown. He had fourteen more steps to go, and he knew he couldn't make it. There was only one thing left.

I'm sorry, Wes, there's no other way. If one of us has to break their neck, then let it be me.

He stood up as straight as he could and fell forward into the flames. They tumbled, rolling down the burning staircase, over and over. He held on to Wes' head, in an effort to support his neck and stop him from snapping his spine. He didn't feel the bumps and jars of the hard stair edges as his body hit them. He was past that, past all of it. He didn't feel the flames even, as they licked around him and burned his body. His wounds had gone numb and were forgotten. Even his amputated legs were forgotten, as he focused all his efforts in a last effort to escape the fire. It was a surreal nightmare, rolling through the flames, Wes' heavy body banging against him every time they rolled over. He hit the landing of the fourth floor, taking a blow on his head, skidded through the flames, and smashed against the opposite wall. And they stopped. They'd made it. He screamed, losing the mouthpiece as the agony returned and surged over him, as if he was still in the flames, burning, dying. But he'd held onto Wes. Someone was shouting, making no sense.

Wes? The guy's arguing with me, for Christ's sake, but his voice sounds different.

"Jack, Jack! We've got him!"

He dimly realized that Kate and Levi were bent over him, trying to extricate Wes' body from his grasp. He let go, and they dragged the big man away and out of the flames. He tried to crawl, but nothing worked properly. It was strange. His limbs had given up, not just the prosthetic miracles Doc Hermann had fitted on him, but his arms had stopped responding to his brain, even his head would only move an inch or two. Levi and Kate rushed back, dragging him out of the flames to an area of the fourth floor that was clear of the fire and laid him next to Wes.

"You're okay now. You're going to be okay."

Yeah, sure! I can't move, so how the hell am I going to scramble down some improvised escape line? And Wes, he's unconscious. They don't get it. They really don't get it.

They removed the air bottle and mouthpiece from him, took off his mask, and pulled off the smoking garments. He could feel Levi beating at the flames from his burning legs. He stared up at him.

"Levi, you may as well save yourself the trouble. You know I'm never getting out of this place."

"What are you talking about, man? They're coming for us."

"Who's coming?"

"The Boston Fire Department. They're parked in the street right now, and they're sending a ladder up to get us out. You're gonna be okay. We'll be out in a few minutes."

He didn't reply. He felt stunned and dizzy. Kate sprayed an extinguisher over him, and he smelt the rank stench of burned clothing, smoldering plastic, with the overlaying stench of acrid, stultifying smoke.

"Wes, how is he?" he managed to croak.

"He's alive, thanks to you. Don't try and talk, Jack. Save your strength until you're out of here."

"Yeah."

He swiveled his eyes to look back at Kate. She didn't know yet he couldn't move, and he didn't want to tell her. He'd done his best, and now his body had packed in completely. He guessed everyone had their limits, and he'd gone way past them. As he watched and waited, he heard the sound of breaking glass as the first fireman entered the building. They fitted Wes on a special gurney and lowered him carefully to the ground. Then, it was his turn, and he watched the ground spiraling nearer as he descended. A pair of medics swarmed over him when he touched down, and they cut off the rest of his tattered and burned clothing. They whistled in surprise when they saw the exposed mechanism, cables, servos, and circuit boards inside the burnt plastic that was all that remained of his legs.

"What are you, some kind of Six Million Dollar Man?"

"I used to be. I guess those days are over."

He nodded. "Is there someone we should call? Someone who knows about this stuff? I mean; it's not something we encounter every day."

He thought about Hermann van Rhoos, but that was in the past. He was a miracle worker, but Taylor knew the damage his body had suffered was too extensive even for him, for anyone.

"No, no one."

They covered him with a blanket and lifted the gurney to place him into the ambulance. The sound of a helo lifting off the burning building, made them look up.

"Christ, there were more people up there. Thank Christ they got away."

"Yeah, it's just as well," his partner replied. "That building ain't gonna last much longer."

Taylor felt a wash of despondency sweep over him.

Have we failed? Did that bastard Arab beat us, after all?

Kate and Levi were standing a few yards away, so they'd got out after him. And then the ground shook. The roar of the exploding helicopter rumbled over the city, and pieces of broken machinery showered down to litter the nearby streets. Taylor smiled, as the paramedic looked out of the open doors in astonishment.

"Jesus Christ, that chopper exploded. My, god, the poor bastards." He looked in concern at Taylor. "You okay, buddy?"

"Yeah. Oh, yeah. I'm good, real good."

CHAPTER TWELVE

He'd been lying in the hospital bed for five days, drifting in and out of a drug-induced stupor. He avoided any mention of Hermann to the medical staff. He knew it was some kind of a death wish that kept him from giving them the name of who had fitted the complex prosthetic legs. The doctors who worked on his body were baffled. It was like seeing something from a science fiction film, and they had no idea of how to start making repairs. In the end, it was Kate who contacted van Rhoos, and within thirty minutes, the MIT genius was bustling into the hospital room, pulling behind him a big, wheeled case that held his equipment, laptop, and spare parts. Taylor watched and gave him a glacial welcome.

"You're wasting your time, Doc. It's gone too far even for you to fix."

Hermann didn't say hello. He'd spoken to Taylor's physician and knew his state of mind. He ignored him completely he began to examining the burned and damaged limbs. He first connected a diagnostic cable to a socket he uncovered above the knee joint, and then sang quietly to himself as his fingers hammered at the keyboard like a concert pianist. Finally, he nodded and looked at Taylor.

"Wasting my time, am I? Did you honestly think you could do this amount of damage to my valuable creations, and I'd just leave you be? No way!"

He looked back to the screen and tapped again at the keyboard. Then he rummaged in his case and came out with a compact circuit board.

"I can make temporary repairs straightaway, and we'll do something more permanent when you come into the lab."

"That's not the problem, Hermann, surely you can see that? Look at my arms. I'm paralyzed."

"Hmm. They are badly burned. I see that, and you have a dressing on what looks like a bullet wound on one hand. I assume that dressing on your side is to cover another bullet wound?"

"Yeah, there were a lot of bullets flying around."

But the guy doesn't see it.

"I'm paralyzed, Doc. Can you see that now? It's over. Thanks for everything you did. It was great, but now I've reached the end. Save it for some other poor bastard who gets his legs blown off," he shouted.

"Is that right? Hmm, try moving your left arm."

Taylor obeyed.

The guy may as well see how pointless it is.

Nothing happened. "See what I mean?"

Hermann nodded thoughtfully. "Yeah, now that's interesting."

"Interesting! That's not what I would call it. Give it up,

Doc."

"Hmm, right, let me take another look inside."

He played around with the cables inside the top of his leg that interfaced it to his central nervous system, and then turned back to his laptop. He spent a full half-hour running what Jack assumed were a series of diagnostic tests. Finally, he nodded.

"Yeah, I see the problem. The stresses of whatever happened inside that burning building were more of a strain on the equipment than I'd anticipated. It's not something I've seen before. It's like you picked up and carried a very heavy weight and overloaded everything. No, heavy doesn't explain it. The weight must have been massive. Do you know what I mean? It's strange, but something weird must have happened in there."

"Oh, he can be pretty stupid, Hermann."

They both looked as Kate came into the room and walked up to Taylor. She bent down and kissed him. At least he felt something, a warmth sending a tingle through his body.

A tingle, but surely I'm paralyzed?

"Do you know what happened to him?" Hermann asked her.

She explained how he'd carried the wounded Wes, their air bottles, weapons, and equipment down two flights of stairs, after he'd been shot twice. "Well, it was almost two flights of stairs. He tumbled down the last few steps with Wes on top of him. Would that be enough to do the kind of damage you describe?"

Hermann nodded thoughtfully. "You mean Wes, the former Seal, who went to see Doc Weinberg?"

She smiled. "That's him, I'd guess he's about two

hundred and twenty pounds of solid muscle."

Hermann grimaced and then nodded. "Then I guess Jack had no choice. It would certainly do the kind of damage he's sustained. Maybe I should have used stronger components. I wasn't anticipating him running down burning staircases carrying two hundred and twenty pounds of dead weight."

He started checking figures on his laptop. Neither of them was sure whether he was serious or joking. Kate stayed next to Taylor, clutching his good hand in hers while they watched Hermann continue tapping the keys and muttering to himself. He ran yet another diagnostic program on his laptop, and Jack felt something tremble in his arm, as if a servo had suddenly come online. But that was ridiculous. The arm was his, not a collection of cables, chips, and motors. There were no servos. Hermann nodded.

"Feel something? Try moving it now."

Taylor tried moving his thumb first. He commanded his brain to send the signal, and he felt his thumb move a little in response.

Hermann looked satisfied. "Jack, your limbs will be stiff for a while, so don't expect miracles until you've exercised the muscles for a time. Try raising your arm."

He sent the signal, and his arm moved up, only a couple of inches. It was slow and sore, but it moved.

If it's sore, the nerves are connected and working.

"That'll do for now, Jack. Let me take a look at the other leg and see what I can do. I'm sure it's the same problem on that side. You overloaded everything in that building, and the legs took rather more punishment than I designed them for."

He spent another half-hour working on the other leg, and indicated that Jack should attempt to move his arm. With a wash of relief, he felt his hand and then the muscles of his bicep responding. His arm rose off the bed, four inches upward. It was hard, and the pain was considerable, but he wasn't complaining.

"Doc, you think I can it all back?"

Van Rhoos looked surprised. "Get it back? Sure, why not? It's just a glitch. Did you think I wasn't up to it?"

Taylor shook his head. "Not for a moment."

He spent three more days in the hospital, and for most of the time, Kate was with him. Levi came to visit each day as well. He was a different person from the inexperienced young man who'd just suffered the loss of his father. Levi Yates had the strength and confidence of a combat veteran.

In fact, that's exactly what he is; he's seen more combat than many men see in a lifetime, Taylor smiled.

Wes was still in a medically induced coma, and on the last full day of his hospitalization the three of them went to visit. Taylor had to submit to being pushed in a wheelchair before the staff would give permission. Wes lay unmoving on a hospital bed in the Intensive Care Unit, covered from head to toe in bandages. He almost seemed to be suspended by the many cables and tubes that passed into his body. The monitors surrounding his bed beat steadily, and Taylor assumed that was a good sign. They stayed with him for a half-hour, willing him to pull through, but there was no response. Eventually, a doctor walked into the room.

"Are you family?"

They looked at each other and at Wes, who despite the

bandages was clearly many shades darker than they were. The doctor reddened.

"I guess not. Look, I don't want visitors in here, right now. It's nothing personal. There's still a high risk of infection. He took quite a beating, this guy." He looked at them, Levi and Kate still displayed the bruises, and Taylor was swathed in dressings. "You were with him when he was hurt?"

"We were with him," Levi replied.

"In that case, you can stay."

"What's the prognosis, the outlook?" Kate asked him.

"It's good," he replied in a confident tone. "Luckily, the bullets missed anything too serious, and once we'd replaced the blood he'd lost, it was a matter of treating the burns and broken bones. The bones were easy, although there were plenty we had to work on. The burns are a matter of time, and there's always the worry of infection setting in. It looks like he tumbled down several flights of stairs. "

"He did," she told him.

"Okay, that explains it. The burns are the real problem. As I said, there's a high risk of infection with that kind of injury, especially as he's weakened with his other injuries. That's why we're happy to keep him under for the time being. The shock could kill him if we bring him round too soon. I would imagine another twenty-four hours should do it. If nothing worsens, we'll bring him round tomorrow."

He eventually left them, and they stayed with Wes for a little longer. It was time for Taylor to return to his hospital room. Levi left and promised to visit when he was out. Then it occurred to him.

"Where will you go when they let you out of here?"

Before he could answer, Kate replied, "To my place, of course. Where else would he go?"

Levi nodded. "Right, I'll give you guys a couple of days and see you then."

After he'd left, Taylor looked at her.

"You sure?"

"Sure? Of course I'm sure. You're not thinking about running out on me, Jack Taylor?"

Her sincerity, her warmth and love, moved him to feel a lump in his throat, a rare emotion for him. He finally understood the kind of girl she was and knew they may even have a future together, more than he'd ever dared to think before. He stared at her disheveled hair and her vivid green eyes. He admired her smooth, creamy skin, and full luscious lips, and for a few moments luxuriated in the nearness of her.

But still, she's entitled to so much more.

"You know it's wrong."

"Fuck you, Taylor!" she erupted, startling a nearby nurse. "I thought you'd know me better by now. After all we've been through, don't you think it's time to let go and relax? How many times do I have to bail out your ass before you understand?" A pause. "And there's something else. I'm not prepared to live without you, Jack. So I'm going to carry on saving your ass, and you'd better get used to it."

He pulled her down to him and kissed her. "Yes, Ma'am. I guess that's one order that won't be too hard to obey. But if things get tough, we'll have to re-look at it all."

"That's not the way it works, buddy. When things get tough is when we pull together, there's nothing to re-look at. I guess you have a lot to learn," she smiled. "But there'll be plenty of time to teach you."

She stayed with him for the rest of the day and through the evening, until the nursing staff almost had to physically eject her. She promised to be back first thing in the morning and said she'd help him get his things together, so he could move into her apartment.

"I put some pants and a T-shirt in your locker," she nodded to a small cabinet at the side of his bed, "if you need to go to physio or something like that. But I didn't leave shoes or a coat," she smiled. "Just in case you try and make a break for it."

"That's pretty cunning."

"Yep. Now you're learning how determined this girl can be."

After she'd gone, he felt exhausted, so he lay back in the bed and tried to sleep. He only managed to doze, as the struggle with Mehdi Hussein and his minions kept flashing through his mind.

I was lucky. We were all very lucky, except for Lincoln Moss.

Kate had talked to his widow and promised they'd do everything to help her. The account of Lincoln's bravery went a long way toward alleviating some of her grief. But the crooked Arab, Mehdi Hussein had come within an inch of escaping, while they could quite easily have perished in the building he'd purposefully set on fire.

It was close, very close, but now it's all over. At least Kate is safe, and I have a chance of a life with her, which is more than I ever thought possible.

He must have dozed off, for someone was shaking him. "Mr. Taylor, Mr. Taylor!"

He looked up and recognized the nurse who normally attended him during the night, an older woman about mid forties, dark hair, dark eyes, and a little overweight. He also knew her as a tough and highly competent nurse.

"Yeah? What is it?"

"I have a call for you. He said it's important. I tried to tell him you were asleep, but he insisted it was life or death. I transferred it to your bedside telephone."

He nodded his thanks and picked up. "This is Taylor."

"Jack?" he recognized Levi Yates. "What is it, Levi? What's wrong?"

"Maybe nothing. I called Kate earlier on to suggest I call round tomorrow and help out with anything you might need. You know the kind of thing, running errands, fetching groceries. There was no reply, so I called the hospital, and they said she'd left about an hour before. I don't know why, but something bothered me, so I went round her place. She's not there. Something's happened."

Taylor was puzzled. There was something more, something Levi wasn't telling him. Maybe it was the drugs he'd taken that day. "What are you trying to tell me?"

"The lock was broken, and the door to her apartment was wide open. I went inside, and it looked as if there'd been some kind of a struggle." He sounded worried, desperate even. "Jack, it looks as if someone has taken her."

Taylor groaned inwardly.

All she's been through, how the hell could this have happened to her, to Kate?

He raced through all the possibilities, stopping when he came to the obvious answer.

Wasim Malouf. The crooked cop who was on the take

from Hussein, the cop who is subject to a Boston PD Internal Affairs investigation. There's no other possible answer, but why take Kate Donovan when he's on the run? What does he have to gain?

The answer struck him like a wave of ice-cold seawater.

"It's Malouf. He wants revenge. I've seen it too many times before."

He remembered his service in Iraq and Afghanistan. Whole families, tribes even, were often targeted by another group of Islamic crazies for insults often so trivial as to be laughable. But it wasn't laughable when those crazies set out to slaughter men, women, and children to satisfy their bloodlust for revenge.

"What do I do?" His young voice sounded despairing and lost.

"Call the cops, Levi. Tell them what's happened. Wait for me at Kate's place. I'll be along as soon as I can get dressed and call a cab."

"But you don't finish your treatment until tomorrow."

"The rules have changed. Do you have any weapons? What about a car?"

"I'm still driving the Lincoln. I didn't know what to do with it after that business at Hussein's building, and I couldn't return it to Lincoln's widow like that. The trunk is still half filled with those guns you put in there. I was waiting for you to come out of hospital and decide what you wanted done."

"That's good. Okay, call the cops as soon as you end this call, and wait for me."

"What are we going to do?"

"We're going to find her, and I'm going to kill Malouf."

He started pulling out the needles and removed

the sensors and catheters linking him to the drips and monitors over his bed. He dug into the locker and grabbed the clothes she'd left him, clean lightweight beige cotton chinos, and a dark green T-shirt with NYU printed on the front. He opened the door and walked out into the corridor, only to bump into the nurse who'd woken him to take the call.

"Mr. Taylor! Where are you going?"

"I have business to attend to. It can't wait."

"No way, Mister. You have to stay in bed until the doctor can see you tomorrow." She looked down. "Besides, you don't even have any shoes."

"Not a problem, Ma'am. I don't have any feet either."

He sidestepped and left her gaping at him, as he ran out through the main entrance onto the street. A cab had just pulled up to deposit a passenger at the ER room. He jumped in through the open door and gave the driver the address of Kate's apartment. The driver twisted around, looking pointedly at Taylor's pants and T-shirt, with bare feet. Hardly appropriate clothing for late at night. He probably thought his passenger was an escaped mental patient.

"You sure about that, buddy? I'm not certain you're okay to leave the hospital."

Taylor stared back at him. "I'll do the worrying, friend. Just drive."

The man nodded. The hard tone carried a message he was too experienced to ignore. They pulled up five minutes later outside the apartment block, and he had to keep the suspicious cabbie waiting while he ran inside to borrow money for the fare from Levi. He paid him and returned to look inside the apartment. It told a story that was clear enough, and it wasn't anything good. He knew from his previous visits that her apartment was immaculate, with tasteful furnishings and everything kept neat and tidy. Now the lock on the front door had been smashed open, and a chair inside the living room had been overturned. The glass top of the coffee table lay in pieces. A couple of her paintings had been ripped from the walls and lay strewn on the floor. It looked to him as if she'd thrown them at her assailant. He turned to Levi.

"What did the cops say when you called them?"

"Not a lot. I told them it looked as if she'd been kidnapped, but they weren't impressed. They said they may send someone along to take a look sometime tomorrow, but it was probably a lover's quarrel, and she'd come home sooner or later."

"Fuck them. Some of those cops couldn't find their own dicks in the dark. I'll call Brad Stutz."

He put the call through and checked the time. It was just after 0100, and he had to let the phone ring for a long time before it was answered. The voice was blurry and full of sleep.

"Yeah? Stutz here, what is it?"

"This is Jack Taylor. Your pal has gone and kidnapped Kate Donovan."

"Malouf? Jesus Christ, Taylor, why are you calling me?"

"Because your fucking department isn't interested, and you're the only one that knows the guy well and has a chance of locating him."

He heard the detective give out a long sigh. Finally, he said, "Okay, I get it. It sounds as if the stupid bastard has finally flipped. Why the hell would he kidnap her?"

"Revenge."

"Revenge? That doesn't seem very logical."

"Believe me, for someone like Malouf, or his paymaster, Mehdi Hussein, revenge is something that runs in their blood."

"Fuck! What do you think he'll do with her?"

"Nothing good, but it's almost certain he'll keep her alive so he can get to me."

"You're still at her apartment? I'll be right over."

The detective arrived thirty minutes later, wearing yesterday's shirt with the buttons wrongly fastened and no tie. His jacket and pants were as crumpled as the shirt. His face was filled with concern as he looked around the messed up apartment.

"If Malouf kidnapped her, he's off his head."

Taylor didn't comment on that. "Where would he take her, Stutz? You must have some idea of the kind of places that are familiar to him. Does he have a cabin somewhere, a favorite Motel maybe where he takes a girlfriend? Think, man, there must be something, somewhere quiet. Maybe even a trailer, or a boat."

Stutz looked up sharply. "A boat! He owns a boat. I know that for a fact. We went fishing on it last year."

"Where does he tie up?"

"Boston Waterboat Marina. He rents a permanent berth there."

Levi's eyebrows rose. "That's only for large craft, and it doesn't come cheap. What kind of boat does he have?"

Stutz cast his eyes down and his face reddened. "She's a Grand Banks 59, an Aleutian."

Levi whistled. "Man, that must have cost around a couple of million dollars. Where the hell did a cop get money like that?"

Stutz didn't look up or reply, and Taylor decided not to embarrass him any more than he already was. He'd obviously been blinded by the senior detective's knowledge and long experience, and failed to see the obvious, until now. The cost of running a craft of that size, kept in an expensive and exclusive yacht harbor, would be astronomical, and out of the reach of any cop, including the Chief; unless you were on the take in a big way.

Levi got the message. "Oh, yeah. Right."

"We'll need the exact location. We're leaving, what about you?" Taylor said, looking at Stutz.

"I ought to contact the precinct and organize a squad to get down there. They may need SWAT if it's a hostage situation."

"Fuck the precinct! We're going in to get her out," Levi shouted.

"Don't forget you're dealing with one of your own people," Taylor cautioned Stutz. "He'll know every trick in the book, including the way SWAT operates. The only way to save Kate is to hit him where he least expects it. That's the way we're going to handle it."

They were both looking at him. He shuffled his feet, and they could see he was thinking furiously. He finally looked at them, his face torn by indecision.

"You know this could get messy?"

Taylor tried not to sigh in exasperation. "Stutz, what the fuck do you think we've been doing with his pal Mehdi Hussein? You don't go see these people and try to reason with them. That's not the way it works and not the way they're brought up. You go in and kick the shit out of them before they see you coming."

"That's the way you did it in Afghanistan?"

"Yes. It's the only way." He looked down at his prosthetic legs and grinned. "Of course, sometimes it goes wrong, but more often than not, it works out. Look, we're leaving right now. Are you in, or are you out?"

"It could cost me my badge, you know that."

Neither of them replied. They left him to work it out. On the one hand a badge, and on the other, the life of a girl kidnapped by his partner. It didn't take him long to make the connections.

"I'm in."

They piled into the Lincoln, Stutz gave directions, and Levi drove them to the harbor. It was an incongruous sight, luxury yachts tied to floating pontoons in the shadow of the towering skyscraper office blocks and hotels of the city of Boston. Levi parked in a slot two hundred yards from the first of the pontoons. He chose the place well. It was tucked into the shadows, and a big refrigerated truck in an adjacent bay gave them a good degree of cover. Taylor opened the trunk and began removing equipment. They had no armored vests remaining, but there was no time to go looking for replacements. Brad Stutz was armed with his police issue Glock 17. Levi had his big Colt 45. Taylor took an HK 416 carbine for himself, with the only pistol left in the improvised armory, a battered Ruger .22. It was lightweight and accurate, but without the stopping power of something heavier. He shrugged inwardly.

It's enough to do the job. I'll kill the bastard with my bare hands if necessary.

At the last moment, he remembered the Baby Glock. So far, he hadn't used the tiny automatic, so they had no idea he carried it. The gun was his ace in the hole, and he reckoned he might well need it. They'd be up against only one man, but Malouf was no fool. He was a tough, experienced cop, and no stranger to dealing with armed intruders. Presumably, he'd be armed with a Glock 17 or something similar, the preferred weapon of many law enforcement officers. But he also had his own ace in the hole, a hostage. Kate Donovan.

No matter what it takes, putting myself between this rogue cop and the girl I love, I'm getting her off that boat, alive!

He gave the two men a quick briefing.

"Remember," he concluded, "this mission is about the safety of Kate Donovan. Everything else takes second place."

Stutz bristled. "Look, Taylor. It's not that simple. There's a warrant out on Malouf. If he is on the boat, I have to try to take him in."

"Just give me a chance to get Kate out first before you do anything, that's all I ask."

He gave Levi an imperceptible nod, and the younger man inclined his head slightly, to show he understood. They didn't get it. Revenge festered in Malouf's blood like a disease. If they didn't finish him, they'd always be looking over their shoulders.

The cop nodded. "I'll take it easy, don't worry. Just remember, I want Malouf alive. Since you've been after that guy Hussein, all my department has seen is a trail of bodies. Wasim Malouf has to answer for a lot of crimes, and we need to have a long talk with him. When he comes off that boat, I want him in handcuffs, not a body bag."

"Sure, he's all yours." He looked at Levi. "You got that? We get Kate out by any means possible, and we'll leave Malouf to Stutz here."

Levi stared back at him with a straight face. "Yep, I got that."

"Good. Let's do it."

The boat was at the end of a long pontoon. The gate was locked, but Stutz went to the nearby harbor office and showed them his badge. Within minutes, a bunch of security guards arrived, four men, all of them looking coldly at the armed intruders.

"You got a warrant, Detective?"

Stutz shook his head. "Sorry, this is a police emergency. I have to reach that boat."

The man, a hard faced guy of about fifty, stared uneasily at Taylor's assault rifle and then back at Stutz. "I understand that, but my orders are clear. Without a warrant, you don't go past that gate."

They stared at each other for long seconds while Taylor studied the men. He could take them, but they were all armed, and it would be bloody. He began to reach for the Ruger when a new voice intervened.

"You got a problem here?"

He looked at the new arrivals. It was a voice he'd heard before. The man who'd spoken was massive, a hugely muscled black man, who resembled Mike Tyson after he'd taken extra steroids. Quint, his dealer. It made sense that he'd have a boat there; a way to relax, away from the constant threats his business put him under. He sure could afford it. Maybe he used it to bring in merchandise unloaded out to sea from a passing ship. Behind him, one of his enforcers was standing and watching carefully, his hand close to the piece he had to have stashed under his coat. He was also black, and only a fraction smaller than his boss. Quint nodded to Taylor, and looked pointedly at the assault rifle.

"What gives, man?"

Taylor decided to take a chance. He told the dealer everything about the kidnap, and how they needed to reach Malouf's boat before Kate died.

"You mean that pretty white chick I saw you with the other day? Damn, she was one classy lady. You say she's held on one of those boats?"

He nodded.

"Damn, that ain't right. No way, ain't nobody treats a customer of mine that way. Not one that pretty, anyway." He winked at Taylor, and then scowled at the guards. "Okay, you guys listen up. You let my man and his friends on the dock, you hear?"

"But, we can't, it's..."

Quint stared at the senior guard. "You shut your mouth, shithead. I didn't ask you nothing. I said let them through. Open it. Unless you want to take it up with me."

The guards stared at the dealer, and Taylor could see what they saw. Quint was death, a mountain of a man who could kill as easily as eating his breakfast. And right then, he looked mighty hungry.

The guard nodded. "Yes, of course, Sir. No problem."

They unlocked the gate.

"That's it, folks." Quint rumbled. "You go get that little lady."

Taylor nodded his thanks. "I appreciate it."

Quint winked in reply. "Anything to help out one of my best customers."

He ignored Stutz's pointed glance. They ran along the long, floating mooring, past millions of dollars of leisure yachts until they were within yards of Malouf's Grand

Banks.

"My God, that's one hell of a boat," Levi breathed. "You see that?"

Proudly painted on the bow was the name of the boat, 'Star of the Prophet'.

"Yeah, that particular prophet's in for a surprise," Taylor murmured. He turned to Stutz. "Give me ten minutes. I'm going on board to find Kate."

"No more, Taylor. Ten minutes, and I'm coming on board to make the bust."

Taylor nodded and started forward with Levi close behind him. He'd known all along that Jerry's son wouldn't miss finishing off what they'd started. Levi blamed Malouf in part for his father's death. He had his own score to settle.

If that means he kills the Arab detective that's just too bad. I don't care what Stutz wants. Shit happens.

They edged down the gangplank. In front of them, the yacht's superstructure loomed large, lit up by the illumination of the harbor lighting. There was a substantial flying bridge, giving the skipper good all-round visibility. On the deck below, he could see a covered walkway running all the way around the boat's superstructure, and portholes lower down in the hull showed there was another substantial deck, probably containing the galley and cabins. Taylor used hand signals, and Levi understood to go left when they were aboard. He would go to the right, so they could circle around the boat for any sign of Kate. But something puzzled him. The craft was almost in darkness. If Malouf was aboard, it should be lit up.

Does it mean we've called it wrongly? Has he taken her somewhere else? There's only one way to find out.

He stepped off the gangplank onto the boat and began searching through the portholes. He went all the way round and met up with Levi, who shook his head. Taylor pointed down to the door leading to the interior of the boat. It was unlocked, and he led the way through and came to a companionway leading down to the next deck. He edged downward, feeling the churning in his guts that told him he was moving into a hot zone. It was never wrong. He reached the bottom of the narrow ladder and put a foot onto the thick carpet of the hallway that led to the staterooms. He could see a dim light shining from underneath the door at the front of the boat, almost certainly the master cabin. He placed his HK 416 out of sight behind the companionway steps. The cramped interior of a pleasure craft was no place for an assault rifle. He went forward and listened at the door. Nothing. Levi was right behind him. He indicated he should stay back out of sight, and his partner nodded, returning to stand hidden behind the companionway steps.

It's now or never.

He grasped his pistol firmly and took several steps back. Then he charged the door, smashed it open with his shoulder, and rolled away the left, out of the direct line of fire if Malouf was inside, waiting. Then he froze. Kate was tied to a huge bed, tied spreadeagled with ropes, gagged, and naked. It was like she was the victim of some bizarre bondage game. At first, there was no sign of Malouf. Then he appeared suddenly in the smashed and broken doorway. He looked shocked, but he had a gun in his hand and snapped off two quick shots. Taylor fired back, and the detective disappeared. Maybe Levi would nail him, although he doubted it. The guy was too tricky to be caught out easily. Taylor bent over and began to unfasten the gag. She looked terrified.

"Kate, are you okay? Did he hurt you?"

"Thank God you come, Jack. The bastard was about to start exploring his weird fantasies with me." She shivered. "Get me out of here. I'll tell you about it later."

He cut the rest of her bonds and pulled her to her feet. She began to pull on her clothes as Taylor looked out the door for any sign of Malouf, but he'd disappeared.

"I'm ready."

He looked at her, and his heart leapt. She was disheveled, a bruise over one eye, and a cut on her hand, but she was alive.

I'm getting her off the boat, no matter what. And despite what I promised Brad Stutz, Malouf is going down. He won't get off this boat alive!

"Let's go, and stay with me."

He stepped into the hallway, pulling her behind him. He listened, but there was nothing, no movement. No rustle of clothing or sound of a footstep. They went forward and reached the companionway stairs. Levi was still standing behind them, partially hidden. Taylor froze. Levi had a gun held to his neck, and a man stood behind him, but it wasn't Malouf.

"Put the gun down, Taylor, or I kill him."

Grant Williams, general manager of MMP, the company he'd put out of business. He looked frightened but determined, a dangerous combination. He froze. The man who faced him stared at him through weak, watery blue eyes. He was living a nightmare and prepared to do anything to get way with his pal, Malouf. He'd have plenty of money stashed in an offshore account, intending to disappear somewhere he could spend his ill-gotten gains, away from the gaze of the authorities.

And now it's all in ruins. Too bad, you should have left it alone.

The man's thinning hair looked almost comical, the comb-over awry, and his chin displayed several days of dark growth. But the Beretta M9 9mm automatic was anything but comical.

Taylor pushed Kate to one side, out of the line of fire, and waited. And watched.

"I said drop it, Taylor, and the girl. I'll give you five seconds, and then your friend dies."

The man's hand was shaking, and it was obvious he'd gone over the edge. Taylor gently put the Ruger on the carpeted deck, and Kate tossed her Makarov to one side. Then he heard someone call out from behind him. A voice that was all too familiar.

"That doesn't look like your kind of gun. I thought you went in for something bigger. I heard a rocket launcher was more your style."

He turned slowly. Wasim Malouf was at the other end of the narrow passageway, his own gun pointed toward them. He was sandwiched between the two men, and the lives of Kate and Levi now hung in the balance.

"You can let them go, Malouf. This is between you and me. It'll mean you'll have a chance to get away, without the cops hunting you down for a murder rap."

"No, no…" Kate sobbed. "They'll kill you."

Malouf laughed, a long, drawn out grating laugh. "You think I care about any of that? Besides, they're hunting me down anyway. I don't give a damn. You're going to die, Taylor, you and your friends. We had a good thing going with Hussein's business, and me watching his back from inside the Boston PD. And a fucking boy scout like you had to go and ruin it, for what? A bunch of no good deadbeats who couldn't make good on their loans."

"Those people you call 'deadbeats', were vets, people who'd fought and been wounded for their country," Taylor spat back. "They didn't need a leech like Hussein to prey upon them when they came back. He deserved to die, and if we hadn't finished him, someone else would have."

"You're crazy! He was making us all rich. You could have joined us, for Christ's sake. Think of the money you would have made."

Taylor knew he was wasting his time. The man only understood shaking down vulnerable people to enrich himself. The concepts of decency and honor were as alien to him as eating pork or imbibing alcohol. They just weren't part of his makeup. He took a half step toward Malouf, but the detective was too wary.

"Hold it right there! Or are you in a hurry to die?"

He stopped. It would need a miracle to get out of this. And a miracle happened. It was as if it occurred in slow motion. A voice came down the companionway.

"Is anyone down there? What's happening?"

Brad Stutz had tired of waiting and came to investigate.

"Get out of here, Brad," Malouf shouted to his partner. "I've got this covered."

"I can't do that, Wasim. You have to come with me. I have to place you under arrest, buddy."

"I'll kill them all!" he shouted back.

There was a short silence as each side considered their next move. Grant Williams was looking up, waiting for Stutz to appear on the steps. Malouf was distracted, trying to warn off his old partner.

Taylor made his move. He dived low, his hand reaching for his ankle holster. He whipped out the Baby Glock. Williams had moved, looking for Stutz, and his head was visible. Praying he wouldn't get it wrong, he aimed and fired a single shot. Levi cried out in shock as Williams' blood and brains splattered over him. He spun around and snapped off two more shots at Malouf. He winced as a round chipped polished mahogany woodwork from the wall next to him, and then the rogue cop was gone. He pushed Kate toward the ladder.

"Get out, fast. Levi, go with her. Get her out of here!"

Levi recovered from his shock, ran around, and started to climb, pushing Kate ahead of him. They reached the main deck just as the interior of the boat echoed to the sound of an assault rifle, firing burst after burst.

Flashes lit up the hallway, and in their light Taylor could see Malouf standing at the other end of the passageway, firing an M16. He managed to dive into an adjacent cabin and peered out the door. Malouf was advancing toward him, firing from the hip. He stopped when his clip emptied. Taylor took the opportunity to snap off several shots in the hope of scoring a hit, but Malouf had stepped into the cover of an alcove that housed emergency equipment, and the shots all missed. Then the rogue detective stepped out with the M-16 and started shooting again. It was no contest, a tiny automatic against an assault rifle, and the man was getting nearer and nearer. And then he ran out of bullets. The Glock clicked on an empty chamber, and Malouf smiled.

"And so it ends, Mr. Taylor."

He pointed the M-16 at him, and Taylor saw the round,

black opening of the end of the barrel, staring at him like some mythic evil eye. Malouf was only feet away from him. He prepared to launch himself at him just before he fired, in a forlorn attempt to save himself, but two shots rang out before he could move, and then another two. Incredibly, he wasn't hit, but Malouf was slammed to the floor by the force of the bullets, blood pouring from his body. Whoever had fired knew his business, two shots to the heart, one slightly lower, and a headshot. But somehow the man was still alive. Taylor ran over to him and kicked away the M-16, which lay next to him on the floor, then bent down to check his vital signs. The Arab's eyes flicked open one last time.

"I'll…see…you…in…hell," he whispered.

The dying man coughed out a spray of blood before he gave out a loud sigh and stopped breathing. Stutz came running down the ladder toward them. Taylor stared at him.

"Thanks, but I thought you said you wanted to take him in."

Stutz knelt by the body, and nodded in satisfaction. He turned, smiling at Taylor.

"Sometimes you just have to improvise. I guess this was one of those times."

"Yeah, I'm glad you saw it that way."

Stutz shrugged. "I guess this'll save the city a packet of money. I think we're finished here."

Taylor nodded. "Yeah, it's ended."

He went up on deck to join Kate and Levi.

* * *

He lay on Doctor Hermann van Rhoos' examination table, feeling like a specimen in a laboratory about to be dissected. It wasn't too far from the truth. Hermann had ordered him to remove his pants, and while he lay still, the prosthetics genius connected his software to Jack's legs and began another lengthy session of diagnostics and software modification. They were partway through when the door opened, and Kate walked in with the psychologist, Sol Weinberg. He felt embarrassed and vulnerable. He usually didn't give a damn about people seeing his prosthetic legs. After all, they were a part of him. But not when they were being worked on modified, overhauled. He felt humiliated, out of control, like a robot on an assembly line. He'd have done anything to stop her seeing him so vulnerable, so helpless. In a position exposing the fragility of his body.

"Can we do this later, Doc?" Hermann ignored him. He went climb off the table, but found he couldn't move his lower limbs. "What have you done? Nothing's happening."

Hermann smiled. "And it's not going to happen, Jack. You were supposed to talk to Doctor Weinberg about your problems with pain. As you failed to turn up, I decided to ask him to come here. Something about Mohammed going to the mountain, if the mountain won't go to Mohammed, I believe is how the saying goes."

"But, my legs!"

"Yeah, while I'm running the program, they're disconnected from your central nervous system. It means you haven't any choice but to listen to Sol."

He felt himself redden as he was forced to suffer the humiliation of two people who loomed large in his life, Kate Donovan and Hermann van Rhoos, listen as Sol Weinberg talked over his problems.

"Of course, it's not the way I normally do it, with third parties looking on," Weinberg explained. "But in your case, it's the only way I can pin you down before you charge off, shooting up half of Boston."

Kate interrupted. "Only the bad guys, Sol. Otherwise, he's pretty nice to know."

Weinberg copped an eyebrow. "Is that right? Does that include the illegal drugs? I take it you buy off the street?"

"No he doesn't," Kate interrupted again." I bought them for him last time around." She stopped speaking as her cellphone rang, checking the display. "Excuse me, I have to take this. It's from work."

She walked out of Hermann's lab, closing the door. The room fell silent, and then Weinberg continued.

"It has to stop," the psychologist looked at him gravely. "Large doses of hard drugs can only have one outcome. You're a clever man, so you must know what that outcome is."

Taylor nodded. "I know."

But at least I feel better. Since it was over, things are different. What began as a chance visit to an old friend from my Navy Seal platoon, developed into a blazing battle on the streets of Boston. Along the way, I met Kate and brought down the Arab crime lord who was turning poorer parts of the beautiful old city into a place of despair. Wes is out of the coma, and I chatted to him yesterday. The terrible injuries did nothing to blunt his recovery from the PTSD that's plagued his life since the explosion in Afghanistan. Once again, he's the man I fought alongside in the filthy, rubbish-strewn hiding places of America's enemies. Levi spends nearly every day with him, talking, and helping him through his recovery.

Probably, he sees in Wes someone to be a father figure. Someone with the same kinds of values his father, Jerry had. The strength, guts, and moral fiber to hunt down his nation's enemies overseas, and no matter how powerful they were, defeat them in battle. There were casualties. Evie, Wes' wife, slaughtered by Hussein's goons; Lincoln, killed by a hand grenade thrown by Hussein's mercenaries. Maybe there were more in the past. They're good people and didn't deserve to die, whereas Hussein and Malouf sure did. Nothing can change the past, though, but they died fighting a worthy battle. What more can anyone give? That's a question for the philosophers.

He glanced at Weinberg.

"Right now, it's not so bad."

Weinberg looked suspicious. "What do you mean? How bad is it?"

He shrugged. "Look, Doc, I have to face it. I can't lose my legs and expect it won't hurt. Sure it hurts. But there's hurt and there's hurt. It really isn't so bad."

The psychologist still looked suspicious. "In my experience, when one of my patients says something like that, it means is they've found some alternative. Like a heroin addict who moves on to crack. Tell me, honestly, Jack, is that what you're on? You've found something else?"

"Hmm, maybe I can help clear this up?"

Hermann had been listening intently to what they said.

"Yeah, go ahead," Sol replied. "What's your take on this? Is he up to something he shouldn't be?"

Van Rhoos looked embarrassed. "Not him, no. Me. I conducted an experiment when I ran that last test. I put some new code into the software. Essentially, what it does is divert some of the pain messages on a different pathway."

Weinberg looked surprised. "That sounds mighty dangerous, Hermann. Is the procedure approved by this institution?"

"Well, no. I mean, they don't know about it, so they can't approve it. But neither can they disapprove it."

"Jesus, I don't know what to say. Jack, how to you feel about it? Tinkering with neural messages to the cerebral cortex. It could backfire. Anything could go wrong, from total paralysis to loss of brain function. It's a hell of a risk. You should have checked with the patient first."

"No!" Taylor interjected. "Hermann knows me better than anyone. I was going down a route that could only end in one way. I was becoming an addict, and what faced me was an early death, either through an accidental overdose, or suicide when it got too much to bear. It's a no-brainer, Doc. Hermann's way gives me a chance of life. My only chance, I reckon." He looked at van Rhoos. "Thanks, Hermann. You know how much I appreciate everything you've done."

He nodded. "No problem, although it's still not perfect. You'll still feel some pain, but a lot less than before. As guinea pigs go, I've grown pretty fond of you, Jack. I didn't want to lose you."

Taylor turned his attention back to Sol. "I found something else as well. Another way to deal with it."

Weinberg's sigh was noticeably loud, "So it is drugs."

Before Taylor could reply, the door opened, and Kate Donovan walked back into the room.

"They're queued up at the law center. It's real busy down there. I have to get back."

He nodded. "I'll finish up here and see you later. You go and sort them all out."

She grimaced. "No, it's not what you think. It's not me they're queuing up to see. It's you."

"Me?"

"Yes. They seem to think you can help them out with the problems that no one else can." She looked at van Rhoos. "Can you get him back on his feet soon? It looks like we're going to need him."

Hermann nodded. "I think I'm about done here. He can go with you. I need five or ten minutes, and he'll be as good as new."

"But I'm not finished," Weinberg spluttered, "You heard what he said. He stopped using one drug, just to go onto something else."

"No, Sol, I don't think it's what he meant at all." He glanced across to where Kate was standing next to Taylor. She'd taken one of his hands in hers. The look that passed between them was more eloquent than words. "That's what I mean. I think we're looking at the something else."

The penny dropped. Sol chuckled.

"I'll be darned. That sure is good therapy. I'll have to recommend that to some of my patients. I guess I'm finished here."

Taylor walked with Kate out of the MIT building and into the bright sunshine of a new day. He turned to her.

"So what's this thing at the law center? I mean; they don't want me to kill anyone."

She laughed. "Certainly not. Everything we do has to be legal." He stayed silent, and she reddened. "Well, more or less legal. First in the queue is an old couple. They run a Mom and Pop store in Southie. They're having trouble with some guys trying to extort protection money."

"Can't they go to the cops?"

"He did. At first they gave him the runaround, but then he ran into Brad Stutz. Brad sent him to us at the law center and told him to ask for you."

"Nice of him. Do we call a cab, or did you rent a car?"

"Something like that."

They rounded a corner, and there stood a gleaming red classic car. A Camaro, fully restored, 1967 vintage. In his opinion it was the best year. He admired the glossy paintwork, Bolero Red, and he knew that underneath the hood beat a 350 cubic inch power plant. It was a very special car, a sleek, shiny, classic Chevy. His Chevy.

"How the hell did you manage to get it out of the parking garage?"

"I sweet talked that lovely boy. His name is Chuck, I believe. He told me there was no way he could ever allow anyone to drive it away without you there, but I managed to persuade him."

"Yeah, I can believe that. The guy is a sucker for a pretty face."

She smiled at the compliment. "I thought you'd like to drive away in style."

She meant drive away into a new life, and they both knew it.

"I do, and it's appreciated."

"You okay to drive?"

" Gimme the keys."

"What are they worth?"

He stared into her laughing eyes. "Name your price. Whatever you want, it's yours."

She handed him the keys. "There's a lot I want from

you, Jack Taylor. I'll think on it, and let you know what I come up with."

"I'm all yours."

"That's all right then. Let's go see these people. I have a feeling you're going to be busy in the near future."

"In or out of bed?"

She gave him a puzzled look. "Why, both, of course. Now get this car moving. We're wasting time."

"Yes, Ma'am."